THE PIONEERS

Also by Jack Schaefer

THE PIONEERS

JACK SCHAEFER

University of New Mexico Press | Albuquerque

To Kit
this book, these stories

© 1952, 1953, 1954 by Jack Schaefer, renewed 1980, 1981, 1982 by Jack Schaefer
All rights reserved. University of New Mexico Press edition published 2017
by arrangement with the Jack Schaefer Trust
Printed in the United States of America
22 21 20 19 18 17   1 2 3 4 5 6

Library of Congress Cataloging-in-Publication Data
Names: Schaefer, Jack, 1907–1991, author.
Title: The pioneers / Jack Schaefer.
Description: University of New Mexico Press edition. |
Albuquerque : University of New Mexico Press, 2017.
Identifiers: LCCN 2016052207|
ISBN 9780826358479 (softcover : acid-free paper) | ISBN 9780826358486
(electronic)
Subjects: | BISAC: FICTION / Westerns. | FICTION /
Short Stories (single author). | GSAFD: Western stories.
Classification: LCC PS3537.C23 A6 2017b | DDC 813/.54—dc23
LC record available at https://lccn.loc.gov/2016052207

Cover illustration: Albert Bierstadt, *Oregon Trail*, 1863
Composed in Adobe Jenson Pro 11/15

Contents

Something Lost

June

This was far up in the mountains and still the great peaks climbed, thrusting up and thinning to the bare bones of rock above the timberline. The high upland valley was lost among them, an irregular pocket caught in the soaring immensity, rimmed by the timeless rock, its glints of meadow green shading into the darker green of forest where it broke into the downward slopes. The figure of the man by the stream near the upper end of the valley, where the water slowed from its rush down the rocks, was unbelievably small in the vastness. He stood stooped by a sandbar where the riffles swung and died in a pool and the slant sunlight flashed on the worn tin in his hands and his shoulders rocked as his arms moved in a circular motion.

The motion stopped and the man bent his head farther to peer into the pan in his hands and the dull gleaming of the flakes there was reflected in the pale hazel irises of his eyes. He straightened and nodded his head in slow satisfaction. He studied the sandbar and the pool where the water slipped into apparent stillness and the silt of years had settled to the bottom. He raised his head and looked at the untouched wilderness about him. The valley lay open around him, a half-mile wide and a mile long, its level floor cut by the swinging course of the stream. At its head the mountain wall rose steeply in huge broken steps that the stream took in rushes and falls as it drove down from the endless snow in the far upper reaches of rock. Along the valley sides the slopes climbed, tree-dotted and thicket-entangled, to stop against the enduring stone, on the near side against a high sharp ridge, on the opposite side against a vast rock buttress towering out to tremendous cliff edge. Between the ridge and the buttress the valley entrance swept out to open parkland that dropped abruptly into jack pine forest covering the downward slopes and divided by the deepening gorge of the stream as it sought the lower levels. And beyond the ground rose again, rising in ridge upon ridge to the high eastward mountain barrier.

The man nodded his head again in slow satisfaction and the sun shone warm on the broad flat planes of his face beneath the wide squared brim of his hat. He took a leather pouch from a pocket and eased the flakes into it. He strode across the carpet of wild flowers bordering the stream and bent to pick up the trailing lead rope of the grazing burro. By the slope of the near valleyside, where a thickening stand of spruce and juniper fringed the valley floor, he stopped and pulled the rifle and ax and short shovel from under the tie ropes and unfastened the pack and picketed the burro on a twenty-foot rope length. He selected a fallen tree, angling up, the upper end wedged in a crotch of another tree. Using this as his ridgepole, he began building his shelter. He shed his jacket and sweat darkened the faded brown of his shirt as his short broad body swung in steady rhythm and the ax blade bit into the springy wood.

Across the meadow green, across the wild-flower carpet and the stream, half a mile across the stretching expanse of valley floor and two hundred yards up the opposite slope where bare rock jutted over a flat ledge, the great bear lay and watched the man. It lay limp on the ledge in the warm slant sun, hind legs sprawled back, front legs stretched forward with the big head, broad and dished to the muzzle, resting on the rock between them. A light breeze ruffled through the short brown fur made ragged by the remaining long still unshed hairs touched with silver on the tips. Its small farsighted eyes followed the man's every move among the distant trees.

Eighty-odd miles away, over the mountain barrier to the east, where a ragged collection of rude log cabins and tents straggled along the side of an almost dry stream bed, men worked at their wooden cradles and sluice boxes and grumbled to themselves and each other. The showings of color that had drawn them there to stake their claims were dwindling. In the oblong tarpaulin-roofed shack that served as store and bar other men spoke of the one who had left, quietly, speaking to no one, abandoning his slow half-worked claim to disappear with his burro into the high distances to the west. Their talk was tainted with envious wondering. They argued with each other in edged monotones. Unrest and disappointment crawled through the mining camp.

Far up in his valley, as the midnight stars wheeled in their slow course, the man stirred on his bed of spruce boughs and sat up, suddenly alert. The embers of the fire outside the open end of his shelter had faded to a dull glow that meant nothing to the moonless dark under the trees. He heard the burro moving restlessly on its shortened picket rope. In the following silence he felt a familiar prickling on the back of his neck as the short hairs there stiffened in response to some instinct beyond reach of the mind. His right hand moved and took the rifle and he was leaning forward to rise when he heard the burro scream and lunge to the end of the rope. He leaped to his feet and stood in the open end of the shelter, baffled by the unrelenting blackness of the night. Gradually he could make out the darker shapes of the trees. He went cautiously toward the burro and found it half choked by the taut rope. He spoke softly and it pushed against him and together they stood in a silence that lived and breathed around them. There was not a single separate discernible sound, yet the prickling persisted on his neck and the flesh of the burro quivered against him. The prickling died and the burro quieted and they stood in an empty silence. The man returned to the fire and piled wood on it and kneeled to blow until flames sprang and a circle of firelight fought back the dark. He shifted the burro closer to the circle before he lay again on his spruce bed.

In the morning the man found the tracks. Those of the forefeet were nearly seven inches wide and nine long, those of the hind feet eight inches wide and fourteen long. The claw marks of all five toes on each were plain. Apprehension crept along the man's spine. His hands tightened on the rifle. The tracks led in a circle around his camp and close in by the shelter and again by the place where the burro had first been picketed. He crawled inside his shelter to the low diminishing end where his meager supplies, depleted by weeks of wandering, were cached behind a barrier of short logs. He took a handful of cartridges and dropped them into a jacket pocket. Outside again, he strode off, steady and unhurried, following the tracks away.

They led him across the stream below the pool and across the level of the valley. He lost them on the edge of a field of slide rock near the lower end of the valley. He skirted the field and could find no further trace. He turned back and began a thorough circuit of the valley.

He found signs in many places, old tracks caked where the ground had dried and fresher tracks in soft ground. He found three rubbing trees with bark worn thin and high up, higher than he could reach, gashes where the bark had been torn open crosswise by big gripping jaws. He found the trail angling up the far slope to the ledge. It was hard-packed by years of use by generations of animals reaching back into the dim past, so packed that the imprints of the big claws were all but invisible scratches on the hard surface. Approaching the ledge, he saw the wide and narrowing crevice behind it leading back to blackness under the overhanging rock. No light could penetrate the inner dark depth. He dropped silently back down the trail fifty yards and crouched behind a big stone and shouted and there was no response except the jeering call of a jay. He shouted again and waited. At last he strode down the trail and across the valley. In a few moments he was stooped by the pool, his arms moving in circular motion as the sun glinted on the pan in his hands. But now he looked up at regular intervals and scanned the expanse all around him and the rifle lay within quick reach not more than a yard from his steady hands.

Out of the valley, eight miles around the jagged sweep of the vast rock buttress that towered above the opposite slope, out where the forest of jack pine below the edging parkland flowed unbroken down to the shore of a small lake, the great bear lay in a patch of sunlight on the soft needle carpet. Already it had forgotten the man and the burro. They were new sights, new scents, never before known, tucked away now in the reservoir of experience and would remain untouched until a fresh encounter summoned remembrance into being. They had been seen and smelled and investigated in the caution of the night and dismissed. There was no challenge in them for the bear to understand.

A marten drifted down the trunk of a nearby tree, stretching its small pointed head outward to stare intently at the bear. The scritch of the small claws in the bark was barely audible a few feet away, yet the bear's head rose. The marten scurried back up the tree. The big head dropped and the bear, full-fed and lazy, drowsed in the sunlight. The tree shadows moved slowly and crept to engulf the bear and it rose and padded softly on through the forest It was obeying its own instinctive calendar of habit moving on the periodic four-day feeding march that took it out of the valley on a wide swing and return through the thirty-seven miles of its mountain-bound range.

July

The man strode up the stretch of parkland that edged the forest and led to the valley entrance. The late afternoon sun was full in his face. Behind him the burro trotted obediently, weighted by the big pack, whose new canvas covering gleamed white in the sunlight. Where the parkland leveled to enter the valley he stopped and turned to look back the way he had come, down the long rolling forested slope sliced by the stream gorge and up and over the first high ridge beyond. Satisfied at last that no one followed, he turned again and led the burro up the valley and across the green carpet to his camp in the spruce and juniper fringe. Everything there was as he had left it eight days before. But in the soft ground by the pool he found the big five-toed tracks crossing the stream toward his camp and going back again. He looked across the valley and up. The steep sideslope curving to the high rock buttress was splendid in the late sunlight and the overhanging rock and the ledge two hundred yards above the valley floor shone rust-red and gray against the green around them. A hawk floated in the air above the scattered clinging trees. There was no other sign of life. He strode back to his camp and began unpacking the burro.

Far to the eastward, over the mountain barrier, where the rude cabins and tents marred the bank of the stream bed, men talked to the keeper of the tarpaulined store and bar, worrying again the worn questions of four days about the one who had returned with his burro and bought supplies and shaken bright flakes out of a leather pouch in payment and disappeared again into the western heights. Already the legend was growing. He had made a rich strike. He was scooping dust out of rich silt pockets by the handful. He had unlimited wealth in dust and nuggets cached in his mountain hideout. The voice of a lean man with narrow hatchet face gashed by a thin-lipped mouth was tinged with bitterness as he told of his failure in following the boot and hoofmark traces into the mountains. A trail that well hidden must have been deliberately cloaked to cover its destination. The talk warmed and eyes glittered and the storekeeper did good business over his hewn-log bar.

Twice in the night the man woke, alert and rising to sitting position on his bed of boughs. There was no sound beyond the barrier of logs with which he had closed the open end of his shelter except an occasional soft movement of the burro in the narrow high-poled enclosure he had built for it. In the morning there were no new tracks. It was the same the next night and the next and early during the night after that thunder echoed through the mountains and lightning laced down through the peaks and enough

7

rain fell in the valley to dampen the ground and renew it for fresh writings by any living thing that walked it. In the morning the man took the rifle and made another thorough circuit of the valley. He found no fresh signs, no five-toed tracks except what remained of the old after the erasing action of the rain. But in the moist sand by the stream where it eddied around rolled rocks well below the pool, he found other tracks, split-hooved, deeply indented. He studied these a long moment. He followed them along the stream and when they faded into the firm sod he kept on down the valley. His stride, long for the length of his legs, gnawed steadily into distance.

Half an hour later he was skirting the vast rock buttress, pausing often to scan the sweep of slope opening below him. He was well around, out of sight of the valley entrance, when he saw the elk, three of them, more than a mile away, on the edge of the parkland that slipped abruptly into the jack pine forest. Patient and steady, he began the long approach, angling down the slope to put the light wind directly in his face.

Far ahead where the forest dipped into a deep ravine, a thin column of smoke floated upward from the inside hollow of the shattered stump of a long dead pine. The slow fire, legacy of the lightning, glowed faintly as it ate into the punklike wood. It edged through a split in the old bark and little flames began to flicker along the side of the stump. It worked down and began to creep through the carpet of brown needles. It crept to the tiny outstretched dried twigs of the branch ends of a fallen tree and moved hungrily along them, reaching for the more solid wood.

The man was on his hands and knees, lifting the rifle carefully and setting it down gently with each forward movement of his right hand. He crawled to the top of a slight rise and lay flat to peer over. He was within rifleshot of the elk. He eased the gun forward and let the sights sink down on the closest of the three. It stood quartering away from him and he aimed a bit behind and below the high foreshoulder and squeezed the trigger. He saw his elk leap a fraction of a second before the others and the three of them swirl and melt like sudden swift shifting shadows into the forest. He rose and went forward and followed. He was well in among the trees when he found the first blood drops, spattered and dark from internal bleeding. He lengthened his stride to follow the trace deeper into the forest Forty minutes later, winded from climbing over and around down timber, he jumped the wounded elk out of a bushed hollow and his bullet, fired almost without aiming in the instant reflex of long experience, broke the animal's neck as it strove with flagging strength to leap away.

Down the slope, farther into the thick of the forest, the great bear prowled, sniffing for rotted logs among a tangle of fallen trees. It heard the second shot, faint yet distinct, a sound foreign and unknown. The big body stopped moving and the big head, unacquainted with fear in any form, rose and turned toward the sound. The bear waited, listening, then the head lowered and the long straight foreclaws sank into the outer shell of a log and, seeming without effort, ripped it open. The tongue, surprisingly small in the big mouth, licked quickly at the scurrying insects and slowed to take the sluggish wriggling white grubs.

The man worked steadily with his knife, quartering the elk carcass. He had already bled and dressed it. He lifted one of the forequarters, testing the weight, and set it aside. He began to cut poles on which to hang the remaining quarters until he could return with the burro. The small of his back ached from bending over and he straightened to rest it, and as his head came up he caught the first faint tang in the air. His body stiffened and the tiny premonitions running through him tightened into awareness. Smoke. Smoke drifting over the forest ceiling and filtering down fine tendrils that could elude the eye but not the nose.

The man stood motionless, testing the breeze. It stirred gently, barely whispering through the branches above him. Disregarding the rest of the meat, he hoisted the one forequarter to a shoulder and steadied it with one hand and look the rifle with the other. He started at a right angle to the direction of the breeze, straight up the slope, the shortest path to the edge of the forest and the open parkland. Steadily he hammered on and the breeze freshened and talked in the branches and smoke began weaving among the tree trunks from the left. He angled toward the right, still climbing, and the smoke thickened, seeming to come from ahead as well as from the left, and at last he stopped, listening between the labored rush of his own breathing. The breeze strengthened and was a wind sighing high overhead and faint and far he could hear, not so much heard as sensed, the sullen roar of the racing fire. Around him he could fairly feel the hurrying of panic, the small life of the forest moving, unseen but known, past him down the slope. A deer bounded out of the smoke and saw him and swerved and was gone. He lowered his shoulder and the meat slid to the ground and without hesitation he turned and struck down the slope.

The smoke thickened and the light dimmed strangely and the roar rose until it was clearly audible and a high crackling breaking over it, and in a short while he was running, using his free hand to help him vault fallen logs, stumbling often and driving downward. The ground leveled and the trees ended and he broke through bushes and tripped full length into the shallow shore waters of a lake. The rifle leaped from his hand and disappeared beneath the surface and he scrambled after it. But the water deepened suddenly a few feet out and he floundered, with his chest heaving for air. He struggled back to the shallow edge and stood quietly while his lungs eased their frantic labor. Smoke rolled around him and he kneeled to keep his head close to the water and the layer of clear air just above it. Fire flared on the rim of the forest to the right and moved toward him and the heat grew until it drove him into the deeper water. He stood stretched upward with his head alone above the surface and looked out over the lake through the rolling smoke clouds. Fifty yards from shore a huge rock showed, humping out of the water like the low ridged back of some vast immobile beast. He swam slowly to it, fighting the drag of his clothes and boots, and crawled up on it and lay flat, while his tired muscles jumped and knotted and relaxed to rest.

The man lay on the rock and watched the fire work its way along the shore. He saw flames spire swiftly up one tree and leap to the next and sometimes, driven by the surge of their own tremendous draft, lunge to engulf several trees at once. The roar of the burning drowned all possible other sound. It was nothing heard, little more than a slight prickling on the back of his neck, that turned his eyes to the water past the other end of the rock. Only the broad head showed, with the muzzle cutting the water, as the great bear swam toward the rock. Quietly the man slipped into the water, stretching out in it with one hand holding to the stone while the other took the knife from its sheath on his belt. Silent in the water, he saw the bear's head rise over the rock opposite him, not more than twenty feet away, the forepaws stretch for footing, the massive shoulders emerge into view. He watched the bear turn broadside and shake and send the drops spattering clear across the rock. He watched it settle on its haunches, facing the flaming shoreline, and let its forepaws slide forward until the broad belly rested on the rock and the big head sank on them. He moved cautiously to look out over the rest of the lake. Through the clear area just over the surface he saw that it was almost ringed with fire and there was no other haven showing above the water. He turned his head back to the rock and his body stiffened. The bear was looking at him. Its head was raised and swung toward him and the small eyes watched. His knees began to flex under him for a swift thrust outward from the rock but the bear remained motionless and while he waited, taut in tenseness, he saw the big mouth open and stretch in a yawn and the white of the great teeth and the lips drawing lazily back and the muzzle crinkling. The jaws closed and the head swung away and dropped on the forepaws again.

The hot air, uncomfortable but not unendurable, beat against the man's face and the chill of the water sank into his body. Cautiously he reached and put the knife between his teeth and placed both hands on the rock and began to draw himself forward and up on it. The bear's head rose and swung toward him and the small eyes watched. He waited and the bear did not move and he inched forward until at last he was on his hands and knees on the rock. Slowly he shifted position until he was sitting cross-legged, ready for an instant scrambling push striking into the water. The bear watched and when he was settled the big head swung straight again and sank down. Gradually the man's muscles softened and the instant alertness eased out of them. The hot air dried his clothes, and the fingers holding the knife now in his right hand relaxed. The smoke clouds rolled and made a strange unnatural dusk and the fire roared through it along the shore. The man's back and buttocks ached with the strain of his position on the hard rock. Slowly he shifted again until he was stretched full length on his side with his face toward the bear and his head pillowed on his left arm. The bear's ears twitched upright but the big head did not move and in a moment the ears eased limp again. The heat in the air lessened slightly and the fire roared dwindling along the shore. Far off it reached the edge of the gorge of the stream running out of the valley and sought to leap across and failed and fell back and was content with the timber it had taken, held now within the limits of the ravine where it had started behind this and the open parkland above and the gorge cutting down the long slope ahead of it and the beginnings of the open rocky climb below where the first ridge of the eastward mountain barrier thrust upward in the new ascent.

The sun, hidden behind the smoke clouds, dropped behind the westward heights and the remaining flames around the lake sent weird lights dancing in the murky dark over the water. The man's eyes closed and opened abruptly and closed again and at last remained closed. The wind died and the smoke trailed away in wisps and the high stars wheeled in the clearing sky above the two silent figures pinpointed together on their rock in the heart of the soaring immensity of the timeless mountains.

The man woke suddenly in the gray dawn of the light before sunrise. He had rolled over in his sleep on his back and the knife had slipped from his opened hand. As awareness flooded him he fought the stiffness in his muscles to turn quickly on his side and fumble for the knife handle. The seeking fingers halted before they found it. The rock stretched away from him empty and open to the sky. The bear was gone. He pushed to his feet and stooped to take the knife and stood straight. The sound of splashing water turned his head toward the near shore. The bear was emerging from the lake onto a short sandy spit. Against the background of rising slope with charred trunks thrusting above blackened floor and thin wisps of smoke still spiraling lazily, it was a miracle of enduring life, enormous and indomitable in the half-light in defiance of the barren desolation. It started inland and drew back with quick mincing steps. There were hot embers under the ashes and flames ready to break forth flickering strong in many places at the push of any breeze. It started to the right along the shore, picking its way in the shallow water. It moved along the shoreline three hundred yards and more and turned inland and disappeared almost in the instant of turning.

The man slipped into the water and swam to the sandy spit. Working from there he made systematic forays into the deeper water until he found the rifle. He washed away the bottom muck and broke it open to blow the barrel and firing chamber clean. Shivering in the first rays of the sun, he moved along the shoreline as the bear had done, stepping slowly but swinging his arms vigorously to warm his muscles. Where the bear had turned he came on a narrow gorge that sliced down the slope to the lake edge with rocky walls guarding a small stream. The fire had done little damage here because there was little to burn and it had leaped over to race on around the lake. The man started the climb, still traveling slowly, and he nodded to himself when he came on the big tracks in soft spots among the bottom stones.

Hidden in an aspen thicket a short way out on the parkland above the stricken forest, the great bear stood over the carcass of a whitetail doe that had fallen in the flight of fear into the upper gorge and broken its neck. The bear had dragged the carcass to the open of the parkland and into the thicket. The big head lifted and the small eyes peered through the thicket. The man was passing, sixty yards away. A low rumble sounded in the bear's throat, soft and deep, not audible to the man and not meant to be. He strode on with the tireless stride of a man long used to the mountains. The bear watched him, its head turning slowly to follow his passing, and when his figure grew small in the distance the big head dropped to feed again.

August

In the clear light of early morning the man stood by the pool and looked at the shallow pan in his hands. The bottom of it was almost covered with the dull gleaming flakes. The pool silt had become richer as he worked deeper into it. He took the leather pouch from a pocket and shook the flakes into it. This was his third panning of the morning and already the pouch was full. He went to his camp and behind it among the trees and stopped by a flat stone. He heaved at the stone to raise one side and braced it against one leg while he set a piece of stout branch to prop it up. In a hollow underneath lay a five-pound salt bag filled to plumpness and another partly filled. He emptied the pouch into the second bag and lowered the stone into place. He went back by the pool and stood slapping the pan gently against his thigh while he looked out over the valley. The air was fresh on his face and mystic cloud shadows wandered on the mountain wall at the head of the valley. He dropped the pan on the sandbar and took the rifle from the grassbank and strode off down the valley with the sun warm in his face. He was close to the valley entrance, where the big boulders of an ancient rockslide had rolled out to become bedded in the ageless sod, when he met the bear, suddenly, coming toward him around one of the rocks.

The bear stopped and the man stopped, thirty feet apart.

Slowly the man swung up the rifle so that his left hand could grip the barrel and his right forefinger slipped around the trigger. The bear watched him and the low rumble, soft and deep, formed in its throat. Slowly the man stepped to the left, moving in a half-circle, always facing the bear, yielding the right of way. The bear watched him, turning its head to follow him until its neck was arched around. When he completed the half-circle the man turned, deliberately turned from the bear, and his will clamped hard on his muscles to hold them to a steady walk away. When he had traveled some forty feet he looked back. The bear had gone forward on its own way and its big, ridiculously tiny-tailed rump was toward him as it overturned scattered stones and sniffed for the scuttling insects.

Five hours later, in the early afternoon, the man returned to his camp, back-packing the dressed carcass of a small whitetail buck. Across the valley the great bear lay on the ledge and watched him. He could see it there, a dark shape on the stone, while he skinned the deer and pegged out the hide for drying. He built a big fire of dry wood and while he waited for it to burn down to glowing embers he began cutting the meat into strips. He looked across the valley and saw the bear rise and disappear into the dark recess of the crevice and he nodded to himself. He knew its habits now. Always when it was in this part of its range it fed at night and in the early morning hours. By midmorning it was lying on the ledge. When the sun was high overhead, sliding into the afternoon slant, it sought the cool darkness of the rock depth.

The man raised poles in a rack over the fire and hung the strips of meat on it. He piled green wood on the fire and retreated from the smoke and sat resting with his back against a tree looking out across the valley. The dropping sun glinted on the pan lying on the sandbar but the man remained still against his tree, rising at long intervals to replenish his fire.

The stream gathered speed as it left the valley and skipped in stony steps down past the edge of the burned-out forest where new green was beginning to rise above the blackened ground. It dropped, gaining momentum, into the deepening gorge that took it farther down and where it raced and whirled in rock pools and raced on. The man stood on the low cliff edge overlooking the gorge. Thirty-five feet below him the great bear lay beside the stream. Its new coat was lengthening and a pale silvery cast was beginning to touch the tips of the thick-grown hairs. It lay limp and relaxed on the pebble strand. Suddenly a forepaw darted and flipped a fat trout flashing through the air and the bear leaped from its lying position to seize the fish as it landed flopping a dozen feet away. Lazily the bear fed, then wandered up the stream to where a smooth rock slanted straight into the water. Standing at the top of the slant, it gave a small bounce and went forward on its belly on the rock with legs outstretched and slid splashing into the stream. The man leaned over the cliff to watch and a soundless chuckle shook him. Lazily the bear climbed again to the top of the smooth rock and rolled over on its back and slid down, tail first, thick legs waving. Its rump struck the water with a spattering smack and the chuckle in the man grew into sound. The bear whirled and rose in the water and looked up. It looked away and inspected the opposite bank in plain pretense that the man was not there. Its head dropped and it shuffled away down the gorge and out of sight around the first turn.

Farther to the eastward, far over the mountain barrier, only a few men worked by the shallow pools that were all that remained of the stream flowing there in the spring and early summer. Most of the cabins were sinking into ruins and only a few tents remained. Under the tarpaulin roof of the store and bar several men argued the failure of prospecting trips into the surrounding country. The storekeeper, short and thick with deep burnt-out eyes in a round bullet head, stood at one end of his bar listening to the low voice of the hatchet-faced man with the thin-lipped mouth. He looked about at his scantily stocked shelves and shrugged his shoulders. Greed and bitterness and discouragement crawled through the mining camp.

Quiet against the sky the man stood on the first ridge outside the valley and saw, small in the vast panorama below him, the great bear stalking an elk. It slipped upwind along a dry gulch and crept out to the shelter of a scrub thicket. The elk grazed closer and the bear broke from the thicket. The elk wheeled into flight, legs driving with the strength of terror. But the bear overtook it and was alongside and reared and a paw flashed in a blur of motion beyond vision and struck the elk's head sideways and snapped the neck like a twig breaking. There had been stillness, a flash of movement, then stillness again, the motionless body of the elk on the grass and the bear standing beside it. The man watched the bear feed slowly then drag the carcass into the gulch and scoop a hole in the soft shale and pull the carcass into this and begin covering it. A small grim smile touched his lips. He turned and started down the other side of the ridge to hunt in another part of the wilderness empire he shared with the great bear.

The chill of the night lingered, gradually giving way to the sun's warmth. The morning air was crystal in its distinct clarity. The man stood by the pool and looked at the pan in his hands. There were only a few scattered flakes in it. The pool was almost worked out. He started to walk along the stream, studying its flow and occasional silt banks. His steps slowed and at last stopped and he looked out over the valley. New color was showing on the clumps of low bushes that dotted the valley floor. Berries were ripening there and along the climbing sides of the valley. Far by the opposite slope he saw the bear rise out of the bushes, settling back on its haunches like a big sitting squirrel, stripping berries into its mouth with its long foreclaws. He strode back to his camp and tossed the pan to one side and lifted the flat stone. Three full salt bags lay there now and a fourth partly filled. He emptied the leather pouch into the fourth bag and lowered the stone in place. Rifle in hand he wandered out through his side of the valley, tasting berries along the way.

September

The green of the valley was changing, darker with a brown cast in barely discernible splotches. The thin cutting edge of fall was invading the air. Among the trees behind the man's camp the flat stone lay undisturbed with grass blades curling over it. The camp itself was neat and orderly. Firewood was stacked in a long pile. A little to one side the pan lay, no longer glinting bright, spotted with dirt and rust. Where the tree fringe abutted the open of the valley the man sat, cross-legged in the sun. Across his lap was a deerskin, tanned with lye from wood ashes and worked to fairly smooth flexibility. Carefully he sliced into the leather, cutting doubled patterns for moccasins to replace his worn boots.

Across the valley, working along the base of the slope and up a short way, the great bear was digging for ground squirrels, ripping into the soil several feet with half a dozen powerful strokes and lying flat on its belly for the final reaching, scraping thrust. The increasing richness of the fur with its silver tipping shone in the clear light. Alternately the man bent to his cutting and raised his head to watch the bear. Suddenly, with the suddenness of decision, he rose and strode back among the spruce and juniper and about, until he found a level space between the trees to his liking. Here he laid out a rough rectangle, scratching the lines with his boot heel. He marked off space inside for a bunk and another rectangle, small and against one end of the other, for a fireplace. He studied his design and nodded to himself and looked around, estimating the standing timber close by. He strode to his shelter and crawled to the low end to inspect what remained of his staple supplies. He came out carrying a small pack and closed the open end of the shelter with its log barrier. He strode to the flat stone and filled the leather pouch from one of the bags. A few moments later he was striding eastward out of the valley with the rifle in one hand, the lead rope of the burro in the other.

A cool wind whipped down the valley, whispering of the winter still hidden far up in the soaring peaks. It moved over the changing green that was darker with the brown splotches plainer and spreading. It moved out the valley entrance and down the rolling slope where the man strode steadily forward, facing straight into it. He was leading a loaded packhorse now and the burdened burro trotted behind. At the crest of the slope he stopped and searched his back trail for long minutes. His head rose higher and his stride lengthened as he passed through the valley entrance and the horse and the burro followed.

Three miles away on the ridge overlooking the last slope, ten feet back in the timber that topped the ridge, two men stood in the tree shadows and watched the three figures entering the valley.

The taller of the two, lean even in his thick mackinaw jacket, had a narrow hatchet face gashed by a thin-lipped mouth. The other, shorter but bulking thick from shoulders to hips, had burnt-out eyes in a round bullet head. The thin-lipped one snapped his fingers and nodded to the other. Together they went back deeper into the timber and mounted the two horses there and rode out and down the ridge, circling to the right toward the high shoulder of climbing rock that would give them a view out over the valley.

Restless on its rock ledge, the great bear lay on the stone and watched the empty camp across the valley. Its ears twitched and the big head rose and swung to the right. It saw the man entering the valley and the horse and burro following. It saw the man stop and look toward it and wave his arms and start forward again. The low rumbling, soft and deep, rolled out from the ledge and died away in the afternoon wind. Quietly the bear watched the man stride toward his camp and begin untying the packs. Quietly it rose and padded on the stone into the darkness of the crevice.

Vigor flowed through the man. The afternoon air of his valley flooded his muscles with strength. His ax leaped in his hands and he felled four trees of the right foundation size and lopped away the branches and cut the logs to the lengths he wanted and notched them. Using the ax handle for a measure he took three pieces of rope and used the three-four-five rule to square the corners as he fitted the logs together. As he straightened from checking the fourth joint he saw first the heavy boots, and as his eyes swept upward he saw the small wicked muzzle of the rifle bearing on his belly and the thin-lipped gash of a mouth in the narrow face.

The two men wasted no time. They asked their questions and when he did not answer they roped him to a thick tree. They searched through his camp and came back by him and built a fire and when this was blazing strong they took his rifle and emptied the magazine and laid it with the barrel reaching into the flames and waited for the metal to heat.

The man stood tight against the tree and the pale hazel of his eyes was startling against the dead bloodless brown of his broad windburned face. He stared out over the valley and his gaze moved upward and stopped two hundred yards up the opposite slope, and the beginning of living color crept into his face. The muscles along his jaw were ridged hard and he waited, cautious in his cunning, until the hot steel was close to his flesh before he spoke. He spoke quickly and bobbed his head toward the far slope. The two others turned. They saw the ledge and the uneven dark outline of the crevice. They spoke briefly together and the burnt-eyed one swung abruptly and started across the valley and the thin-lipped one sat hump-kneed on the ground and picked up his rifle and set it across his lap.

The man tight against the tree and the thin-lipped one hump-kneed on the ground watched the other move out and across the valley floor. They saw him stop at the base of the opposite side and look around for the trail and find it. They saw him start up, hurrying now, and reach the ledge almost running and disappear into the crevice.

Time passed and they watched, each in his own intentness, and nothing moved across the way. The ledge under its overhanging rock slept in its own quietness in the afternoon sun. The thin-lipped one rose and unloosened the rope holding the man to the tree and ordered him ahead and prodded him in the small of the back with the rifle. The man led and the thin-lipped one followed and they started across the valley floor.

Deep in the crevice darkness the great bear stood over the

crumpled body. The big head with the small eyes, red-rimmed now, swung slowly from side to side. The sound of running steps had brought it from sleep into instant alertness. The forward leap out of the inner darkness into the dimness near the crevice entrance and the incredibly swift slashing stroke of forepaw had been instinctive reactions to the challenging affront of invasion. Silently it had dragged the body back into the protective darkness and stepped over it, facing the entrance. The scent of the body, familiar yet unfamiliar, rose in its nostrils and caution at an experience never before known held it waiting in the darkness, listening for further sound out beyond the rock opening.

Striding steadily, the man led the way up the trail. His face was a fixed mask and his muscles bunched in tight tension. When the bear broke from the crevice, red-rimmed eyes blinking for swift focus in the sunlight, the man leaped sideways off the trail and down the steep slope, falling and rolling over the sharp rocks and hard against the trunk of a sturdy spruce. He scrambled to his feet and jumped for the first limb and swung his legs in to the trunk and began climbing.

Above him on the trail the thin-lipped one swung up the rifle and fired and the bullet thudded into the bear's left shoulder and scraped the bone and bore back along the side under the skin. In a silent rush the great bear drove down the trail and the thin-lipped one screamed and turned to run and a crashing forepaw crushed his spine forward into his breastbone and raked tearing down through the muscles of his back. The big jaws closed on the already lifeless body and shook it and flung it twenty feet away.

Close against the trunk, the man peered through the thick tranches of the spruce. Below him the great bear quartered the ground like a huge dog on a hunt, moving with a silent flowing deadliness, raising its head often to test the wind. It limped slightly, favoring its left foreleg, and the recurrent pain from the flesh wound in the shoulder swelled the steady rage within and brightened the reddened rims of the eyes. It worked back along the trail near the valley floor and looked across at the man's camp. Abruptly it swung and with steady purpose went up the trail to the ledge and passed along the slopeside and faded into the tangled growth near the head of the valley.

Safe in his spruce, the man watched it go and disappear from his sight. He waited. At last he climbed to the ground and scrambled up to the trail and grabbed the rifle there. Quickly he ejected the spent cartridge shell and pumped another cartridge into the firing chamber. Quickly he checked the magazine and saw it was almost full. Cautious and alert he slipped down and started across the valley.

The packhorse and burro grazed by the camp, quiet now after the brief startling from the single shot across the way. In the fringe of trees behind them and around the camp nothing stirred except the wind whispering its endless murmur through the evergreen branches. As the man approached, downwind, he stopped often to peer forward and swing his head to scan the whole long fringe of trees, searching with his eyes every possible cover. It was the drumming of the horse's hooves as it pounded to the length of its picket rope and jerked around, strangling, that whirled him toward the sound. The great bear streaked toward him out of thicket shadow and he fired in the instant, instinctively—aiming as rapidly as he could pump the gun. The first shot bored into the junction of neck and right shoulder and shattered the bone there and the second smashed into the massive breast and ripped back through the lungs. The great bear drove ahead, uneven in bounding stride with a deep coughing tearing its throat, and the third shot struck through the mouth and back into the spine. The man leaped aside and the bear's rush took it past and it crumpled forward to the ground. The man stood by the bear's body and stared down. It was smaller with the life gone. The muscles of the man's shoulders shook a little and he swung his head slowly from one side to the other and the flat planes of his face were hard as the rock formations ringing the valley.

He stood by the rectangle of notched logs a long time. Quietly he turned and went to the flat stone and took the plump salt bags from under it and carried them over by his shelter and began to prepare his packs. Half an hour later he strode across the valley floor and the packhorse and the burro followed. The sun, dropping below the far peaks, was behind him. The chill rising wind beat against his back. Unbelievably small in the vastness he strode out of the valley, and with him went a new loneliness and a sense of something lost.

Leander Frailey

New Calypso was getting to be a real town when Baldpate
Frailey settled there. It wasn't tucked away so far in a corner of Nebraska that you couldn't find it on a map if you looked
hard enough. On a big map. It bumped out with a fair quota of low
buildings and squared-corner roads on each side of the railroad
and twice a week a freight train stopped and when the station
agent sold a ticket he could set the signals and one of the two-a-
day one-each-way passenger trains would squeal to a halt instead
of chugging straight through. The local farmers shipped there in
harvest season and the local cattlemen too and supplies came in
for the whole surrounding countryside. Yes, New Calypso had
grown to town-size when Baldpate Frailey stepped off the train
with the tools of his trade in a black leather valise and set up shop
in a squat two-room shack between a saloon and a sprawling
feedstore.

Baldpate was a barber. Maybe it was peculiar for a man without
a hair on his own long thin head to make a living out of other
men's head-crops, but he was a fair-to-middling barber who could
trim your hair without nicking your ears and scrape away your
stubble leaving most of the skin intact. His shop was on the wrong

side of the tracks. Well, wrong side to some people. It was on the side with most of the saloons and the stockyard and the warehouse and the basket mill and the in-and-out squatters' shacks. It wasn't on the side with the saloon that had upstairs rooms to rent and called itself a hotel and the prosperous livery stable and the good retail stores and the solid respectable houses of the solid respectable townsfolk. That side already had a barber shop that had already caught the fancy trade with its neatly painted pole out front and its big mirror behind the two chairs and its shiny brass spittoon that its proprietor called a cuspidor. Baldpate started with a makeshift chair that he could raise and lower with a wooden lever. He finally acquired a real barber chair secondhand out of Lincoln. He finally acquired a small mirror and a black-painted spittoon. But he couldn't compete with the other shop and he didn't try. He got the fringe trade, the men who worked on the same side of the tracks and an occasional cowboy nursing his nickels and trainmen stopping off and the squatters, who sometimes could pay and sometimes couldn't. He had to be content with that and he was. He didn't ask much out of life.

When Baldpate stepped off the train he wasn't alone. He had two boys with him, his sons, Leander and Greenberry. Leander was the older, already stretching long and thin in body and head with such a meager scraggly topknot of hair you could tell he wouldn't be wearing a man's pants long before he'd be bald as a bean. He took after his father. Greenberry was a pair of years younger, considerably shorter but plumper, with a waving tangle of hair that would have made a fine big floor mop. He must have taken after his mother, who had quietly checked out of the Frailey family and the whole of this world some years before.

The three of them lived in the back room of the shop. Baldpate did the barbering and Leander did the housekeeping and

Greenberry did nothing. Nothing except eat hearty, wander around town with other boys, and sit lazy in the sun, which was what he liked best after the eating. Old Baldpate favored Greenberry, maybe because of that mop of hair, and was always telling Leander to take care of him and watch out for him. So naturally it was Leander not Greenberry who began to be snapping the shears at the chair in the afternoons when Baldpate grew tired and felt the arthritis creeping into his joints. And then one night along about the time the boys had their full growth Baldpate sat up on his cot in the dark and called across the little room, "Leander. You mind me now. You take care of your brother." And old Baldpate lay back down and rolled his head on the pillow and died.

You can forget about Baldpate Frailey now. He's not important to this story. He brought the family to New Calypso and started the family business and told Leander what to do and died and that's enough said about him. It's Leander and Greenberry we're interested in.

Leander first. He was a good boy, quiet and steady, so naturally he became a good man, quiet and steady still. The only thing unusual about his growing stage was the stretch he spent a lot of time drawing pictures with a thick surveyor's pencil he'd found somewhere, on any scrap of paper that came to hand. Nobody paid any attention to that. Nobody except Greenberry, who just looked and laughed and settled back to more lazing in the sun. But anyone who paid real attention might have noticed that Leander liked to draw heads, men's heads, with plenty of hair on them and sideburns and all kinds of mustaches and beards. Then he didn't have time for that because he was helping with the barbering as well as doing the housekeeping and then his father was dead and he had full-time barbering to keep him busy. He didn't need to draw heads after that. He had real ones to work with.

It wasn't long before folks on the wrong side of the tracks knew they had a prize barber there who wouldn't be worrisome about being paid on the dot as long as they brought him heavy manes of hair or thick crops of whiskers to be sheared. They gave him plenty of practice and by the time he had his techniques worked out it was a treat to be barbered by that Leander. He'd set you in that one chair and stand back and circle you slowly, studying your head from all around. Then he'd pick up the right tool and go to work. Sometimes it'd be the handclippers. He could do a whole handsome haircut with those clippers alone. Sometimes it'd be the heavy shears or again the light scissors or an alternating of them. Whatever it was, there'd be a wonderful snipping rhythm soothing about your ears. Leander had more than rhythm. He had positive melodies matching the work in hand. If your hair was coarse and strong, you'd hear a marching tune from the flying blades as the locks fell. If your hair was light and fluffy, you'd hear something like a delicate dance tune. His combing was right in time and his soft old brush with the powder on it would be dusting dainty about your neck at the exact second the cut tag ends of hair might be beginning to get itchy and threatening to slide down under your shirt. And when he'd lower the chairback and lather your face and take the right razor out of old Baldpate's box that had one marked for each day in the week, then you knew you were in the hands of a master. His razors were always so sharp the toughest whiskers surrendered without a struggle. His strokes were so deft you weren't certain you felt them. When he raised the chairback again and stepped away and circled you again, you sat still and waited for the verdict. Maybe he'd shake his head and snatch up his scissors and make a fresh attack on your hair or mustache or beard or even eyebrows and by that time you'd not even think of interfering because you knew that when he was finished you'd look better than you ever did before. Let him do it his way and Leander could make anybody look like somebody.

As good as his barbering, some people said, was the effect he had on his customers. He wasn't a talking barber and that marked him as different right away. He was usually so intent on the portrait he was making out of the raw material of features and hair and whiskers in his chair that he might not even hear you if you spoke to him. But if you listened closely you might hear him muttering to himself, not much and not often, just a few words now and then. "Interesting head to work on . . . now these are eyebrows . . . no sense hiding that chin," things like that. No matter how low and picayune you felt going into the shop, you had the feeling coming out that maybe the face you presented to the world had a point or two in its favor.

The first the folks on the right side of the tracks began to have some notion what had been developing over on the other side was when Osgood R. Buxton, proprietor of the Big Bargain Mercantile Establishment and president of the New Calypso Bank, was stranded there with a half-hour to kill. The day had started bad for him. All through breakfast his wife had complained again about the wide drooping mustache that had taken him years to cultivate into the kind of upperlip canopy he thought impressive. "Makes you look like a seasick mastiff," she said and was so delighted at her comparison that he stomped out madder than usual. Then he went down to the freight office to check the shipment he was expecting and found it wasn't in and the train would be half an hour late. He stomped up and down the dirt street kicking at the dust, and the unfairness of it all hit him so hard he decided to strike back in some drastic way. Through the open door of Leander's shop he saw the barber chair empty and stomped in and planked himself in it. He took hold of his mustache with both hands. "Shave this thing off," he said.

Leander didn't pay any attention to the words. Leander was padding around him in a circle studying his head from all sides. Buxton slapped both hands on the chair arms. "You hear me?" he shouted. "I said shave this cookie duster off me!"

Leander focused on him as someone speaking. "No," Leander said. "It belongs there."

Buxton subsided with a blowing gurgle that waggled the mustache. "Belongs there?"

"Yes," Leander said. "It just needs a little pointing so it won't fight with your forehead."

"Fight with my forehead?" Buxton said in a small voice. He relaxed in the chair and a big piece of checkered cloth covered him up to the neck and was tied behind and a clipping rhythm began about his head and something like a cheery marching tune tickled his ears. When the cloth came off he stood up and peered into the little mirror. His hair had been thinned along the sides so suddenly it seemed thicker on top. His eyebrows had acquired a faintly quizzical air. His mustache was almost the same yet remarkably different. It had a slight upward twist suggestive of jauntiness without being aggressive and the side tips somehow pointed your glance upward to notice the broad forehead. The whole effect was that of a man who could do things in the world and was of consequence in his community. When he walked out the door Buxton was snapping his knees in long strides, and though the train was another half-hour late he spent the time chatting cheerfully with the station agent and trying to catch the light right so he could see his reflection in a window.

With a beginning like that and a booster like Buxton only a few months were needed for Leander to have a steady clientele from the right side of the tracks. There were those who remained faithful to the other shop and that was sensible because even Leander couldn't have kept the entire masculine quotient of New Calypso in trim. But he had all the trade he could handle, fancy and fringe, and it was all the same to him. A customer was a customer regardless of where he lived or how full or empty his pocket. Leander would do as artistic a job on a stray tramp as on Osgood R. Buxton himself. He stayed right on in the same one-chair shop and made only the one change of buying a bigger mirror. New Calypso became real proud of him and Gus Hagelin, who ran the *New Calypsan Herald-Gazette*, ran items about his shop once in a while and kept notes on some of the stories about him to be included someday in a history of the township.

You've probably never heard the one about the haircutting contest with Polkadot City's best entry. New Calypsans rarely talked about that one. Some of them got to blowing boastful over Polkadot City way about Leander's speed with the shears, which was silly because speed with Leander was just a part of his skill and not a purpose in itself. But anyway that started an argument and the upshot was that the New Calypsans bet that Leander could trim down two shaggy heads before the best barber Polkadot City could find could finish one. The bets were heavy before Leander heard about it. He didn't like it but he couldn't let any of his regulars lose money on him by default so he said he'd make the race. They thought he ought to go into training, practice finger exercises and things like that, but he just said to tell him when and went on with his regular barbering. When they came for him on the day he just picked up his clippers and a comb and dropped them in a pocket and went along.

They had three men lined up on kitchen chairs and those were really shaggyheaded. The other barber had a tray ready with half a dozen pairs of scissors laid out. Leander shrugged his shoulders and took out his own old clippers and waited. At the start-off gun the two of them went at it, and it was Leander's race all the way. While the other barber clacked his shears and tangled himself in the hair and nipped his own fingers in his hurry, Leander skimmed along, swift and sure, and a fine racing-fast jigtime tune played around the two heads he was working on, first one and then the other. There wasn't any waste motion. Each cut was exact and true. He was carving out neat haircuts with his clippers like a sculptor chipping a statue.

He was going strong and about finished when the inevitable happened. He started muttering to himself. He had the two heads trimmed in a way that would have made any ordinary barber proud when he stepped back and made a circuit of his two men and shook his head. He didn't even hear the shoutings of his supporters and he stepped close again and started the final little delicate polishing strokes that would bring out the best-barbered points of those two men. While the New Calypsans groaned the other barber made a last jagged slice and claimed a finish, and considerable argument developed but the judges gave him the decision. And Leander wasn't even aware of the argument. He was quietly padding around his two subjects and nodding satisfied to himself. The New Calypsans paid their bets grumbling and in time most of them conceded that Leander couldn't have done anything else and still been Leander but they never talked much about that contest. They preferred telling the stories like the one about the time the Governor was worried over re-election and as a campaign stunt came all the way to New Calypso for some of Leander's barbering and Leander touched him up so noble and convincing that he won with a thumping majority. But you've heard that one. Everybody has.

It's Greenberry's turn now. Just as Leander kept on the way he had started, growing longer and thinner and balder and more energetic, so Greenberry kept on the way he had started too, growing plumper so that he seemed shorter, and thicker-haired and lazier. He sprouted whiskers at a remarkably early age and they weren't sparse and blond like Leander's, which had to be shaved off because they were such poor specimens. No, Greenberry's whiskers were stout and dark and close-sprouting and he showed prodigious power in producing them. By time he was old enough to vote, if he'd ever bother to do anything taking that much energy, he had the biggest, bushiest beard in New Calypso. And it kept right on growing. No razor, not even a pair of scissors, had ever touched the main body of it. The only clipping he gave it was a mere minor pruning around the mouth to keep the way clear for his frequent intake of food. It roamed around his face from ear to ear and down over his chest like a magnificent stand of underbrush and merged above into his dark waving hair crop so that his upper cheeks and eyes and forehead peeped out like someone hiding in a thicket. Maybe he clung to that wondrous beard because he realized it represented his one real accomplishment. Some backbiting folks said he did it because he was mean and worthless and was trying to shame his brother and in a figurative sense thumb his nose at the very family business that enabled him to stay so plump and well fed. That couldn't have been true. Greenberry Frailey wasn't mean. Maybe close to worthless. But not mean. He was just lazy. He was just trifling. Matter of fact, he was as proud of Leander as anyone in New Calypso and if arguing hadn't been too much trouble he'd have been ready to argue with anyone that Leander was the best brother and the best barber in the country.

All the same it was peculiar to see the most amazing crop of hair and whiskers anywhere in civilized captivity sitting day after day in the sun on the little porch of a barber shop. That was what Greenberry did every day the sun shone. Nobody ever knew whether he would have tried to do any barbering if the shop had had another chair. Probably not, because Leander hinted about getting another one once and Greenberry promptly pointed out there wasn't room enough. So Greenberry took over the chore of meals, which was somewhat to his liking, and after breakfast he'd settle on the porch till time for his midmorning snack and then settle again till time for lunch and after that settle again till time for his midafternoon jaunt all the way next door to the neighboring saloon. Just before this last he'd go into the shop and around Leander by the chair and pull open the money drawer under the scissors shelf and slip into his pocket one dollar, never any more and never any less. When that dollar was in the hands of the bartender he would come back for the evening meal. If his taste had been for the good liquor at a quarter a shot, he'd still be able to navigate among the dishes and play a fair game of backgammon with Leander after supper. If it had been for the cheap liquor at ten cents a shot, he'd likely soon be snoring on his cot and Leander would have to be the cook. Those times Leander might begin to worry he wasn't doing right by his brother and shake him awake and try telling him he ought to get a job of some kind and Greenberry would simply say, "Why? We're doing all right, aren't we?" and Leander wouldn't know what to say because they were.

There they were, Leander doing his barber's magic inside the shop and Greenberry raising whiskers on the porch and they might have continued that way indefinitely if Leander hadn't acquired an obsession that started as a small notion and grew until it was so bad it could quiver in his fingertips. He had all his regular patrons in the New Calypso territory well in hand, each fitted with the hair styles and whiskery facial adornments or lack of same that would make the emphatic most of their natural endowments. The task now was simply to keep them trimmed that way. There was no challenge left in them, no demand for fresh creative effort. He welcomed stray strangers who wandered in with positive delight. But they were few and long between. He began to feel frustrated and barren of inspiration. And then he stood on the little porch one afternoon and looked at Greenberry snoozing in the sun and a breeze waggled the long soft ends of Greenberry's beard and the small notion was born. By evening it was so big in him that he could hardly look at Greenberry across the supper table. During the next days it swelled to such proportions that it interfered with his barbering. He had to shake his head sharp to rid it of the image of that magnificent shock of raw material and the rhythmic melody of his cutting would break as his fingers quivered on the clippers. And then Greenberry all unknowing tripped the trigger of the trap awaiting him by taking on ten shots and coming home and falling asleep.

Leander closed the shop door at five o'clock as usual and padded into the back room and saw Greenberry gently snoring and a sudden little tremor ran through him. He rocked on his feet a moment and closed his mouth with a sudden snap. He padded into the shop and returned and laid out his tools on a chair by the cot, the clippers and the scissors, big and small, and a comb and the right razor and the brush and the soap mug. Carefully he raised Greenberry's shoulders with one arm and slipped two pillows behind them. Carefully he spread the checkered cloth over

Greenberry's plump middle and raised Greenberry's beard to slide the upper edge of the cloth under it. For a long time he stood staring at the huge thatch of wondrous hair and whiskers framed against the cloth and the top pillow. He was not studying the head, because he did not need to. He knew every possible configuration hidden inside that thicket, every feature that everyone else in New Calypso had long forgotten. He was tasting the sweet tangy ecstasy of anticipation. At last he carefully set another chair by the cot side and sat down on it and leaned forward. With a soft sigh of complete contentment he picked up the clippers and went to work.

Greenberry stirred once at a slight tugging on his chin but a rich majestic melody of snipping blades was playing about his head and it soothed him even deeper into slumber. He woke late in the evening in the lamplight and was surprised that Leander had not roused him to supper. He was more surprised when he saw Leander limp on the other cot, asleep, and on his long thin bald-topped face the beatific smile of a man who has made a supreme effort and found it good. Greenberry heaved to his feet and was so befuddled he was not aware that he was a changed man. Out of sheer habit he ate five big sandwiches and did not notice the new freedom of access to his mouth and lay down again and slept once more. He was still unaware in the morning despite the secretive proud glances Leander gave him and awareness did not touch him until he went out the back door and took hold of the two-wheeled pushcart there and started off on his weekly food-shopping jaunt to Oscar Trittipoe's General Grocery Store.

He never reached the store. Not on that trip. He was accustomed to being ignored by most people passing and that pleased him because it saved the energy of a return greeting. He was accustomed to having those who did speak make humorous references to his beard. But this time neither thing happened. Everyone noticed him. Very definitely. They stared at him as if they had never seen him before and turned to watch him go by. And no one spoke about his beard. No one spoke at all. Most of them nodded to him, respectful and deferential, and some of the men involuntarily tipped their hats. It was too much for Greenberry's somnolent mind to grasp all at once. He hurried back to the shop, went in and turned to Leander, puttering at his instrument shelf, and in the turning saw himself in the big mirror.

Not himself. Someone else. A man of amazingly impressive presence. A thick shock of hair tamed and disciplined to dignity yet with the inherent vitality plain in every faultless wave. Strong eyebrows subtly arched to emphasize the width and nobility of the brow. A sturdy mustache, firm and short-cropped, speaking of confidence and self-assurance in itself and somehow also pointing out the out-thrust power of the nose above. Rugged sideburns clipped close yet with a faint flaring that suggested breadth of mind. And a beard, deep under the chin and reliable, short but not too short, wide but not too wide, a solid foundation for the face proclaiming serenity and wisdom with every sturdy hair.

Greenberry shook with the shock. He threw Leander one look of frenzied reproach and fairly ran into the back room and closed the door. He sat on the edge of his cot and leaned the superb portrait that was now his head forward into his plump hands and let the frightening knowledge that he was marked with distinction sweep over him. It was characteristic that he never once thought that a few strokes with scissors could reduce him again to a scraggly nonentity. He would have had to make those scissor strokes. He sat motionless a long time. At last his head rose and he made a few exploratory motions with his hands around his chin and cheeks. He stood up and placed himself in front of the little mirror that had once served in the shop and his mind was braced now for what he would see. He studied himself, turning his head sideways and rolling his eyes to catch the splendor from various angles. Unconsciously he stood straighter and pulled in his bulging waistline and puffed out his chest. By noontime the new Greenberry Frailey, fortified with a full lunch, was ready to face the world.

The new Greenberry Frailey. That is precisely what he was. A new man. A changed man. In all outward semblance at least. The very first day he discovered what his impressive appearance could accomplish in promoting prompt, actually scurrying service and the choicest cuts of meat from the formerly lackadaisical and almost contemptuous Oscar Trittipoe. On the third day he learned the ease with which he could obtain virtually unlimited credit at the Big Bargain Mercantile Establishment and forthwith arrayed himself in what was to be thereafter his unvarying uniform, black trousers and black frock coat and gorgeous gray vest and white shirt and celluloid collar and black-string bow tie, unseen beneath that now disciplined matchless beard except when he thrust his chin outward and fluffed the beard up in a gesture calculated to draw attention to its perfect proportions. By the end of the first week he had even acquired a gold-headed cane and his voice had dropped several notes to a deepening resonance and he was developing a flowing almost courtly manner. By the end of the second week he was settled in his new role, rapidly becoming another New Calypsan institution, a monumental figure seen every clear day on the center bench between the town watering trough and the town flagpole across from the post office. You can assay the true measure of Leander's art when you understand that already the New Calypsans were forgetting the old

39

Greenberry who sat in his ancient red-plaid shirt and split-seam dungarees on the porch of the little shop and were drifting so completely under the spell of the new Greenberry that they accepted his benign nods as benedictions and felt that their town was a better place because such a towering testament to the dignity and nobility of the human race dwelt among them. When he had snoozed on the shop porch he had been a shiftless disgrace to be ignored. Now, when he drowsed on the bench, serene and nodding in the sun, he was a philosopher thinking deep thoughts and pondering grave problems and giving tone to the community. Why, it's a fact there was not even a noticeable chuckle when he began calling himself J. Greenberry Frailey.

It was Osgood R. Buxton himself who launched Greenberry on his public career. The time came when Buxton was a mite worried about the New Calypso Bank. More than a mite worried. The bank had overreached itself in granting loans and the cattle market was wobbly and a lot of the loans might have to be carried over and a few rumors got to skipping about and Buxton was worried what would happen if a run started. He sat at his desk by the bank's front window worrying and stroking the mustache Leander had saved for him and out the window he noticed with a sudden idea-prompted push the never failing impressiveness of Greenberry on the bench. Five minutes and a brief talk later Buxton was on his way to Gus Hagelin with an item for the *Herald-Gazette* to the effect that J. Greenberry Frailey had kindly consented to become a director of the New Calypso Bank. The only immediate change for Greenberry was the addition of ten dollars a month to his pocket and a slight shift of sitting quarters, from the bench by the flagpole to a bench in front of the bank where the sun was even better and his presence was a steady reassurance to troubled depositors. The monthly meetings were no real chore. All he had to do was attend and sit quiet and murmur "Hmmmm" in a thoughtful tone when an important decision was posed, and the other directors would proceed exactly as they would have done without him, buttressed now with the feeling that they were being wise and judicious indeed. But this first gesture into the realm of actual activity encouraged other people to draw him into other things. He discovered the lure of speechmaking. The deep roll of his voice combined with the overpowering benignity of his appearance to produce hypnotic effect on his audiences. The words were unimportant. It was the impression that prevailed. He auctioned the box lunches at town dances and could obtain good prices for those prepared by the most unattractive unattached females. He presided at the annual Strawberry Festival and the Stockmen's Show and was the Fourth of July orator. There was no doubt about it. With little real effort on his part he had become an unofficial public functionary.

And Leander? Well, Leander was content. He had done what old Baldpate told him to do. He had taken care of Greenberry in the most important way and what remained of the taking care was merely a matter of helping to maintain Greenberry in the style to which he had become accustomed. That was simple because Greenberry was not active enough to wear out clothes rapidly and ate, if anything, less than before and his drinks were almost invariably supplied by admirers more than willing to pay for the privilege. Leander now had constantly before him the inspiration of his finest masterpiece, the one perfect portrait that he never tired of retouching and keeping in perfect trim. And Greenberry, in his way, was properly grateful. His innocent trust that Leander would take care of him had been justified in a surprising and superlative degree. He never failed, when extolling the glories of New Calypso in his occasional orations, to include some mention of the tonsorial wizardry of that far-famed prince among barbers, my brother Leander. He continued to grace the little shop building with his presence as his eating and sleeping quarters. He continued to spend his spare evenings playing backgammon with Leander. So complete was his hold on the town that many people regarded this as somewhat of a condescension on his part.

Yes, Leander had worked out a way of life for himself and Greenberry that satisfied them both and was a double-weight asset to New Calypso. Then enter the serpent, Worthington P. C. Stimmel. That was the name in Old English lettering on his calling cards and he carried his cards in a cardcase. They also stated, in smaller but no less compelling type, that he was President and Corresponding Secretary, the Amalgamated Association for the Betterment of American Communities. This Stimmel had long since made an interesting discovery. He had learned that when towns attained some size they found themselves needing such modern improvements as sewers and cobblestone pavements and those ingenious means of public transportation, horsecars. He had discovered that sometimes the people of an ambitious small town could be persuaded that the process would work in reverse, that if they would sell bonds to themselves to raise the funds and draw plans for new streets and install sewers and pavements and horsecars, then their town would automatically attract newcomers and grow swiftly and become boomingly prosperous. It was unfortunate that the promotional expenses and the cost of this Stimmel's invaluable services always approximated most if not all of the funds raised. But by time the townsfolk learned that in full eye-opening force this Stimmel would be far away planning the improvement of another community in another part of the country.

A man of Worthington P. C. Stimmel's experienced discernment could see at once the splendid future that awaited New Calypso. He could recognize with equal facility the unusual opportunity offered by J. Greenberry Frailey's bewhiskered magnificence. He had not been in New Calypso ten days before stationery was printed and bonds were being engraved and both stationery and bonds proclaimed the fact that J. Greenberry Frailey was Chairman of the New Calypso Progressive Citizens' League, the latest chapter of the A.A.B.A.C. There was some opposition led by Oscar Trittipoe, who was by nature an obstinate individual, and Gus Hagelin, who had acquired from his newspaper work a suspicious trend of mind and some knowledge of human frailties. But obstinacy and suspicion could not prevail against the majesty of the Greenberry whiskers. The N.C.P.C. League gained momentum like an avalanche moving and the date was set for the public meeting that would launch the bond sale.

All this bothered Leander not at all. He never interfered in Greenberry's doings. His own doubts about the League project were overwhelmed by Greenberry's contagious optimism. To him the thought of a bigger and more booming New Calypso was pleasant because that might mean new and unfamiliar customers. He went quietly on with his barbering. And then Worthington P. C. Stimmel made a mistake. Operating on the principle of when in Rome doing what the Romans do, he went into the little shop for a hair trim.

"Heard about you from your brother," this Stimmel said in his best patronizing manner. There was no reply. Leander was circling the chair, studying him from all sides. The first eager small smile on Leander's face was fading into a tight-lipped frown. Muttonchop whiskers. Leander had never liked muttonchop whiskers and refused to permit them on any regular customer. They were not right for any decent human head. They could have only one purpose, to hide or draw attention away from other things. Correct. These muttonchops gave a broadness and solidity to this head that was not really there. They obscured the whole sinister, greedy, calculating cast of the countenance. Leander picked up his big scissors and they hovered about Stimmel's head, and the rhythmic tune they played in their first warming-up skirmishes in the air was a stern and resolute one. But they never touched a hair or whisker. Leander stopped and laid them down. He could not do it. He picked up the small scissors and for the first time since he was a boy relieving old Baldpate in the afternoons he gave an ordinary haircut, merely trimming into neatness the original portrait presented to him.

That was all that happened then in the shop. But afterward Leander did what he had never done before. He closed the shop during working hours and went to see Gus Hagelin and what he learned there added more worry to what he had learned in the shop and he tried to talk to several League members and they laughed and told him to stick to his harboring and he tried to talk to Greenberry that evening and Greenberry laughed too and at last grew huffy and said he'd move to a room at the hotel if Leander didn't stop harping on something he knew nothing about. So Leander kept his worry to himself and it grew till it was a new obsession in him and he kept remembering what old Baldpate had said and realizing that Greenberry was in this slick Stimmel scheme and in a sense the kingpin of it, the asset that could push it through. And so at last when he had worried himself thinner and the time was short, he did something else he had never done before. On the day before the public meeting he went to the saloon next door and bought a bottle of the cheap liquor and had it on the table when he played backgammon with Greenberry that evening.

He poured more into Greenberry's glass whenever that was empty and his own slick scheme succeeded. By eleven o'clock Greenberry was snoring soundly on his cot. Leander padded forward into the shop and returned and laid out his tools on a chair and spread the checkered cloth over Greenberry's chest. For a long time he stood staring down at the finest portrait he had ever achieved. With a soft sigh of torment he picked up his clippers and a slow sad melody of snipping blades began to play around Greenberry's head.

Greenberry slept straight through the night and well into the morning. He woke slowly and then focused suddenly on the old clock on a shelf. Five minutes past ten. The meeting had begun five minutes ago and he was not there. No time even for breakfast and that was a drastic thing to happen to him. He shrugged as quickly as he could into his frock coat and grabbed his gold-headed cane and hurried out through the shop past Leander sitting mournful in his own barber chair. He hurried out the front door disregarding Leander's calling to him, and hurried up the street and across the tracks and to the crowded space behind the flagpole where a bandstand had been erected and the four-piece New Calypso band was seated and Worthington P. C. Stimmel was standing erect delivering his practiced spiel.

There on the stand this Stimmel, talking against time, saw with relief the magnificent wavy shock of Greenberry's hair moving toward him through the assembled people. He shifted smoothly into remarks introducing that almost legendary repository of wisdom and civic foresight, that peerless pillar of New Calypsan community life, J. Greenberry Frailey, and waved to the approaching pillar to ascend the stand. And Greenberry burst out of the crowd and went up the steps and took his dignified stance and thrust his head forward a bit and reached up in the strange hushed silence that had gripped the whole scene to fluff his beard.

It was that gesture that released the first of the sniggering chuckles into loud and contagious guffaws. Greenberry's hand came up in the familiar movement to fluff his beard and there was no beard for him to fluff. There was only what the New Calypsans had long ago forgotten, the ridiculous small and round little-boyish dimpled chin that the beard had hidden. As the laughter rolled around the flagpole and New Calypsans thumped each other on the back, Worthington P. C. Stimmel, that man of experienced discernment, slipped down from the stand and away and Gus Hagelin, that man aware of human frailties, leaped up on the stand and shouted at the band and raucous music began to blare. And through the midst of the overall merriment came a long and thin and bald-headed figure, stoop-shouldered and sad and ashamed, to take care of his brother and lead him home.

All the rest of the day the little shop was closed. The next day it was open and time had gone backward. A plump figure in a red-plaid shirt and split-seam dungarees sat on the little porch in the sun. But inside there were no mere snipping melodies. There was only the plain pedestrian plodding of routine cutting. Greenberry sat in the sun and some of the time actually snoozed and Leander went on with his barbering inside, but it was an ordinary barber's barbering. He had used his art to destroy and not to create and the magic was gone from his fingers.

In midafternoon Greenberry rose and went into the shop and pulled open the money drawer and took out a dollar and reached and took another and looked at Leander patiently working his scissors in dull routine and put the second dollar back and plodded out. It was a ten-shot session for him and he returned barely able to navigate and lay down on his cot and in a few moments was sleeping, and almost anyone seeing him there would have said that was all he was doing.

But he was doing something else. All unaware he was doing the one thing that he could do better than anyone else in New Calypso. Leander saw it when he came into the back room from the shop and started to prepare some supper. He saw what he, a barber, had actually forgotten. He saw the dark stubble emerging on Greenberry's chin and remembered Greenberry's prodigious talent for raising whiskers. His eyes brightened and small rhythmic melodies began to stir again in his finger muscles. He had not failed old Baldpate. Not yet. He could try again and, if necessary, again. It would not take long, not with Greenberry so obligingly concentrating even in his sleep on that one wondrous accomplishment.

Already Leander could begin to see the next portrait. Not dignity and thoughtfulness and deep wisdom this time. No. A portrait built around a short, stubby, square-cut beard, the beard of a man steady and dependable and competent at whatever work he might have in hand.

That Mark Horse

Not that horse, mister. Not that big slab-sided brute. Take any or all of the rest, I'm selling the whole string. But not that one. By rights I should. He's no damn good to me. The best horse either one of us'll likely ever see and he's no damn good to me. Or me to him. But I'll not sell him . . .

Try something, mister. Speak to him. The name's Mark . . . There. See how his ears came up? See how he swung to check you and what you were doing? The way any horse would. Any horse that likes living and knows his name. But did you notice how he wouldn't look at me? Used to perk those ears and swing that head whenever he heard my voice. Not anymore. Knows I'm talking about him right now and won't look at me. Almost ten months it is and he still won't look at me . . .

That horse and I were five-six years younger when this all began. I was working at one of the early dude ranches and filling in at the rodeos roundabout. A little riding, a little roping. Not too good, just enough to place once in a while. I was in town one day for the mail and the postmaster poked his head out to chuckle some and say there was something for me at the station a mite too big for the box. I went down and the agent wasn't there. I scouted around and he was out by the stock corral and a bunch of other men too all leaning on the fence and looking over. I pushed up by the agent and there was that horse inside. He was alone in there and he was the damndest horse I'd ever seen. Like the rest around I'd been raised on cow ponies and this thing looked big as the side of a barn to me and awkward as all hell. He'd just been let down the chute from a boxcar on the siding. There were bits of straw clinging to him and he stood still with head up testing the air. For that first moment he looked like a kid's crazy drawing of a horse, oversize and exaggerated with legs too long and big stretched-out barrel and high-humped withers and long-reaching neck. The men were joshing and wondering was it an elephant or a giraffe and I was agreeing and then I saw that horse move. He took a few steps walking and flowed forward into a trot. That's the only way to put it. He flowed forward the way water rolls down a hill. His muscles didn't bunch and jump under his hide. They slid easy and smooth and those long legs reached for distance without seeming to try. He made a double circuit of the corral without slowing, checking everything as he went by. He wasn't trying to find a way out. He just wanted to move some and see where he was and what was doing roundabout. He saw us along the fence and we could have been posts for all the particular attention he paid us. He stopped by the far fence and stood looking over it and now I'd seen him move there wasn't anything awkward about him. He was big and he was rough-built but he wasn't awkward anymore even standing there still. Nobody was saying a word. Everyone there knew horses and they'd seen what I saw. "Roast me in the eternal pit," I said. "That's a horse." The agent turned and saw who it was. "Glad you think so," he said. "It's your horse. This came along too." And he stuck a note in my hand.

It had my name on it all right. It was from a New York State man who ran some sort of factory there, made shoes I think he told me once. He'd been a regular at the ranch, not for any dude doings but once a summer for a camping trip and I'd been assigned to him several years running. It wasn't long. It said the doctors had been carving him some and told him he couldn't ride again so he was closing his stable. He'd sold his other stock but thought this horse Mark ought to be out where there was more room than there was back east. Wanted me to take him and treat him right.

I shoved that note in a pocket and eased through the fence. "Mark," I called and across the corral those ears perked stiff and that big head swung my way. "Mark," I called again and that horse turned and came about halfway and stood with head high, looking me over. I picked a coil of rope off a post and shook out a loop and he watched me with ears forward and head a bit to one side. I eased close and sudden I snaked up the loop and it was open right for his head and he just wasn't there. He was thirty feet to the left and I'd have sworn he made it in one leap. Maybe a dozen times I tried and I didn't have a chance. The comments coming from the fence line weren't improving my temper any. Then I noticed he wasn't watching me, he was watching the rope, and I had an attack of common sense. He was wearing a halter. This wasn't any western range horse. This was one of those big eastern crossbreds with a lot of thoroughbred in them I'd heard about. Likely he'd never had a rope thrown at him before. I tossed the rope over by the fence and walked toward him and he stood blowing his nostrils a bit and looking at me. I stopped a few feet away and didn't even try to reach for the halter. He looked at me and he was really seeing me the way a horse can and I was somebody who knew his name out here where he'd been dumped out of the darkness of a boxcar. He stretched that long neck and sniffed at my shirt and I took hold of the halter and that was all there was to it . . .

That was the beginning of my education. Yes, mister, it was me had to be taught, not that horse. The next lesson came the first time I tried to ride him. I was thinking what a big brute he was and what a lot of power was penned in him and I'd have to control all that so I used a Spanish spade bit that would be wicked if used rough. He didn't want to take it and I had to force it on him. The same with the saddle. I used a double-rig with a high-roll cantle and he snorted at it and kept sidling away and grunted all the time I was tightening the cinches. He stood steady enough when I swung aboard but when we started off nothing felt right. The saddle was too small for him and sat too high-arched over the backbone and those sloping withers. He kept wanting to drop his head and rub his mouth on his legs over that bit. At last he sort of sighed and eased out and went along without much fuss. He'd decided I was plain stupid on some things and he'd endure and play along for a while. At the time I thought he was accepting me as boss so I started him really stepping and the instant he understood I wanted him to move that was what he did. He moved. He went from a walk into a gallop in a single flowing rush and it was only that high cantle kept me from staying behind. I'm telling you, mister, that was something, the feel of those big muscles sliding smooth under me and distance dropping away under those hooves.

Then I realized he wasn't even working. I was traveling faster than I ever had on horseback and he was just loafing along without a sign of straining for speed. That horse just liked moving. I never knew another liked it as much. It could get to him the way liquor can a man and he'd keep reaching for more. That's what he was doing then. I could feel him notching it up the way an engine does when the engineer pushes forward on the throttle and I began to wonder how he'd be on stopping. I had an idea twelve hundred pounds of power moving like that would be a lot different from eight hundred pounds of bunchy little cow pony. I was right. I pulled in some and he slowed some but not much and I pulled harder and he tossed his head at the bit, biting, and I yanked in sharp and he stopped. Yes, mister, he stopped all right. But he didn't slap down on his haunches and slide to a stop on his rump the way a cow pony does. He took a series of jumps stiff-legged to brake and stopped short and sudden with his legs planted like trees and I went forward, bumping my belly on the horn and over his head and hanging there doubled down over his ears with my legs clamped around his neck. That Mark horse was surprised as I was but he took care of me. He kept his head up and stood steady as a rock while I climbed down his neck to the saddle. I was feeling foolish and mad at myself and him and I yanked mean on the reins and swung him hard to head for home and that did it. He'd had enough. He shucked me off his back the way someone might toss a beanbag. Don't ask me how. I'd ridden plenty horses and could make a fair showing even on the tough ones. But that Mark horse wanted me off so he put me off. And then he didn't bolt for the horizon. He stopped about twenty feet away and stood there watching me.

I sat on the ground and looked at him. I'd been stupid but I was beginning to learn. I remembered the feel of him under me, taking me with him not trying to get away from me. I remembered how he'd behaved all along and I studied on all that. There wasn't a trace of meanness in that horse. He didn't mind being handled and ridden. He'd been ready and willing for me to come up and take him in the station corral. But he wasn't going to have a rope slapped at him and be yanked around. He was ready and willing to let me ride him and to show me how a real horse could travel. But he wasn't going to do much of it with a punishing bit and a rig he didn't like. He was a big batch of damned good horseflesh and he knew that and was proud of it and he had a hell of a lot of self-respect. He just plain wouldn't be pushed around and that was that and I had to understand it. I claim it proud for myself that I did. I went to him and he waited for me as I knew now he would. I swung easy as I could up into the saddle and he stood steady with his head turned a little so he could watch me. I let the lines stay loose and guided him just by neck-reining and I walked him back to the ranch. I slid down there and took off the western saddle and the bridle with that spade bit. I hunted through the barn till I found a light snaffle bit and cleaned it and put it in the bridle. I held it up for him to see and he took it with no fuss at all. I routed out the biggest of the three English saddles we had for eastern dudes who wouldn't use anything else and that I'd always thought were damned silly things. I showed it to him and he stood quiet while I slapped it on and buckled the single leather cinch. "Mark," I said, "I don't know how to sit one of these crazy postage stamps and I'm bunged up some from that beating. Let's take it easy." Mister, that horse knew what I'd said. He gave me the finest ride I ever had . . .

See what I mean, the best blamed horse either of us'll ever see? No, I guess you can't. Not complete. You'd have to live with him day after day and have the endless little things happening tally up in your mind. After a while you'd understand as I did what a combination he was of a serious dependable gent and a mischievous little kid. With a neat sense of timing on those things too. Take him out for serious riding and he'd tend strict to his business, which was covering any kind of ground for you at any kind of speed you wanted. The roughest going made no difference to him. He was built to go at any clip just about anywhere short of straight up a cliff, and you'd get the feeling he'd try that if you really wanted him to. But let him loaf around with nothing to do and he'd be curious as a cat on the prowl, poking into every corner he could find and seeing what devilment he could do. Nothing mean, just playful. Maybe a nuisance if you were doing a job where he could get at you and push his big carcass in the way whiffling at everything or come up quiet behind and blow sudden down your shirt collar. Let him get hold of a bucket and you'd be buying a new one. There'd not be much left of the old one after he'd had his fun. He'd stick his nose in and flip the tiling and do that over and over like he was trying for a distance record then start whamming it around with his hooves, tickled silly at the racket. And when there'd be no one else around to see how crazy you were acting he'd get you to playing games too. He liked to have you sneak off and hide and whistle low for him and he'd pad around stretching that long neck into the doggonedest places looking for you and blow triumphant when he found you. Yes, mister, that horse liked living and being around him'd help you do the same.

And work? That horse was a working fool. No. There was nothing foolish about it. The ranch was still in the beef business too in those days and he'd never had any experience with cattle before. He was way behind our knowing and he knew it. So he tried to balance that by using those brains of his overtime and working harder than any of the others. He'd watch them and try to figure what they were doing and how they did it and then do it himself. He'd try so hard sometimes I'd ache inside, feeling that eagerness quivering under me. Of course he never could catch up to them on some things. Too big. Too eager. Needed too much room moving around. He couldn't slide into a tight bunch of cattle and cut out the right one, easing it out without disturbing the rest much. And he wasn't much good for roping even though he did let me use a western saddle for that soon as he saw the sense to it. Lunged too hard when I'd looped an animal and was ready to throw it. Maybe he'd have learned the right touch in time but he didn't get the chance. The foreman saw us damn near break a steer's neck and told us to quit. But on straight herding he couldn't be beat. He could head a runaway steer before it even stretched its legs. He could scour the brush for strays like a hound dog on a scent. He could step out and cover territory all day at a pace that'd kill off most horses and come in seeming damn near as fresh as when he started. I used to think I was tough and could take long hours but that horse could ride me right out of the saddle and act like he thought I was soft for calling a halt.

But I still haven't hit the real thing. That horse was just plain honest all through. No, that's not the exact word. Plenty of horses are that. He was something a bit more. Square. That's it. He was just plain square in everything he did and the way he looked at living. He liked to have things fair and even. He was my horse and he knew it. I claim it proud that for a time anyway he really was my horse and let me know it. But that meant too I was his man and I had my responsibilities. I wasn't a boss giving orders. I was his partner. He wasn't something I owned doing what I made him do. He was my partner doing his job because he wanted to and because he knew that was the way it ought to be with a man and a horse. A horse like him. Long as I treated him right he'd treat me right. If I'd get mean or stupid with him I'd be having trouble. I'd be taking another lesson. Like the time along about the second or third week when I was feeling safer on that English saddle and forgot he wasn't a hard-broke cow pony. I wanted a sudden burst of speed for one reason or another and I hit him with my spurs. I was so used to doing that with the other horses that I couldn't figure at first what had happened. I sat on the ground rubbing the side I'd lit on and stared at him watching me about twenty feet away. Then I had it. I unfastened those spurs and threw them away. I've never used the things again ever, any time on any horse . . .

Well, mister, there I was mighty proud to have a horse like that but still some stupid because I hadn't tumbled to what you might call his specially. He had to show me. It was during fall roundup. We had a bunch of steers in the home corral being culled for market and something spooked them and they started milling wild and pocketed me and Mark in a corner. They were slamming into the fence rails close on each side. I knew we'd have to do some fancy stepping to break through and get around them. I must have felt nervous on the reins because that Mark horse took charge himself. He swung away from those steers and leaped straight at the near fence and sailed over it. He swung in a short circle and stopped looking back at those steers jamming into the corner where we'd been and I sat the saddle catching the breath he'd jolted out of me. I should have known. He was a jumper. He was what people back east called a hunter. Maybe he'd been a timber horse, a steeplechaser. He'd cleared that four-foot fence with just about no take-off space like a kid skipping at hopscotch. I'm telling you, mister, I had me a time the next days jumping him over everything in sight. When I was sure of my seat I made him show me what he really could do and he played along with me for anything within reason, even stretching that reason considerable. The day I had nerve enough and he took me smack over an empty wagon I really began to strut. But there was one thing he wouldn't do. He wouldn't keep jumping the same thing over and over the same time out. Didn't see any sense in that. He'd clear whatever it was maybe twice, maybe three times, and if I tried to put him at it again he'd stop cold and swing his head to look at me and I'd shrivel down to size and feel ashamed . . .

So I had something new in these parts then, a jumping horse bred to it and built for it with the big frame to take the jolts and the power to do it right. I had me a horse could bring me some real money at the rodeos. I wouldn't have to try for prize money. I could put on exhibition stunts. I got together with some of the old show hands and we worked up an act that pleased the crowds. They'd lead Mark out so the people could see the size of him and he'd plunge around at the end of the shank, rolling his eyes and tossing his head. He'd paw at the sky and lash out behind like he was the worst mean-tempered man killer ever caught. It was all a joke because he was the safest horse any man ever handled and anyone who watched close could see those hooves never came near connecting with anything except air. But he knew what it was all about and he made it look good. The wranglers would get him over and into the outlaw chute with him pretending to fight all the way. They'd move around careful outside and reach through the bars to bridle and saddle him like they were scared green of him. I'd climb to the top rails and ease down on the saddle like I was scared too but determined to break my neck trying to ride a terror of a bucking brute. We'd burst out of the chute like a cannon going off and streak straight for the high fence on the opposite side of the arena. All the people who'd not seen it before would come up gasping on their seats expecting a collision that would shake the whole place. And at the last second that horse Mark would rise up and over the fence in a clean sweet jump and I'd be standing in the stirrups waving my hat and yelling and the crowd'd go wild.

After a time most people knew what to expect and the surprise part of that act was gone so we had to drop it. But we worked up another that got the crowds no matter how many times they saw it. I never liked it much but I blew too hard once how that horse would jump anything and someone suggested this and I was hot and said sure he'd do it and I was stuck with it. He never liked it much either but he did it for me. Maybe he knew I was getting expensive habits and needed the money coming in. Well, anyway, we did it and it took a lot of careful practice with a slow old steer before we tried the real thing. I'd be loafing around on Mark in the arena while the bull riding was on. I'd watch and pick a time when one of the bulls had thrown his rider and was hopping around in the clear or making a dash across the open. I'd nudge Mark with my heels and he'd be off in that forward flowing with full power in it. We'd streak for the bull angling in at the side and the last sliced second before a head-on smash we'd lift and go over in a clean sweep and swing to come up by the grandstand and take the applause.

Thinking of that since I've been plenty shamed. I've a notion the reason people kept wanting to see it wasn't just to watch a mighty good horse do a mighty difficult job. They were always hoping something would happen. Always a chance the bull might swerve and throw us off stride and make it a real smash. Always a chance the horns might toss too high and we'd tangle with them and come down in a messy scramble. But I didn't think about that then or how I was asking more than a man should expect in a tight spot that can't be avoided from a horse that's always played square with him. I was thinking of the money and the cheers and the pats on the back. And then it happened . . .

Not what maybe you're thinking, mister. Not that at all. That horse never failed in a jump and never would. We'd done our stint on the day, done it neat and clean, gone over a big head-tossing bull with space to spare and were just about ready to take the exit gate without bothering to open it. Another bull was in the arena, a mean tricky one that'd just thrown his rider after a tussle and was scattering dust real mad. The two tenders on their cagey little cow ponies had cut in to let the rider scramble to safety and were trying to hustle the bull into the closing out pen. They thought they had him going in and were starting to relax in their saddles when that brute broke away and tore out into the open again looking for someone on foot to take apart. While the tenders were still wheeling to go after him he saw something over by the side fence and headed toward it fast. I saw too and sudden I was cold all over. Some damn fool woman had let a little boy get away from her, maybe three-four years old, too young to have sense, and that kid had crawled through the rails and was twenty-some feet out in the arena. I heard people screaming at him and saw him standing there confused and the bull moving and the tenders too far away. I slammed my heels into Mark and we were moving too the way only that horse could move. I had to lunge forward along his neck or he'd have been right out from under me. There wasn't time to head the bull or try to pick up the kid. There wasn't time for anything fancy at all. There was only one thing could be done. We swept in angling straight to the big moving target of that bull and I slammed down on the reins with all my strength so Mark couldn't get his head up to jump and go over, and in the last split second all I could think of was my leg maybe getting caught between when they hit and I dove off Mark sidewise into the dust and he drove on alone and smashed into that bull just back of the big sweeping horns.

They picked me up half dazed with an aching head and assorted bruises and put me on some straw bales in the stable till a doctor could look me over. They led Mark into one of the stalls with a big gash from one of the horns along his side and a swelling shoulder so painful he dragged the leg without trying to step on it. They put ropes on the bull where he lay quiet with the fight knocked out of him and prodded him up and led him off. I never did know just what happened to the kid except that he was safe enough. I didn't care because when I pushed up off those bales without waiting for the doctor and went into the stall that Mark horse wouldn't look at me . . .

So that's it, mister. That's what happened. But I won't have you getting any wrong notions about it. I won't have you telling me the way some people do that horse is through with me because I made him smash into that bull. Nothing like that at all. He doesn't blame me for the pulled tendon in his shoulder that'll bother him long as he lives when the weather's bad. Not that horse. I've thought the whole business over again and again. I can remember every last detail of those hurrying seconds in the arena, things I wasn't even aware of at the time itself. That horse was flowing forward before I slammed my heels into him. There wasn't any attempt at lifting that big head or any gathering of those big muscles under me for a jump when I was slamming down on the reins. He'd seen. He knew. He knew what had to be done. That horse is through with me because at the last second I went yellow and I let him do it alone. He thinks I didn't measure up in the partnership. I pulled out and let him do it alone.

He'll let me ride him even now but I've quit that because it isn't the same. Even when he's really moving and the weather's warm and the shoulder feels good and he's reaching for distance and notching it up in the straight joy of eating the wind he's doing that alone too. I'm just something he carries on his back and he won't look at me . . .

My Town

Ask pardon, gents, but heard you talking. Seems a strange boasting. About cemeteries. The boothill brand. Now in my town . . .

Me? Nobody much. Just a lonesome passing through, plain and peaceable. Always get to wondering when talk swings around to towns and how many folks in each catch lead poisoning awearing their outdoor boots. Always wonder why burying's cause for boasting. About a town's toughness that is. Seems silly. Take my town now. Not much of a place. But the toughest town its size this side the devil's fireplace. More shooting there than in all your towns together. But no folks being planted. All enjoying life too much . . .

One man's responsible. No. Two. Two men. Have to divvy it between them but one's a mite more responsible than the other. That one's Samuel J. L. Claggett. Our sheriff. Sandburr we call him. Sandburr Sam Claggett. Started calling him that a time back because when he goes after a man he sticks to the trail like a sandburr to a mule's tail. Come to think of it he hasn't done much trailing for quite a stretch now. No need to. Folks in my town behave. Behave sensible that is. No one wants Old Sandburr sticking to his trail. Now a man like that can do things with a six-gun you wouldn't believe not having seen him do them. He's long and he's lean and kind of double-jointed all over and he's about the gentlest and kindliest man you'd bump into in a month's riding. And the toughest.

Maybe not quite that last. Wilbur Morriston Burton is plenty tough too. He's the other man. Black Ace he's called. Black Ace Burton. Can see you've heard of him. Most folks have. Maybe don't know the Wilbur Morriston part but when they hear the Black Ace they tumble. Probably wonder why tales about him aren't running anymore. That's because he's living in my town, plain and peaceable like the rest of us. Used to be about the fastest gunfighter ever to hit these territories. Still is. Fast as Old Sandburr himself. Still doing plenty shooting. But not the kind you'd hear about . . .

Yep. All this starts the day Black Ace rides into town. He rides in, big and brawny on his horse with that black stubble scratching around his chin, and looks the place over and doesn't think much of it. He meanders into Willie Lord's saloon and soaks up a few. Reaches in his pocket where he carries his silver and the pocket's empty. Bottom frayed out. Cusses some and tells Willie wait a minute he'll go get some cash. Willie's heard the cussing and seen the two big guns hanging down his flanks so Willie says forget it, the drinks are on the house. No, Black Ace says, he's not particular about some kind of debts but a drinking debt is one he always honors. He meanders out and looks the place over again and meanders into the little frame bank building. Tells the clerk there he needs some cash and his name being Black Ace he figures he won't have much trouble getting it. The clerk hears the name and looks around wild and sees there's no one else handy and drops quiet in a faint on the floor. Black Ace is a mite peeved at having to go around behind into the wire cage himself but does so and scoops up what he wants. Meanders back to the saloon and pays Willie and out to his horse and rides on. It's maybe twenty minutes later the clerk has come to and run to the sheriff's office and waked Sandburr Sam out of his early afternoon nap and Sandburr has strapped on his own guns and hit the trail.

Black Ace is easing along casual when he sees Sandburr's dust back along a loop. Hell, he tells himself, being as there's only one of them the only way he can have fun out of this is make it a race. He larrups his horse and skitters off into the hills and Old Sandburr, catching the scent, swings his quirt and skitters after him. They have themselves a time for maybe two hours, tearing up the landscape, working deep into the hills, where the big rocks climb, playing hide-and-seek all over the rough ground. So busy skittering around they don't know they're not the only two-legged critters in the neighborhood. Black Ace can't shake Sandburr and finally gets tired chasing around. Enough's enough, he tells himself. Too bad having to knock over a man can stick after him like that but he can't play games all day. Picks a spot and drops off his horse and waits where he figures Old Sandburr'll have to come at him straight and it'll be a square scuffle. But Sandburr's an old hand at this kind of business too. He's stopping now and again to listen. Notes the other horse has quit running so he drops off his horse and slips in among the boulders on foot. Moves so quiet Black Ace can't hear him and Black Ace gets restless and slips in among the boulders himself. Same thing. He moves so quiet Old Sandburr can't hear him. Hard to believe, but those two are so eternal damned good at slipping around quiet they spend maybe half an hour in and around those boulders without once tagging each other. Both get to thinking the same. That the other's gone.

Both holster their guns and start back where they left their horses. Sandburr's up higher among the boulders and tries to short cut over a big one and skids and comes coasting on his rump and bounces and lands flat on his back not ten feet behind Black Ace, who whirls quick and there are two mighty surprised men astaring at each other in a hollow among those boulders. Old Sandburr is stretched out spread-eagle looking along his own length and over his boot toes at Black Ace and Black Ace is looking down over those same boot toes at Sandburr's lean old face. They're caught like that for a second of surprise and in another tiny tick of time those two, maybe the fastest gunfighters ever slapped leather, might be blazing at each other but in that same second there's a wapping sound and an arrow bounces off a boulder close to Black Ace and lots of whoops whistle in the air and more arrows are wapping around and in a flash of movement that's a dead heat for them those two maybe the fastest gunfighters ever wore boots are showing their skill in another kind of action. They're side by side behind boulders and they're talking back to the arrows in a right hearty gunshot tune.

It isn't really a fair fight. There's only twenty-three of the redskins. Could be why Old Sandburr and Black Ace never talk much about that scuffle. Doesn't take them long. There's a moment when a redskin pokes up quick way over to the right and Sandburr sights him out the corner of his right eye and flicks his right-hand gun around without seeming to aim and that redskin rubs a dead nose in the dirt "Nice," Black Ace says. "Very nice." There's another moment when another redskin behind a rock gets careless and lets a foot show a fraction of a second and Black Ace nicks it and that makes the redskin jump and his head bobs up about two inches over the rock and down again and has a hole in it when it goes down. "Pretty," Old Sandburr says. "Very pretty."

They're really beginning to enjoy themselves when the four redskins left alive fade off glad to go. Black Ace turns his guns up and blows the smoke out the barrels and looks at Sandburr and Sandburr does the same and looks at him and they both grin. But Black Ace's grin dwindles. "Disappointed," he says. "Saw you miss one. When he peeked around that flat rock there. Missed by two feet. Saw that other rock beside there chip where your bullet hit." Old Sandburr just chuckles. "Certain it chipped," he says. "Meant it to hit there. Had to bounce it off that second rock to get it around behind the first one and drill him where it'd count." Black Ace grunts. "No," he says. "I'm the only man can pull a stunt like that. Maybe you tried but your angle was wrong." Old Sandburr chuckles again. "Wrong from where you're standing," he says. "Not from here. There's a dead redskin behind that rock. Shot through the left side about over the fourth rib."

He leads the way over and he's right even to the rib and Black Ace looks at him long. "So there's two of us," Black Ace says. "Too bad I've got to kill you." And Old Sandburr just chuckles again. "Try to, you mean," he says. "But that reminds me. How were we when this little interruption interrupted?" Black Ace is reloading his guns. "You were patting the ground with your backside," he says. "Well, how'll we do this? Pace it off and arrange a signal?" Old Sandburr is reloading his guns too. "No," he says. "Maybe I'm old-fashioned but want things like this done right. Get over where you were when I landed." Black Ace is puzzled but does as he's told. Sandburr finds his own spot and lays down flat on his back and spraddles out his arms. "This the way I was?" he says and Black Ace nods. "All right," Sandburr says. "See that bird on that bush? When he pops off that branch we'll both start fanning."

Black Ace isn't anywhere near grinning now. "You mean," he says, "you're agoing to lie there and give me the advantage?" Old

Sandburr isn't near grinning either. "Certain I do," he snaps. "This is the way I was." Black Ace is beginning to sweat some though the weather's cool. "Maybe you don't know," he says. "I'm Black Ace Burton." Sandburr just shrugs his shoulders there on the ground and Black Ace sweats more. "You've heard of me haven't you?" he says almost plaintive. "Certain I have," Sandburr snaps. "Don't care if you're Old Nick himself." Sweat is standing out plain on Black Ace's forehead. "But I'll drill you," he says. "You won't have a chance scrabbling against the dirt." Old Sandburr shrugs again. "Maybe I won't," he says. "Again maybe I might. I'm right pert with a gun too. But if I go I'll go right. Keep your eye on that bird. It's getting restless."

Yep. There they are, Sandburr flat on his back and Black Ace standing facing him and the bird is twiddling its feathers like it might take off any time and sweat runs down Black Ace's face and he groans and sudden he reaches both hands high up over his head. "Can't do it!" he shouts. "You confounded old he-buzzard! Can't kill you! Not like that!" Old Sandburr pushes up till he is leaning on one elbow. "Son," he says, "are you surrendering to me?" Black Ace looks surprised and then thoughtful. "Reckon I am," he says. "Can't see any other way out of this, you being so damn stubborn." It's Sandburr's turn to look thoughtful. "Can't take you in," he says. "Can't lock up a man won't draw because he thinks it ain't square. Let's mosey to town and you hand back the money and we'll call it quits." Black Ace lowers his hands and hooks them in his belt. "No," he says. "Used part for a drinking debt. Need the rest for more the same till I get me another stake. Got it on the strength of my name, and not giving it up." Old Sandburr snorts. "Who's being stubborn now?" he says. Gets to his feet and scratches an ear. "Only one way out of that. You sign a note for the money and that's still using the strength of your name only a bit different way and maybe the same because you being you the bank won't dare refuse it. I'll put you on the payroll as a deputy till you've squared it off." Black Ace's jaw drops. "Me?" he says. "Me be a sheriff's man?" Sandburr snorts again. "Certain. It ain't so bad. Another thing. You'll promise me not to use those guns on any man 'less I give the word. Just till this is squared of course." Black Ace snaps his jaw tight. "No," he says. "Now you're on your feet let's shoot this out fair." But Old Sandburr flops quick again down on his back. "Shoot it," he says. "But it's got to be this way." There they are, Sandburr down and staring up and Black Ace up and staring down, and sweat starts again on Black Ace's forehead and he can't see any other way out, not with him being what he is and this old he-buzzard what he is too. "All right," Black Ace Burton says and the words are bitter on his tongue and his face is long and disgusted under the black stubble all the while he and Sandburr find their horses and start toward town.

They jog along and Sandburr notes that disgusted look and worries over it and after a time has an idea. He swoops down one side his saddle and picks up a plump little pebble. He holds the pebble so Black Ace can see it and tosses it in the air ahead. Black Ace watches it rise in an arc and start to fall and sudden gets the notion. There's a blur of movement maybe an eagle might catch but nothing else could, and a gun is in his right hand and it blasts and that pebble goes spinning crazy before it hits the ground. Black Ace drops the gun back in its holster and looks at Sandburr and Old Sandburr looks at him and they both begin to grin and they both hop off their horses and gather a handful of pebbles each and mount. Whenever Black Ace thinks Sandburr may be off guard he tosses out a pebble and Sandburr gives that funny little wriggle of his and a gun seems to come out of the air into his hand and the pebble takes a beating. The same happens whenever Sandburr tosses a pebble and the two of them jog along enjoying themselves. First time either one has come on a man good as himself and they get to showing off like a pair of colts. Black Ace gets tricky and whams a pebble twice before it hits ground and whams it again there before it stops rolling and Old Sandburr lifts his eyebrows and worries a moment. Then he smiles and holds up two fingers and when Black Ace tosses two pebbles at once Old Sandburr drops his reins and wriggles and both his guns show and he hits both pebbles simultaneous. They jog along, grinning foolish at each other, and by time they reach town each one knows he's found a man he'd stand back to back with against the whole eternal damned world . . .

Yep. That's the way it starts. Black Ace fits into town in no time to bother over. Rest of us are a mite upset at first having him around but get over that. Find he's a quiet soft-spoken gent a lot like Old Sandburr long as nobody rubs him the wrong way. Only thing that shows the toughness inside is that black stubble around his chin. Doesn't shave it because can't shave it. Razors nick too fast working at it. Can't keep it trimmed close even with scissors. Carries a small pair of wire cutters and uses them once a week. Sunday mornings.

   With him there as deputy folks behave even better'n before. Town's quiet except for an hour each afternoon right after Old Sandburr's nap. He'll come out his office and look up Black Ace and the two'll go into the big old barn standing empty behind Willie Lord's and close the doors and for about an even sixty minutes there'll be queer noises and bursts of shooting coming out the place. Then the two'll walk out, grinning foolish at each other, and their holsters'll have a scorched look from having hot guns dropped back in them. Things drift like that till the day this smoke-eating young gun toter hits town.

He's built like a young bull and has his hair cropped close over a hard hatless head and he wears two big guns low down along his flanks with the holster tips tied tight. Everything about him speaks toughness till you study him some and see he's younger than he seems and he's worked long to get that tough look and it ain't full natural yet. He's a maverick hankers to be a gunfighter and wants to get a reputation quick by knocking off somebody with a big name. That's plain soon as he struts into Willie Lord's and starts talking. "Hear Black Ace Burton's hanging around here," he says to Willie. "That right?" Willie nods and points where Black Ace is sitting at a table dealing himself poker hands that always somehow give him the ace of spades. This young maverick squints his eyes at Black Ace and snorts and turns to the four-five rest of us there. "Name's Poison Pete," he says. "Poison Pete Humphrey. My folks gave me the Pete but gave myself the Poison. Know why? Because I'm poison to any galoot whose face I don't like and I'll be cursed if I see anything to like about that black-whiskered baboon over there likely cheating himself with those cards."

Black Ace looks up, takes in this Poison Pete, looks back at his cards. "You hear me?" says Poison Pete throwing his words direct at Black Ace. "That face of yours makes my trigger finger itchy." Black Ace looks up again, breathes hard, gets a hold on himself. "Don't like it myself," he says mild. "But do the best I can with it." Poison Pete feels he has the edge and starts crowding. "Bet even your mother couldn't stand that face. Probably took off in a hurry after one look." Black Ace crumples a card in his hand then catches himself and straightens it out careful. "Matter of fact," he says, "she did." Poison Pete is pushing in hard now. "Bet she mixed with a lot of men to produce a scrambled-up phiz like that. Bet you don't even know who your father was." Black Ace stacks the whole deck together and rips it across in half and sets the torn deck on the table. "Matter of fact," he says still mild, "you're right. But never worry who my father was. Just worry who I am myself." Poison Pete throws about for what to try next. "Those guns you're awearing," he says. "Bet just for show. Bet you don't even know which end a bullet comes out."

Black Ace stiffens and stands up. He's had himself and his folks mean-talked. He's taken that. But this young maverick has talked low about his guns and that's one thing he can't take. He stalks to the swinging doors and pushes them wide. "Sandburr!" he bellows. "Sandburr you he-buzzard! Get along down here fast!" And up the street in the sheriff's office Old Sandburr stirs out of his early afternoon nap and has his guns buckled on before he's blinked the sleep out his eyes and starts dogtrotting toward the saloon. He comes in puffing and there's this Poison Pete strutting by the bar thinking he's made Black Ace Burton crawl and there's Black Ace standing by the door chewing a knuckle. "Sandburr," says Black Ace, "ain't asked you a favor yet. Asking one now. Let me off that promise just a little part one second so's I can eliminate this young nuisance that's been braying around here like an ornery jackass." Old Sandburr looks at this Poison Pete who's thinking sudden maybe now he'll have a shooting scuffle after all and is dropping into a kind of crouch with his head thrust forward and his arms out in half-circles with the hands clawed ready by his gun handles. Sandburr shakes his head like he can't quite believe what he sees and Black Ace speaks up again. "Sandburr," he says, "this jackass has been prodding me something fierce. Look at him. Ever see a self-respecting gunfighter take a position like that?" And then Black Ace says what maybe he's never said to another man. "Please," he says. "Please, Sandburr, let me kill him. Cart the carcass away myself so you won't have to bother any." And Old

Sandburr looks at Poison Pete and something tickles around in his mind and he soars up somewhere to the heights of pure genius.

Yep. That's when our Sandburr does it. He prowls forward and pads soft in a circle around this Poison Pete, looking at him from every side. "Think you're good with those guns, eh?" he says and Poison Pete snarls in his throat and tries to look tougher and glares around. "All right," Sandburr says, "we'll give you a chance to prove it. Come along outside." He heads straight for the door and tips a wink at Black Ace and Black Ace begins to get him and swings to follow. Poison Pete paws the floor some and snarls in his throat again but there's nothing for him to do but follow too, which he does muttering how he'll take them both on and fill them so full of lead it'll take three men to lift them into coffins. No need to mention the rest of us follow too. Man ain't been born yet wouldn't.

Sandburr leads around back to that old barn and pushes the doors wide and then we're all inside. Not much in there. Pile of old boards and a couple weird contraptions and plenty of space. Sandburr picks the broadest board he can find and sets it upright at the other end of the barn. Takes a piece of chalk out a pocket and sketches quick on the board the outline of a man. Draws a little heart in the right place and comes to join the rest of us by the open doors. Poison Pete is looking disgusted but Black Ace is grinning. He has Old Sandburr complete now and is ready to play it the way he's likely the only man could. "Ain't much of an artist," he says. "Forgot to give that thing a face." He doesn't seem to more than shrug his shoulders a little but his guns are in his hands and both aroaring and sudden two holes for eyes and two close together for a nose and four in a line for a mouth appear on the board spaced just right in the chalk-line head. There's a gulp from Poison Pete but Old Sandburr just chuckles. "Too grim for my liking," he says.

He gives that little wriggle and his guns are in his hands and both blast once and two more holes appear just tipping the mouth on each end so it seems to turn up in a kind of grin. Poison Pete gulps again. But he's game and isn't going to be bluffed. He pulls a gun and he's fair fast but you can see him doing it and he blasts at the board and a hole shows in the middle of the figure there. "Belly button," he says. But Black Ace just shakes his head sorrowful. "Ain't polite," he says, "to make that chalk fellow naked like that. Reckon he needs clothes." Out of somewhere one of Black Ace's guns, reloaded, is in his right hand and his left hand fans the hammer so fast the six shots are one long blast and across the middle of the figure where the belly button was appears a line of holes making a belt.

Poison Pete seems to shrink some. He's forgetting to work at being big and tough. He chews a lip and shakes himself back to size. "If you're through playing games," he snarls, "let's get—" But Old Sandburr has fixed him with a cold eye. "Boy," Sandburr says, "me and Black Ace has a regular date each day about this time to amuse ourselves here. You'll wait and if you're still of a mind then reckon I'll have to let Black Ace take care of you." He beckons to Black Ace and the two of them take a stand with their backs to that board figure the length of the barn away. "Willie," Sandburr says, "when you feel the urge call 'shoot.'" Willie Lord bugs his eyes and sudden starts to say "shoot" and gets out the "shoo" part but hasn't finished forming the "oot" part before Old Sandburr and Black Ace have whirled and each has a gun in a hand and those guns have blasted and a hole shows dead center in that chalk heart, and if you peer sharp you can see it's a bit bigger than one bullet would make.

"Yippee!" yells Old Sandburr. "That one's aready for burying! Acey son, I've thought up a new one. Can you follow me on this?"

His other gun's popped into his other hand and both start blasting and holes appear in the lower left corner of the board forming
a neat letter R. Black Ace scratches his head with the barrel of the
gun in his right hand and looks puzzled. Then a grin spreads
through his black stubble and his other gun pops into his other
hand and both start blasting and a neat letter E shows next to the
R. Then the two of them are at it, reloading and firing in rapid
succession and alternating on the letters. In maybe a minute
they've spelled it out: REST IN PEACE. And then the two of them
really cut loose.

No sense telling all they do. Nobody'd believe didn't see it.
They do things like setting up a couple small boards with nails
started in them and racing each other driving those nails clear in.
They do things like fastening calendar sheets on the wall and taking turns with one calling out numbers in crazy order and the
other shooting out those numbers as called. They do things like
setting up a grooved plank on a slant with a nest of pool balls in a
box at the top with a little catch door on the box with a string tied
to it so each time the string's pulled a ball pops out and rolls quick
down the groove. Idea is for one to take the string and yank it
whenever he has a mind and the other stands there guns holstered
and the instant a ball shows tries to draw and smack it before it
reaches the floor. Old Sandburr knocks his balls off one after the
other and not a one gets past the three-foot mark down the groove.
Black Ace takes his stand and grins a bit devilish. "Aiming for a
record," he says and be eternal damned if he don't knock all but his
last ball off ahead of the two-foot mark and that last one, which
he misses, just knicking it a slice, he smacks with another bullet at
about the three-and-a-half-foot mark and is just peeved enough to
keep it popping all over the barn floor till he's emptied both guns.

They do things like that and others a man wouldn't dare tell less he be named a liar till their gun barrels glow red and you can smell the scorched leather of their holsters and finally Old Sandburr calls enough. He sort of shakes himself back into realizing the rest of us are still there. Poison Pete is leaning limp against a support post. All the poison's long since oozed out of him. Now he isn't trying to look and be tough. He's a likable young galoot who has been shook so far down inside him he can't stand alone. Old Sandburr fixes him with a cold eye. "Seem to recall," he says, "some unfinished business was worrying you some."

Poison Pete pushes out from his post and fights with himself till he can stand without wobbling. He stares at Old Sandburr and he stares at Black Ace and at last he gets his hanging lower jaw under control so he can close his mouth. Yep. Poison Pete makes his play then and it's a good one. He pulls out his guns slow and easy so no one can mistake what he's doing and he looks down at his hands and the guns in them and he shakes his head and bends and lays the guns on the floor and straightens and walks over till he's in front of Black Ace. "Mr. Black Ace," he says, "I know when I'm beat, and not just in shooting. Can't call that face of yours handsome but ready to admit things about it are mighty impressive. Now I've said my sorries and I'm ready to do anything you say might square my foolishness."

Black Ace looks at him and scratches at his stubble and right then Black Ace does some soaring of his own. Looks over at Old Sandburr and grins at what he's remembering and turns back to Poison Pete. "Son," he says, "there is something you can do. You can sign on as deputy with me and Sandburr here." Poison Pete jumps back a step. "Me?" he says. "Me be a sheriff's man?" Black Ace just grins. "It ain't so bad," he says. "Another thing. You'll promise me not to use those guns of yours on any man 'less I say you can." Poison Pete twists his mouth like he's tasting bitter and throws his mind at this proposition and can't see any way out because he's give his word. He gulps and nods his head and his face is long and disgusted. But Old Sandburr and Black Ace note that disgusted look and close in on him. Sandburr is on one side. "You'll do plenty shooting, son," he's saying. "You've got the makings. Just a kink or two in that draw of yours. Take them out easy. Just tuck your elbows in and glide up smooth and curl your—" And Black Ace is on the other side. "Only thing wrong with your aiming," he's saying, "is your hand's too tense. Hold firm without squeezing on the butt and flip your barrel like it was—" And Poison Pete is bouncing his head from one to the other, young and eager and with a new kind of pride sprouting in him . . .

That's my town. That's all you need know about it. Because it's only a few weeks and Poison Pete is living there like the rest of us, plain and peaceable, and giving Old Sandburr and Black Ace a run for their money in that empty barn. Might say he leaves the student class and graduates the day he shows those two a stunt he's worked up all himself. Does it with empty whiskey bottles. Sets them on their sides on a rack he's made with the necks pointing toward him. Backs off. Gives a little combination wriggle and shrug that's his own brand now and a gun's in his hand and he works swift down the line of bottles sending his bullets right through the open necks without nicking the glass and blowing out the bottoms of the bottles behind. Sandburr looks at Black Ace and Black Ace looks at Sandburr and both lift their eyebrows and both grin so foolish you'd think they'd done it themselves. And that's the way things are going till the day this big-jawed rustler with red hair hits town.

He's tired and dusty and full of meanness because he's had a hard three days shaking a posse down southwest somewhere. Too many of them for him to shoot it out so he had to scat and that's made him edgy and looking for a scuffle to give him a feeling of being back to size again. Climbs off his horse and loosens the two big guns in the low-cut holsters he wears kind of high on his hips which is his style. Stalks into Willie Lord's and rakes his throat with straight stuff and looks around for a likely. Misses Black Ace and Old Sandburr playing casino at a side table. Sees Poison Pete inspecting pictures of tooled-leather boots in a mail order catalogue at the other end of the bar. Spots Pete's two guns and licks his lips. "Sonny boy," he says, "that's a lot of fancy hardware you're packing." Pete looks at him peeved at the sonny-boy business, catches himself, grins pleasant. "Not so fancy," he says. "Just plain ordinary everyday sort of guns." This rustler sticks his big jaw out. "Rawhide Red, that's me," he says. "Tough as rawhide with a liking to see red blood running. Where I come from we don't let little boys run around wearing guns like that." Pete holds tight to his temper. "Good notion," he says. "They might get hurt." This rustler ain't tired anymore. He's scenting what he wants. "Right," he says. "So if they don't show they can use them, we pop our little boys over our knees and paddle their cute little backsides." He pushes out his jaw till it's jutting like a rock ledge. So busy thinking Pete's quietness means he's scared he doesn't notice the sound of a couple of chairs scraping the floor. Is some surprised when a long lean kind of double-jointed man and a brawny black-stubbled other one prowl up and pad around him in circles looking at him from all sides. "Think you're good with those guns, eh?" says Black Ace Burton. "We'll just give you a chance to prove it," says Old Sandburr Sam Claggett. "Come along outside. You too, Petey son. While you're at it bring along some empty whiskey bottles . . ."

Yep. That's my town.

Harvey Kendall

My father had two pair of boots. He had a pair of shoes too but he wore those only when my mother made him, to church on Sundays and to funerals and the like. The boots were what you'd call his regular footwear. One pair was plain, just rough and ready old-style cowboy boots, nearly knee high, made of stiff cowhide with canvas pulling-straps we used to call mule ears that dangled and flapped on the outside when he walked along. He wore those at work on weekdays. He was cattle inspector at the local stockyards, where the ranchers for quite a stretch around brought their stuff to be checked and weighed before being shipped out. He'd pull out of bed in the morning and pad around the house in his socks, or when Mother got after him, in the slippers she'd bought for him, until after breakfast and then he'd squat on the edge of a chair and heave and yank at those boots till they were on and tuck his work pants down inside the tops and stand up and stretch and say, "Another day, another dollar," which was sort of silly because he earned more than a dollar a day, and out the door he'd go with those mule ears flapping.

We lived a short ways out of town and sometimes he'd walk in those boots down to where the stockyards spread out beside and behind the station about a half-mile away, and sometimes he'd saddle his old cow pony and ride down and maybe during the day circulate some through the pens helping the handlers move the stuff around, which he didn't need to do because he wasn't paid for that. "Can't let this Mark horse get too lazy and fat," he used to say but that was only an excuse. The truth was he plain liked the feel of that horse under him now and again and the tickle of dust rising up in a man's nose saddle high and the fun of shooing a few steers through some tricky gates. It reminded him of the old days when he was a free-roaming cowhand with a saddle roll for a home before my mother herded him into the same corral with a preacher and tied him down to family responsibilities.

Those cowhide boots were just everyday knockabout working boots. The others were something else again. They didn't reach quite as far up the legs but they had high narrow heels that curved under in back with a real swoop and they were made of soft calfskin that fitted like a glove over the feet and ankles and then opened out some to take care of the pants if those were folded over neat and tucked in careful. The tops were curved up on the sides with little leather pulling-straps that stayed out of sight inside and those tops were made of separate pieces of the calfskin darker brown in color than the bottoms and they had a clever design of a rope loop stitched into them. He wore those boots on Sundays after he came home from church and on special occasions like meetings of the stockmen's association and when he was riding old Mark near the front in the annual Fourth of July parade. They reminded him of the best part of the old days, the times he was representing whatever range outfit he was with that season in the early rodeos and showing the other cowhands from the whole country roundabout what a man could do with a good horse and a good rope.

When he wore those calfskin boots my father always wore the belt that went with them. It was made of calfskin too and it was so wide my mother had to fix new belt straps on every pair of new pants she bought for him. It had a big solid slide-through silver buckle that had three lines of printing engraved in the metal. The first line said "First Honors" and the second line said the one word "Roping" and the third line said "Cheyenne 1893." That belt and that buckle, tight around his waist above those calfskin boots, reminded him of the best thing of all about the old days, the time he set a record busting and hog-tying a steer, a record that stood seven years before anyone beat it and then it was beat only because they shortened the run some and changed the rules a bit and fast work was really easier to do.

Anyone knows anything about kids knows which pair of those boots I liked. Cleaning and polishing both pairs with good saddle soap to keep the leather in right condition was one of my regular chores every Sunday morning before church. I'd get out the soap and a moist rag and if my father wasn't around watching I'd give those old cowskin boots a lick and a promise and then I'd really go to work on those calfskins even though they didn't need much, not being worn often. Sometimes I wouldn't do more than just run the rag quick over the old cowskins and figure my father wouldn't notice I'd let them go because that old leather was rough and stiff all the time anyway and then like as not I'd be enjoying myself on the calfskins and sudden I'd look up and there my father would be watching me with his eyebrows pulled down till they about met over his nose. "Gee-rusalem, boy," he'd say. "One of these days you'll rub those boots clean through. It's the others need the limbering so my feet don't ache in them. Get busy on them now afore I sideswipe you one."

Mention of sideswiping points to maybe one reason I didn't like working on those old cowskins. Whenever I'd done something wrong, broke one of the rules my folks made for me or messed up some chore when I should've known better, my father would come after me from behind and hop on his left foot and turn his right foot toe outward and swing his right leg so that the side of his foot swiped me hard and hurting on my rump. He'd sideswipe me a good one or two or three according to how bad it was that I'd done and until I began to get some size there were times he raised me smack off the ground. Just about every time he did that he had those old cowskins on. But likely that didn't have too much to do with my feeling about them. I never was mad after a thumping or went around being sulky. My father sideswiped me only when I had it coming and he'd do it quick and thorough and tell me why, and then to show it was over and done and he was ready to forget about it he'd tell me to stick close around after supper and we'd saddle old Mark and he'd let me sit the saddle and get in some practice throws roping a fence post before dark.

The truth was I didn't like working on those old cowskins because they were tough and hard to do anything with and old-fashioned and pretty well battered and they didn't mean a thing to me. Working on those others, those fine-looking calf-skins, meant plenty. I'd rub away on that soft dark-shining leather and talk proud to myself inside. Not many boys had a father who had been a roping champion and in country where roping was real business and a man had to be good at it just to hold an ordinary ranch job. Not another boy anywhere had a father who had made a roping record that stood seven years and might still be standing if changes hadn't been made. I could work on that leather and see in my mind what I never saw with my eyes because all that was over and finished before I was born, my father on old Mark, young then, firm and straight in the saddle with the rope a living thing in his hands, my father and young Mark, working together, busting the meanest toughest trickiest steer with the hard-and-fast method he always said was the best. I could see every move, as he had told them to me over and over, young Mark reaching eager for speed to overtake the steer and knowing what to do every second without a word or a touch on the reins and my father riding easy and relaxed with the loop forming under his right hand and the loop going forward and opening and dropping over the wide horns and Mark slowing as my father took up the slack and pulled the loop tight and Mark speeding again to give him slack again enough so he could flip the rope over to the right side of the steer and then Mark swinging left in a burst of power and speed and the rope tightening along and down the steer's right side and pulling its head around in an outside arc and at the same time yanking its hind legs out from under it and making it flip in a complete side-winding somersault to lie with the wind knocked clean out of it and then all in the same motion Mark pivoting to face the steer and bracing to keep the rope taut and my father using that pivot-swing to lift and carry him right out of the saddle and land on his feet and run down the taut rope with his pigging string in his hand and wrap it quick around three of the steer's legs and draw it close and tie it and Mark watching and keeping the rope taut ready to yank and make that steer behave if it started causing trouble and then easing some slack at the right instant so my father could cast the loop loose and stand up to show the job was done and walk casual back to Mark without even looking at the steer again like he was saying in the very set of his head on his shoulders that's that and there's a steer hog-tied for branding or earmarking or anything anybody's a mind to do with it.

Well, what I'm telling about this time had a lot to do with those boots and that belt and my father and old Mark too but mostly my father. It began the night before the sort of combination fair and rodeo at our town that year. The committee running things had some extra money available and they'd telegraphed and persuaded Cal Bennett to agree to come for the price and they'd plastered the town with bills saying the topnotch champion roper of the big-town circuit would be on hand to give some fancy exhibitions and everybody'd been talking about that for days. We were finishing supper, my father and my mother and me, and I notched up nerve enough and finally I said it. "Father," I said, "can I wear your belt tomorrow? Just a little while anyway?"

My father settled back in his chair and looked at me. "What's on your mind, boy? Must be something special."

"I'm sick of it," I said. "I'm sick of all the other kids talking about that Cal Bennett all the time. There's a new kid too and I was trying to tell him about you setting a record once and he won't believe me."

My father kept on looking at me and his eyebrows pulled down together. "Won't believe you, eh?"

"That's it," I said. "If I was to be wearing that belt and let him see it then he'd know all right."

"Expect he would," my father said and he leaned back further in his chair, feeling good the way he usually did with a good meal inside him, and he said in a sort of half-joking voice, "Expect he would even more if I was to get out there tomorrow and swing a rope in the free-style steer busting and show everyone around here a thing or two."

That was when my mother started laughing. She laughed so she near choked on the last bite she was chewing and my father and I stared at her. "Gee-rusalem," my father said. "What's so blamed funny?"

My mother swallowed down the bite. "You are," she said. "Why it's eleven years since you did anything like that. You sitting there and getting to be middle-aged and getting thick around the middle and talking about going up against young fellows that are doing it all the time and could run circles around you nowadays."

"Oh, they could, could they?" my father said and his eyebrows were really together over his nose.

"That horse of yours too," my mother said and to her it was still just something to chuckle at. "He's the same. Getting old and fat and lazy. He couldn't even do it anymore."

"He couldn't, eh?" my father said. "I'll have you know being young and full of sass ain't so all-fired important as you seem to think. It's brains and know-how that count too and that's what that horse's got and that's what I've got and like riding a bicycle it's something you don't ever forget."

He was mighty serious and my mother realized that and was serious too. "Well, anyway," she said, "you're not going to try it and that's final."

"Gee-rusalem," my father said and he thumped a fist on the table so hard the dishes jumped. "Just like a woman. Giving orders. Tie a man down so he has to keep his nose to a grindstone getting the things they want and start giving orders the moment he even thinks a bit about maybe showing he still can do something."

"Harvey Kendall," my mother said, "you listen to me. I saw you near break your neck too many times in those shows before we were married. That's why I made you stop. I don't intend to have anything happen to you."

They were glaring at each other across the table and after a while my father sighed and looked down and began pushing at his coffee cup with one finger the way he always did when they'd been having an argument. "Expect you're right," he said and he sighed again and his voice was soft. "It was just an idea. No sense us flaring at each other over a little idea." He turned to me. "Wear the belt," he said. "All day if you've a mind to. If your feet were big enough you could wear the boots too."

In the morning my father didn't go to work because that day was a local holiday so we had a late breakfast and he sat around quiet like he was thinking things over in his mind the way he'd been all the evening before after supper. Then he pulled on the calfskin boots, looking a bit different in them without the belt on up above, and he went out and saddled old Mark and rode into town to help with the preparations there. I couldn't go along because just before he left he told me to stick close to my mother and watch out for her, which was a backhand style of putting it because she would really be watching out for me and that was just his usual little scheme to tie me to her so I wouldn't be roaming around and getting into any devilment. Soon as he was gone I got out the belt and put it on and it went around me almost twice but I could fix it so the buckle was in the middle in front as it should be and I stood on a chair to admire that part of myself in the little mirror my father used for shaving. I waited while my mother fussed with her good dress and the trimmings, doing the things women do to make themselves look what they call stylish, and then the two of us, my mother and me, walked the half-mile into town and the day's activities.

We stopped at all the exhibits and saw who had won the prizes for jams and jellies and raising vegetables and the like and we spent some time looking over the small pens where the prize-winning stock animals were. I stood on one foot and then the other and chewed molasses candy till my jaws were tired while my mother talked to women and then more women and I didn't get a chance to roam around much and show off that belt because she was watching out for me just about every minute. Three or four times we bumped into my father busy circulating all over the place as the cattle judge and one of the local greeters of out-of-town folks and he'd stop and talk to us some and hurry away. He was enjoying himself the way he always did at these affairs, joshing with all the men and tipping his hat to the women, and he was developing a sort of glow from a drink or two with the other greeters.

He joined us for a quick lunch at the hotel. He was feeling good again and he joked me over being about half hidden inside that belt and as soon as we were through eating he hustled us out and to the temporary grandstand along one side of the main stockyard pen so we all could have good seats for the rodeo doings. He picked a place in the third row where he always said you could see best and he sat in the middle with my mother on one side of him and me on the other and it wasn't till we had been there a little while and the two of them were talking hearty with other folks around that I had my chance to slip away by sliding through and under the grandstand and go find some of the other kids so I could strut and show off that belt. I went hunting them proud and happy as I'd ever been and I found them and in maybe five minutes I was running back under the grandstand as mad and near crying as I'd ever been too. I knew where to crawl up through by my father's boots and I did and he felt me squirming through against his legs because the stand was filled now and he took hold of me and pulled me up on the seat beside him. "Quiet now, boy," he said. "We wouldn't want your mother to know you've been slipping away like that." He swung his head to look at her on the other side and saw she was busy talking to a woman beyond and he swung back to me and saw my face. "Gee-rusalem, boy," he said. "What's eating at you?"

"Father," I said, "he doesn't believe it about you."

"Who doesn't believe it?" he said.

"That new kid," I said.

"Did you show him that belt?" my father said.

"Yes," I said. "But he just laughed. He said it's a fake. He said if it isn't you just found it somewhere or got it from some old pawnshop."

"Found it?" my father said. His eyebrows were starting to draw down together but the people all around were starting to buzz louder and things were beginning out in the big pen that was the arena for the day. "All right, boy," my father said. "We'll do something about that when this shindig's over. Maybe a good sideswipe'd do that kid some good. Be quiet now, the bronc riding's coming up." He didn't pay any more attention to me because he was busy paying attention to what was happening in the arena but not all his attention was out there because he kept fidgeting on the plank seat and every now and then he was muttering to himself and once he did it loud enough so I could hear. "Pawnshop," he said and kept on fidgeting around and didn't seem even to know he was doing that.

Plenty was happening out in the arena, the kind of things I always enjoyed and got excited about, but I wasn't in any mind to enjoy much that day and then sudden there was an extra flurry of activity and the main gates swung open and the people began to shout and cheer. A man came riding through the gateway on a beautiful big buckskin that was jouncing with each step like it had springs in its feet and you could tell right away the man was Cal Bennett. He was slim and tall and straight in the saddle and he was mighty young-looking and mighty capable-looking all at the same time. He had on boots just like my father's calfskins, maybe not exactly the same but so close to it there wasn't much difference, and a wide belt like the one I was wearing, and sitting there so easy on that jouncing saddle like he was glued to it he was about the best-looking figure of a man I ever saw. He had a coiled rope in his hand and he shook out a loop as he came forward and began spinning it and it grew bigger and bigger and sudden he flipped it up and over and it was spinning right around him and that buckskin and sudden he flipped it again and it was spinning big and wide in front of the horse and he gave a quick little wriggle with his heels and the horse jumped forward and he and that horse went right through the loop and it was spinning behind them and then the people really went wild. They shouted and clapped and stomped their feet. Cal Bennett let the loop fall slack on the ground and bowed all around and took off his big hat to the women and put it back on and coiled in his rope and rode over to the side of the arena where he'd wait for time to do his real roping stunts and still the people shouted and stomped. And my father sat there beside me and pulled up straight with his head high, looking around at the shouting people, and his face got tight and red and he shrank down till he was hunched low on the seat and he sat very still. He didn't fidget anymore or mutter to himself. He just sat still, staring out at the arena and things happened out there, and then the announcer was shouting through his megaphone that the free-style steer busting for the local championship was next and sudden my father turned and grabbed me by the arm. "Hey, boy," he said, "take off that belt."

I fumbled with it and got it off and handed it to him and he stood up right there on the grandstand and yanked off the ordinary belt he was wearing and began slipping that big belt through the special pants straps my mother had sewed for him. She saw him looming up there beside her and what he was doing and she was startled. "Harvey Kendall," she said, "just what do you think you're going to do?"

"You keep out of this," my father said and the way he said it would have made anybody shy away. He pulled the belt tight through the buckle and started down toward the arena, pushing through the people in the two rows ahead. He stepped to the ground and turned to look back at my mother. "Just keep your eyes on that arena," he said, "and you'll see something."

He squeezed through the fence rails into the arena and went straight to the little bunch of men who were acting as judges for the rodeo events. He was reaching in his money pocket as he went and he took out two dollar bills. "I'm in this one," he said to the men. "Here's my entry fee."

They all turned and stared at him. "Lookahere, Harve," one of them said. "You want to show us how you used to do it, that's fine. That's wonderful. We'll be proud to have you. But don't you go trying to do it racing against a stop watch."

"Shut up, Sam," my father said. "I know what I'm doing. You just take this money." He pushed the bills into the man's hand and swung away hurrying and by time the other entries were lined up he was back leading old Mark and with a good rope he'd borrowed somewhere in his hand. He took a place in the line and the judges put all the names on slips of paper in a hat and pulled them out one by one to get a running order and my father's name was one of the last. He stood there among those younger men and their young horses, quiet and waiting by old Mark, just running the rope through his hands to see it had no kinks and coiling it careful and exact, and all the while the excitement was building up in me, and my mother sat still and silent on the plank seat with her hands tight together in her lap.

One after another the others made their runs, flipping their steers and dashing in to hog-tie them, and they used a lot of different methods, some forefooting the steers and some going straight for the heads and quick pull-arounds, some risking long throws to save time and some playing it safer and chasing till they were close in, and some of them were good and some maybe better than just good but you could tell easy enough none of them were in the real champion class, and then it was my father's turn. He led old Mark out and walked around by old Mark's head and reached up a hand to scratch around the ears and he whispered something to that old horse nobody could hear and he came back around and swung up to the saddle. Seeing him there, straight and sturdy in the saddle, I couldn't hold it in any longer. I jumped standing right up on the seat. "Father!" I shouted. "Father! You show them! The whole bunch of them!" My mother pulled me down quick but she was just as excited because her hands trembled and out there in the arena my father didn't pay any attention to anything around him. He sat quiet on old Mark checking the rope again and a hush spread over the whole place and off to the side Cal Bennett reined his big buckskin around so he could watch close and sudden my father let out a whoop. "Turn that critter loose!" he yelled and the bars on the chute were yanked away and a big rangy steer rushed out into the arena and as it crossed the starting line the timer slammed down with his hat and old Mark was leaping forward. Not three jumps and there wasn't a person watching didn't know that old horse knew what he was doing and maybe he was a mite slower than the young cow ponies that'd been performing but he was right up there in the champion class with the know-how. The steer was tricky and started twisting right away and old Mark was after it like a hound on a hot scent, keeping just the right distance to the left of it and closing in steady. My father was riding high in the stirrups and a loop was forming under his right hand and while he was still a ways back the loop whipped forward fast like a snake striking and opened out over the steer's head and the steer twisted and the loop struck on one horn tip and fell over the other horn and pulled off.

"Gee-rusalem!" My father's voice roared out over that whole arena. "Stick with him, Mark!" And old Mark was hard on that steer's tail with every twist and turn and my father yanked in the rope and whipped out another loop and it settled smack over the horns and head and he pulled it tight and flipped the rope over to the steer's right side and old Mark swung left, head low and plowing into the sudden strain coming, and that steer spun like a cartwheel somersaulting as it spun and was down flat and old Mark pivoted to face the steer and keep the rope taut and my father tried to use that pivot swing to lift him out of the saddle and his foot caught on the cantle going over and he went sprawling on his face in the dust. He scrambled up and scrabbled in the dust for the pigging string and started down the taut rope trying to run too fast and stumbled and went down again. He came up this time puffing with his face dark red and ran on and just about threw himself on that steer. He grabbed at the legs and got the string around three of them and tied it quick and jumped to the steer's head and old Mark eased some on the rope and he loosened the loop and threw it off and straightened up. He didn't even turn to look at the timekeeper. He didn't look around at all. He just looked down at the ground and walked slow toward old Mark. And while he was walking there, slow and heavy-footed, the one thing that could rule him out even if he'd made good time and was the worst thing that could happen happened. The steer had some breath back now and was struggling and the knot had been tied in such a hurry that it slipped and the steer got its feet free and pushed up hot and mad and started after my father. Maybe it was the shouts that warned him or maybe it was old Mark shying back and snorting but anyway he turned and saw and dodged quick and began to run and the steer was right after him and sudden a rope came fast and low to the ground and the loop in it whipped up and around that steer's hind legs and tightened and the steer hit the ground again with a thump and at the other end of that rope were Cal Bennett and his big buckskin.

The people went wild again and they had a right to because that was about as fast and tricky a job of roping as they'd ever seen anytime and it wasn't just a show-off stunt, it was serious business, but my father didn't pay any attention to the shouting or even to Cal Bennett. He just stopped running and looked around once and started walking again toward old Mark, slow and heavy-footed with those calfskin boots all dusty. He reached and took hold of the reins and went right on walking and old Mark followed him and he remembered the rope dragging from the saddle horn and stopped and unfastened it and coiled it in and went on walking and old Mark followed and together they went to the outside gate and someone opened it enough for them to go through and he left the rope hanging on a gatepost and they went outside and along around the fence toward the road, the two of them alone together, my father walking like an old man and sweaty old Mark tagging with his head low. I felt plain ashamed of being me, of being a boy with a father who'd made a fool of himself like he had, and I wanted to crawl away somewhere and hide but I couldn't do that because my mother was standing up and telling me to come along and starting down out of the grandstand right in front of all those people. She had her head high and she looked like she was just daring anyone to say anything to her. She marched along in front of the grandstand and around the side toward the road and I had to follow, trying not to look at anybody. She hurried a little and came alongside my father and he kept staring at the ground ahead of him and didn't seem to notice but all the same he knew she was there because he put out a hand and she took hold of it and they walked on along the road toward our house like that, neither one of them saying a word.

It was sad-feeling and mournful around our place the rest of that afternoon. My father was as silent as if he'd forgotten how to speak. After he took care of Mark he came in the house and pulled off those calfskin boots and tossed them in the hall closet with the other pair and put on his slippers and went out and sat on the back steps. My mother was just as silent. She hustled around in the kitchen and it looked like she was baking things but for once I wasn't interested in that. I didn't want to be anywhere close to my father so I took the front steps and I sat there whittling some and chewing on my knuckles and being miserable. I was mad at what he'd done to me, made me feel ashamed and fixed it so the other kids would have something to torment me about and so that new kid never would believe it about him. "He ain't so much," I said to myself. "He's just an old has-been, that's all he is."

Then we had supper and we were all just as silent as before and Mother had fixed the things my father liked best, which was kind of a waste because he only picked at the food and didn't seem to be tasting it. But he perked some and at last he looked up at her and grinned a sick little grin and looked down and began pushing at his coffee cup. "I told you you'd see something in that arena," he said. "Well, you did."

"Yes," my mother said. "I did." She hesitated a moment and then she found something to say. "And I've been to a lot of those shows and I never saw a steer slapped down as hard and thorough as that one."

"That wasn't me," my father said. "That was Mark." He pushed up and turned away quick and went out again to the back steps.

It was only a while later and I was on the front steps again when

I saw something that made me jump up and my heart start to pound and what I saw was a big buckskin coming along the road and turning in at our place and sitting easy in the saddle was Cal Bennett.

"Howdy, bub," he said. "Is your father handy?"

"He's around back," I said. He nudged the buckskin and started around the house and all at once it came rushing up in me and I had to shout it at him. "Don't you dare make fun of him! He was better'n you once! He made a record nobody's ever really beat!"

Cal Bennett reined in his horse and leaned over toward me and his eyes were clear and bright looking down at me. "I know that," he said. "I wasn't much bigger'n you are now when I saw him make it. That's what started me practicing." He straightened in the saddle and went on around the house. I stood still in the surprise of his words and then I had to follow him and when I went around the rear corner of the house there was my father sitting on the steps looking up and there was Cal Bennett on that big buckskin looking down and they were holding a silence there between them for what seemed a long while.

My father shifted a little on the steps. "Nice of you to come around," he said. His voice was taut and careful. "I forgot to thank you for pulling that steer off me this afternoon."

"Shucks," Cal Bennett said. "That wasn't much. You've done it yourself many a time. There ain't a man ever worked cows ain't done it often for another man out on the range."

They kept looking at each other and the tightness that had been in my father's face all those last hours began to ease away and when he spoke again his voice was steady and friendly the way it usually was. "I sort of messed it up out there today, didn't I."

"Yes," Cal Bennett said. "You did kind of hooraw it some." He chuckled and sudden my father chuckled too and then they both grinned like a pair of kids.

"From what I hear," my father said, "you're good. You're dog-gone good."

"Yes," Cal Bennett said and his voice was easy and natural and he wasn't boasting at all. "Yes, I am. I'm as good as a man named Harvey Kendall was some years back. Maybe even a mite better."

"Expect you are," my father said. "Yes, I expect you are." He leaned backward on his elbows on the steps. "But you didn't come here just to chew that kind of fat, pleasant as that can be as I used to know."

"No," Cal Bennett said. "I didn't. I've been figuring. This rodeo business is all right for a young fellow long as he's young but there ain't any future in it. It's getting to be more fancy show for the crowds and less real roping all the time anyway. I've been saving my money. With what I collected in town a while ago I've got the tally I was aiming at. Now I'm figuring to get me a nice little spread somewhere in this territory and put some good stock on it and try raising me some good beef."

"Keep talking," my father said. "There's a lot of sense in what you're saying."

"Well, now," Cal Bennett said. "I figured to ask you to help me some getting started."

My father straightened on the steps and he cocked his head to one side, looking up. "Tell me something, Bennett," he said. "There's a woman mixed up in this somewhere."

"Yes," Cal Bennett said. "There is."

"And she wants you to quit risking your fool young neck showing off with a rope in front of a lot of shouting people."

"Yes," Cal Bennett said. "She does."

"And she's right," my father said. "And now you tell me something else. Why did you come to me?"

"Simple," Cal Bennett said. "I been asking questions round

about for some months. Found out a few things. Found out there's one name signed to a checklist on a cattle shipment that'll be accepted without question anywhere the rails run and that name's Harvey Kendall. Heard people say and for quite a ways around these parts that when you want good stock picked out and straight advice on how to handle them right you go find that same man. Heard them say that man never did another man dirt and never will. Heard them say—"

My father put up a hand to stop him. "Whoa, now," my father said. "No need to pile it on too thick. Of course I'll help you best I can. You knew that before you started all that palaver. Stop being so damn formal up there on that horse. Hop down and squat on these boards and tell me just what you have in mind."

And there the two of them were side by side on the steps talking quiet and friendly and the buckskin wandered off far enough to find a few grass tufts by our little pasture fence and whiffle some over the rails at old Mark and I was standing by the house corner with the strangest feeling in me. Somehow I didn't want to disturb them or even let them notice I was there and I stepped back soft and around the house again, wondering what was happening to me, and then I knew what I wanted to do. I went in through the front door and past my mother sitting quiet in the front room with our old photograph album in her lap and I went straight to the hall closet. I hardly even looked at those calfskin boots even though they were mighty dusty and could stand a cleaning. I took out the rough old cowskins and I got the saddle soap and a moist rag and I went over by the back door, where I could sit on a stool and hear them talking, and I really went to work on those old boots. I wanted to make that hard old leather comfortable as I could for his feet. I wanted to make those old boots shine.

Cat Nipped

Corporal Clint Buckner ambled slowly across the flat baked surface of what would someday be the parade ground of Fort McKay. He carried a stubby cavalry carbine in the crook of his left elbow and patted the stock affectionately with his right hand as he walked. The hot Kansas sun beat full strength upon him and upon the double row of tents that flanked one side of the level space and upon the three sod-walled structures that stretched at a right angle to mark another side. The sun beat with equal untiring fervor upon the sweating bodies of Sergeant Peattie and a crew of half-naked privates piling strips of sod one on another for the walls of the first of the structures that would line the third side.

Corporal Clint ambled in a slow curve to pass near Sergeant Peattie and his sweating crew. He paused to yawn and wipe imaginary dust from the carbine and ambled on. The dripping privates stopped their work to watch him move past.

"Ain't he the brave hunter, toting that big gun."

"Takes nerve to go after those critters like he does."

"Yep. Tumble dangerous when wounded."

Chuckles and a climbing guffaw disturbed the afternoon quiet. Corporal Clint paid no attention to them. "Envy makes a mighty strong poison," he remarked to no one in particular. He ambled on and to the doorway of the middle of the three sod-walled structures and into the shaded interior.

Outside the sun beat down with steady glare. Inside Corporal Clint widened his eyes to look through the relatively cool dimness. He stood in a semblance of attention and raised his right hand in a limp salute. Angled across from him in a corner Lieutenant Henley, acting commissary officer, was perched on a stool using an upturned packing box as a desk. Lieutenant Henley waggled a hand in what could have been a languid salute or a mere greeting and returned to pencil-figuring on a piece of wrapping paper. Corporal Clint perched himself on another stool with his back to the wall where he could look along the rough ground-floored aisle between two long piles of grain in bags. He set the carbine across his knees.

Partway down the aisle between the grain bags a prairie mouse crept out and into the open and darted back and crept out again. Corporal Clint raised the carbine and aimed with casual ease and fired. There was a smudge on the ground where the mouse had been. Over in his corner Lieutenant Henley looked up. Corporal Clint nodded at him. Lieutenant Henley reached with his pencil and made a mark beside many other marks on a piece of paper tacked to the side of his box desk. He sighed and returned to his figuring. Corporal Clint took out of a pocket a linen cartridge holding its lead ball and powder and reloaded the carbine. He inspected the percussion cap. He set the carbine on his knees and watched the aisle in quiet content.

Outside the sun beat down upon the laboring soldiers. Inside was shaded silence punctured only by the occasional sharp blast of the carbine and the sighs and some soft new anguished grunts from Lieutenant Henley. Corporal Clint smiled drowsily to himself. A mouse slipped into view. Corporal Clint raised the carbine.

"Stop that infernal racket!"

Corporal Clint jumped to his feet. He snapped to attention. Off in his corner Lieutenant Henley did the same. Captain McKay stood in the doorway mopping his face and peering into the dimness.

"How's a man to get a report written or even take a nap wondering when that damn thing's going off again?" Captain McKay waved Corporal Clint aside and sat on the stool by the wall and stretched out his legs. "An infernal nuisance."

"You're right, sir." Lieutenant Henley came forward with his paper in his hand. "And useless, sir. Utterly and completely useless."

"Yes?"

"Well, sir, I've been doing some figuring." Lieutenant Henley's voice was weighty with overtones of awe. "According to that animal book these damn mice have four to ten young ones at a time and it only takes them six weeks to have them. Worse than that, they start breeding soon as they're six weeks old." Lieutenant Henley sighed and stared down in somber fascination at his paper. "Well, sir, you take a middle figure for that litter number to be on the safe side and you just say only half each litter is females and you say again only half those females live to breeding age and all the same starting with just one pair after ten generations you've got close to half a million of those damn mice ruining my commissary and all of them busy breeding when they're not eating and they're averaging about a bag of grain a day already and making holes in all the bags. They're multiplying fifty times faster than Buckner here could kill them if he was triplets and every one of him as good a shot."

Captain McKay mopped his face again. "A formidable enemy, the way you put it."

"Beg pardon, sir, but it's no joke." Lieutenant Henley waggled his piece of paper. "We'll run short of feed for the horses and they're getting into our own provisions. We could try wooden bins but we can't get any good wood out on this damned prairie and they'd gnaw through it anyway. I just don't know what to do."

"Cats," said Corporal Clint.

Captain McKay slumped in his chair and drummed fingers on the onetime kitchen table that was his desk. From behind the hanging canvas partition that marked off his one-room living quarters in the same sod-walled building came a soft melodic humming and other small bustley noises as his wife moved about engaged in some incomprehensible feminine activity. The humming annoyed him. Two months they had been out here on the empty prairie creating an Army post out of next to nothing with supplies always short and no new appropriation to draw on for things needed and he didn't even have decent quarters for her yet because he was an old-line Army fool who believed in taking good care of his men first and still she was cheerful and could hum silly tunes and never once complain. By rights she ought to complain. And because she wouldn't, he couldn't, not even in the bosom, so to speak, of his own family and had to go on pretending to be a noble soul who enjoyed hardship for the sake of duty nobly done.

His fingers stopped drumming and he looked down again at the canceled requisition that had been returned in the fortnightly mail. Clipped to it was a note in vigorous handwriting: *Mac— Lucky I caught this before it went any higher. Cats! You're starting a post out there not a blooming menagerie. Next thing you'll be asking for slippers and dressing gowns and a squad of nursemaids.*

The chair squeaked as he shifted his weight. "Nursemaids," he muttered. "I'll nursemaid that jackass when I see him again. Even if he does outrank me."

The finger-drumming began again. It stopped short as Captain McKay realized he was keeping time with the humming from behind the partition. He stood up and strode to the doorway and looked out where his sweating sod crews were raising the walls of the second barracks. "Buckner!" he bellowed. He saw the solid chunky figure of Corporal Clint Buckner turn and start toward him and he swung back to his table desk.

The side edge of the canvas partition folded back and the cheerful face of Mrs. McKay appeared around it. "You be nice to that boy. He found me some more flowers this morning."

"Boy?" said Captain McKay. "He's seen thirty years if a day. Spent most of them doing things a boy wouldn't. Or shouldn't. I don't mean picking flowers."

Sweat gleamed on the broad face and dripped from the broad chin and rolled in little streams down the bare peeling chest of Corporal Clint as he came to attention before the table desk. Not even the heat had wilted the jaunty manner that often stirred in Captain McKay brief memories of his own cocksure youth. "Rest," said Captain McKay and Corporal Clint relaxed all over and began to appreciate the shaded interior of the room.

Captain McKay clasped his hands behind his head with his elbows flung wide. He noted that the canvas hung undisturbed but there was no humming behind it. He noted too the wary what's-coming-now look on Corporal Clint's face. "Buckner," he said. "How many times have you been busted and had to earn that stripe all over again?"

"Not so often, sir. Only about four times, sir."

"And how many times have you been in line for a sergeantcy and missed it for some damnfoolishness or other?"

Corporal Clint had the tone pegged now. His face exploded in a grin. "Reckon I've lost count on that, sir. But I'll make it yet."

"Maybe," said Captain McKay. "At least I'm giving you a chance. I'm giving you ten days and fifteen dollars and telling you to go find me some cats. Go easy on the money. It's coming out of my own pocket. My guess is there ain't a cat yet in the whole of Kansas Territory. But it was your notion and now you're stuck with it. You bring me some cats and the other stripe's yours."

Corporal Clint Buckner woke with the first light of dawn through the open doorway of the dugout. He lay on a thin matting of straw on the dirt floor of this one place that offered any accommodations at all for thirty miles in either direction along the wagon trace outside. He was not alone. His host, a beard-matted trader, was snoring two feet away. A pair of lank and odorous mule skinners lay like logs on the other side of the doorway. And the straw had a moving multitude of its own inhabitants.

Corporal Clint sat up and ruffled bits of straw out of his hair. Four of his ten days and a large part of the fifteen dollars were gone. It was time to start looking for cats in earnest. He had covered considerable territory already and made casual inquiries but there had been no pressure in the search. Two whole days he had wasted in the one settlement within a hundred miles of the post. Well, not exactly wasted. The settlement boasted no cat but it did boast a pert waitress at the false-fronted building called a hotel. She had slapped him the first time he kissed her. She had forgotten to slap the second time. He might have been there yet if her husband had not come home with a wagonload of potatoes and turnips and a positive itch to lambast anyone interested in her. Corporal Clint had no aversion to fighting, any place and any time, but it was against his principles to fight husbands.

Outside by the well he stripped himself bare and sloshed himself thoroughly with several buckets of water. While his skin dried in the early morning air he conducted a careful search through his clothes to eliminate any visitors from the straw. "Wouldn't want to kidnap any of these critters," he said. "Now if they were only cats . . ."

Dressed again, he caught his horse in the small-pole corral by the dugout and saddled and started off. He was traveling light in boots and pants and shirt and hat. His saddle roll consisted of a blanket, a razor, and an empty grain bag with a few holes punched near the top. He had a vague notion of carrying any cats he might collect in the bag. His armament consisted of a standard cavalry pistol in a snap-shut holster on his left hip and the cherished carbine in a saddle scabbard. He had a long day's route mapped in his mind to cover the far-scattered squatters' roosts and ranch stations within a wide radius.

The welcome slight coolness of evening found Corporal Clint Buckner atop a long rolling ridge that gave him a view of several hundred square miles of catless Kansas. He was a tired and downcast man. As usual the more tired and downcast he was, the more determined he became. "Legwork won't do it," he said. "Like hunting a needle in one devil of a big haystack without even knowing a needle's there. This calls for heavy thinking."

He dismounted and let the horse graze while he studied the problem. There were several villages of friendly Indians within reaching distance but Indians didn't have cats. They likely wouldn't even know what a cat was. Only white settlers who might bring them from back east would ever have cats. At that only a few would do it. Cats weren't good travelers like dogs. They had to be carried in the wagons and were a nuisance. They wandered off and were left behind or got lost or some bigger animals made meals of them. But settlers offered the only possible chance. New settlers, those fresh out from back east a ways.

In the cool of the dark Corporal Clint dismounted and picketed his horse. He was ten miles farther south near the deepening road ruts of the main route of the emigrant wagon trains heading farther west to pick up the Santa Fe Trail. He lay quiet, rolled in his blankets, and watched the nearly full moon rise over the left-hand ridge. "Just one of the scratching little brutes," he said, "and I'll make the old man give me that stripe."

Refreshed and jaunty in the morning sun, Corporal Clint rode along beside the wagon ruts. As he rode he hummed a small wordless tune. He had breakfast with an emigrant family, exchanging advice on the best route ahead for his food and edging around at last to the subject in hand. "Cats?" said the man. "Why sure, we had one. Coyote got it two days back."

Corporal Clint rode on, jauntier than before. "On the right track now," he said. He began humming again and after a while his small tune had words.

> I'm hunting a feline critter
> Some people call a cat.
> To me any day it's a sergeant's pay—
> A new feather in my hat.

Ten hours, seventy miles, three wagon trains, and two ranch stations later, no longer jaunty, Corporal Clint dismounted by a small stream and unsaddled before he led the horse to the water. There were several hours of daylight left but the horse was done for the day. He could have pushed it farther but he had the true cavalryman's respect for his mount. He fastened the picket rope and sat on a slight rise near the stream and chewed on the sandwiches he had collected at his last stop. "There ain't a cat between here and Missouri," he said. "Wonder if a gelded skunk might do."

He finished the sandwiches and plucked a blade of grass and chewed this long and thoughtfully. Far to the east along the rutted trail a small dust cloud rose and grew and drifted in the freshening breeze. It came closer, always renewed, and beneath it and moving in it were men on horseback and oxteams straining into yokes to pull a motley collection of wagons. They came closer and swung past in an arc to line up and stop along the bank of the stream.

Corporal Clint chewed on his grass blade and watched the wagons swing past. The third wagon was driven by a faded woman in a faded sunbonnet and beside her on the seat sat a brighter, sharper-colored copy with no sunbonnet to cramp a tumbled glory of dark brown hair. Corporal Clint forgot to chew and stared at this second woman. "Man alive," he said, "that's a mighty attractive sight." He leaned forward and stared some more. "Yes, sir," he said. "Without any argufying or equivocating whatsomever that's the most attractive sight I ever sighted." The woman had seen him on his knoll and had turned to look at him as the wagon swung past. Curled in her lap was a cat.

Corporal Clint Buckner was helpful to have around. He helped the man unyoke the third wagon and water the oxen and picket them along with the man's horse by some good grass. He was expert at finding buffalo chips for the fire in places overlooked by previous overnight campers. And he was a contagious and shrewd talker. By time cooking smells were drifting around he had adequate information in hand. The man and the faded woman, his wife, were headed for California. The other woman was the wife's sister. Her name was Ellen. The cat belonged to her and it was a damn nuisance too. The man didn't think much of this sister business. She was too independent and she thought she knew all there was to know and she made too much fuss over animals and she was another mouth to feed, but his wife had nagged him into letting her come along.

Corporal Clint squatted on his heels and sniffed the cooking smells. "Why sure, ma'am," he said to the faded woman, "I've only had four meals so far today so of course I'll join you. Ain't often I get me real woman's cooking."

Corporal Clint squatted on his heels by the stream bank and watched the sister rinsing off the dishes. "Miss Ellen," he said, "that cat must be a trouble to you on a jaunt like this. If you're so minded I'd do you the favor of taking it off your hands. Give it a nice home at my quarters."

Corporal Clint leaned against a wagon wheel and looked down at Miss Ellen on a stool plying a needle with knowing skill. "Tell you what," he said, "I always was seven kinds a fool. I'll give you a dollar for that cat."

Corporal Clint stood straight and solid and indignant and glared at Miss Ellen shaking out blankets before making up beds under the wagon. He calculated what remained in his pocket. "Miss Ellen," he said, "you're the obstinatest female I ever met. That cat's just a scrawny, mangy, piebald sort of thing. But I'll give you four dollars and thirty-seven cents for it."

Miss Ellen faced him, not as solid but just as indignant. "Mr. Soldier. That's a good healthy cat and you're a mangy sort of thing to say it isn't. I've told you and told you it's not for sale. It's my cat. It stays with me. It goes where I go. Now you go do some soldiering and stop bothering me."

Corporal Clint lay sleepless in his blanket on his knoll and watched the almost full moon climb the sky. "Could sneak down there now they're asleep," he said. "Nab the critter, leave the money, make some tracks." The moon climbed higher. "No," he said. "Can't do that to a woman." He lay on one side for a while and then on the other and the ground seemed uncommonly hard. "If I'm going to get places in this damned Army," he said, "I got to get started soon. I need that stripe." The moon arched overhead and started its downward sweep and still his eyes remained open. "So it goes where she goes," he said. "Got to keep that in mind." He squirmed on the ground and sat up and hunted under the blanket and removed a small stone and lay quiet again. "Awful lot to ask of a man," he said, "just to get hold of a cat." The moon dropped toward the horizon and he began figuring the time he had left. Four days. One would be needed for the return to the post. Three days. Nights too. It would work out about right. In that time, the way the train was headed, it would be close to a meeting with the regular mail wagon bound for the post. "Shucks," he said. "She's unattached and she's a woman. That's plenty of time. Even got me a full moon coming on schedule."

In the early light of morning Miss Ellen held fast to the handle of a bucket of water as Corporal Clint Buckner tried to take it from her. "I'm quite capable of carrying this myself. And if you say one word about my cat I'll dump this water right over your grinning head."

"Cat?" said Corporal Clint. "Oh, you mean that pet of yours. Shucks, ma'am, I was only pretending to be interested in that cat trying to please you, you're so fond of it. Took one look at you coming along in that wagon and haven't been able to think of a thing else ever since but trying to please you."

Corporal Clint Buckner was very helpful to have around. He was on hand wherever help was needed along the wagon line, particularly in the neighborhood of the third wagon. Neither heat nor dust dimmed his cheerfulness. He knew the best camping places. He knew every kink in the trail and a cutoff that saved ten miles. He rode away across the prairie and out of sight and Miss Ellen watched him go with a speculative look in her eyes. He rode back with the carcass of an antelope over the withers of his horse and Miss Ellen watched him come back with a half-smile on her lips and found her hands fussing with her hair. Corporal Clint knew his way around in many ways. Walking with her in the moonlight he wasted no time talking about cats.

In the relative cool of approaching evening Corporal Clint stood by the unyoked wagon and watched Miss Ellen and her sister making antelope stew. He felt a familiar warning prickling on his skin and looked down the arc of bedded wagons and saw two men coming toward him, the two men, youngish and healthy and hefty in the shoulders, who herded the milk cows and spare oxen that tagged the train. He had the notion from the way they had looked at him now and again that their opinion of him was not flattering. They were looking at him now and their forward tread was full of purpose.

"Soldier," said the first one, "me and Bert been talking about you. We been watching you. We don't like it. We decided a couple weeks back Miss Ellen was going to have one of us and she'd have to pick which when we get where we're going. We decided now it's time you—"

"Oh-h-h-h," said Miss Ellen. "I guess I have something to say about that."

No one paid any attention to her, not even Corporal Clint. He was inspecting the two men and his eyes were beginning to brighten.

"That's right," said Bert. "We just don't like it. Three days you been hanging around Miss Ellen. Last night was my night and night before was Jeb's but when we come looking she wasn't around. She was gallivanting off with you somewheres. We decided you better start traveling."

"Well, well," said Corporal Clint. "Ain't it too bad I don't feel any traveling urge."

"We decided mebbe you wouldn't," said Bert. "We decided we'd just have to give it to you."

They stepped forward. Corporal Clint stepped to meet them. With a grin on his face and a gleam of joy in his eyes Corporal Clint moved into battle. He bent low and drove his broad head like a cannonball into Bert's middle and straightened and swung to work on Jeb with experienced fists. Bert rolled on the ground and groaned.

"Oh-h-h-h," said Miss Ellen and ran to bend over Bert, "you poor man. Did he break your ribs?"

Corporal Clint heard. He saw. His blows began to go wild. They missed Jeb entirely or when they hit they no longer carried a powerful jolt. He winced when Jeb struck him and began to retreat. Jeb rushed at him, hot with encouragement, and Bert struggled to his feet and gulped in air and plunged to join Jeb. Together they battered Corporal Clint. The air hummed with sweeping fists. Corporal Clint went down. He groaned. He staggered to his feet. He went down again. His groan was a plaintive and appealing sound. His body twitched and was still.

"Oh-h-h-h," said Miss Ellen. She stood beside his prone body and smacked at Bert and Jeb with her words. "You cowards! Two of you beating him!"

Bert and Jeb stepped backward. "Why, Miss Ellen," said Jeb. "We just decided—"

"Who cares what you decided?" said Miss Ellen. "I hate the sight of both of you. You get away from here and back with those cows which is just about all you're fit to associate with." As Bert and Jeb retired in confusion she ran to the wagon and dipped a cloth in the water bucket and ran back to raise Corporal Clint's limp head with one hand and wipe off his bruised dusty face with the other. Corporal Clint opened his eyes. "You have such nice hands," he said and groaned again, a small satisfied groan, and closed his eyes.

Half an hour later, limping painfully, Corporal Clint edged around the wagon. Out of sight behind it, he strode off toward the rear of the line of wagons. The limp disappeared and he strode with purposeful stride. He found Bert and Jeb squatted by a fire downing third cups of coffee in sullen discouragement. "Stand up, boys," he said. "We'll take up now where we left off." With a grin on his bruised face and a gleam of joy in his half-closed eyes Corporal Clint moved into battle. Seven minutes later he looked down upon Bert and Jeb reclining dazed and much more discouraged on the ground. "Take a bit of advice," he said. "Don't go deciding to interfere with the Army again." He strode back the way he had come behind the line of wagons and as he went the limp began once more and became more pronounced with each step and as he limped he caroled his small tune to himself with new words.

> I found me a feline critter—
> A lady's personal pet.
> Goes where she goes but I'm one knows
> It won't be hard to get.

Walking with Miss Ellen in the moonlight he endured his limp with gallant fortitude. It forced him to lean some on her for support and to put an arm over her shoulders.

The light mail wagon rolled steadily over the prairie. Fifty yards ahead the escort, two privates and a lance corporal, trotted steadily forward and with them, happy at freedom from constant sitting on a board seat, trotted the regular driver astride Corporal Clint Buckner's horse. In the wagon, jaunty and cheerful with the reins in his hands, sat Corporal Clint and behind him, between the mail bag and a box, was a woman's trunk and beside him sat Miss Ellen and curled in her lap was the cat.

The miles slipped away under the wheels. "Clint," said Miss Ellen, "my head's been in such a whirl I didn't think before. Is there a preacher at the post?"

"Preacher?" said Corporal Clint. "Whatever for?"

"Why, to marry us, silly."

"Shucks," said Corporal Clint. "We don't need a preacher. The old man, that's the captain, he's got authority to do the job tight and even better."

"A military ceremony!" said Miss Ellen. "That'll be fun. Will they cross swords for us?"

"Sabers," said Corporal Clint. "I ain't a commissioned officer so it won't be too fancy."

More miles slipped away. "Clint," said Miss Ellen, "you're a sergeant, aren't you? You said so. But there's only one stripe on your sleeve."

"Well, I am," said Corporal Clint, not quite as jaunty as before. "In a manner of speaking I am. I mean I will be when I get back there."

"Oh," said Miss Ellen. "You're being promoted you mean. I knew you'd be the kind of man who gets promotions. What did you do to get this one?"

"Shucks," said Corporal Clint, "nothing much. Just a little special duty." He began to notice that it was a hot and dusty day.

They stopped for a midday meal and to rest the horses. Corporal Clint strutted some giving orders because he was the ranking man present but his voice lacked its usual confident clip. He chewed in a strange silence, very thoughtful. The cat wandered about forty feet away, intent on its own individual business. Corporal Clint leaped to his feet and raced to grab it and bring it back. He smiled weakly at Miss Ellen. "Dangerous country," he said. "Coyotes and things around."

They drove forward again and Corporal Clint was restless on the wagon seat. Miss Ellen did not notice. She had missed most of her sleep the night before and the slight swaying of the wagon as it rolled easily along the trace among the grass tufts made her drowsy. She pulled his right arm about her and snuggled close and rested her head, half dozing, on his shoulder. Corporal Clint could feel her hair blowing softly against his cheek in the breeze of their movement and his shirt suddenly felt too small around his chest and this was very nice hair brushing his cheek and he knew he should be pleased but he was too bothered by troublesome thoughts to appreciate the pleasure.

The miles dropped away beneath the hooves and the wheels and they came to a shallow stream and splashed into it. The front wheel on Corporal Clint's side hit a stone and rose up on it tilting the wagon. Miss Ellen slid on the seat squealing and clutching at him and the cat tumbled out of her lap into the water. Corporal Clint yanked on the reins and dropped them and scrambled past Miss Ellen to follow the cat. He landed on all fours in the eight inches of water and scrabbled about in it and rose dripping with the cat in his arms.

"Good grief!" said Miss Ellen. "You didn't even bother about me but just that cat."

"Might have been a pool over on this side," said Corporal Clint, trying to smile at her and failing. "Might have been real deep water."

"Silly," said Miss Ellen. "Maybe cats don't like water but they can swim all right if they have to. Well, I suppose it's nice you worrying so about that cat just because I like it so. I hope you don't catch the sniffles now."

"It ain't sniffles I'm worried about catching," said Corporal Clint.

The afternoon sun was low on the left as the mail wagon topped the last swell of the prairie that gave a clear view of the beginnings of Fort McKay in the distance. "That's it," said Corporal Clint Buckner with little of a prospective bridegroom's joy in his voice. His eyes brightened. "Maybe I'd better get on my horse and hurry on in ahead to sort of prepare the way some."

"And leave me?" said Miss Ellen. "I think we should drive in together. I want to see how surprised everyone is, too. And don't worry what I'll think about how you behave. I know you have to salute and stand at attention and things like that."

The escort dropped respectively to the rear to tail the wagon in. Corporal Clint's face grew pale as he saw they had been sighted coming and the entire personnel of the post was assembling for a good view. It grew paler as he saw that Captain McKay, contrary to custom at this hour, was not in his quarters but was standing outside with Mrs. McKay beside him. Corporal Clint sighed. Then he straightened on the seat and snapped back his shoulders and cocked his head at a jaunty angle. He urged the team into a faster trot. He pulled up close to Captain McKay with a flourish and jumped to the ground. His salute was a gesture of swift and precise perfection. "Reporting for duty, sir. Right on the tenth day, sir. Brought a young lady with me, sir, who has done me the honor of consenting to become my wife, sir. With your permission of course, sir. I'm asking for same now, sir. And to perform the ceremony yourself, sir. As soon as—"

"But—" said Captain McKay. "But—but—"

"Awfully sudden, sir," said Corporal Clint. "But it had to be that way. Begging your pardon, sir, but I can report later. Bring her around for official introduction later too, sir. Really ought to be fixing her some quarters right away, sir. It's been a long drive. And dusty. She'll want to rest first, sir, and clean up some before a formal meeting. If you'll just let me have a tent, sir, I can fix—"

"But—" said Captain McKay. "But—but I sent you out to get some cats."

"Oh-h-h-h-h-h," said Miss Ellen.

"I told you I'd report later, sir." Corporal Clint had taken another breath. "Explain everything then, sir. I've done my duty. Done the best I could, sir. Things kind of happened and turned out this way. All for the best all around, sir. If you'll just let me have a tent—"

"Shut up!" bellowed Captain McKay. "I don't know what particular breed of devilment you've pulled this time but I know it's all of a piece with past behavior. Send you out with orders to find some cats and you come back bringing another woman to this heaven-forsaken place that ain't fit—"

"But she's got a cat, sir," said Corporal Clint.

"Oh-h-h-h," said Miss Ellen. "So that's why you were so interested in my cat! And jumping after it all the time without caring what happened to me! Talking about marrying just to trick me into coming here so maybe you could steal it!"

"I did not," said Corporal Clint. "That's not right. That's—"

"I hate you," said Miss Ellen. "I just plain utterly despise you. Taking me away from the only folks I had and making it all sound so nice when it isn't at all. I wouldn't marry you now even if—well, I just wouldn't—I wouldn't—" Suddenly Miss Ellen was crying and she was ashamed to be crying in front of a group of startled and embarrassed men and she put her head down in her arms and the cat slipped out of her lap and retreated over the seat into the rear of the wagon and she was sitting there with her shoulders shaking.

"Humph!" snorted Mrs. McKay. "A fine mess you men've made now. But then you always do. Where a woman's concerned anyway. Yelling at each other. Blathering about cats. A nice lovely girl like that too." She marched to the wagon and cooed soft reassurances at Miss Ellen and helped her down from the seat. In a silence made ominous by the expression on Captain McKay's face she led Miss Ellen into the captain's quarters. They disappeared from sight.

"Buckner," said Captain McKay. His tone was mild and deadly. "You have committed so damn many offenses under the military code from the moment you started yapping at me before I gave you permission to speak that I won't even try to list them now. God only knows what devilish things you've been doing while you were gone but I intend to find out. You're under arrest. Go to your quarters and stay there till I decide what to do with you. While you're there improve your time taking that stripe off your sleeve."

Captain McKay wiped his forehead and turned to go inside and face Mrs. McKay and Miss Ellen. Surrounded by his fellows and a babble of jeering and commiserating and even envious voices, Corporal Clint moved toward the double row of tents. The mail escort rode forward and one of them dismounted and climbed to the wagon seat to drive it over by the stable. "Wait a moment," said Lieutenant Henley, pushing out from the shade of one of the sod-walled buildings. He leaned over the backboard of the wagon and reached inside and lifted out the cat.

Private Clint Buckner sat on a three-legged stool in the end tent of the front row facing the stretch of level ground that would someday be the parade ground and stared out into the morning sun. Somehow it was hotter under the canvas than it would have been outside under the open sun with a sod crew. The heat was personal, oppressive, made so by the silence, the solitude of that particular corner of the post, and his complete ignorance of what was happening in Captain's McKay's quarters and adjacent areas.

He twisted on his stool to get a better view. Across the way there was a flurry of unusual activity. Sergeant Peattie appeared with a squad of fast-stepping privates carrying various things and walking beside him, pert and chipper with her dark brown hair a tumbled glory about her head, was Miss Ellen. Private Clint could see that Sergeant Peattie was unusually neat and natty and was strutting to good effect and barking orders with obvious relish. The squad stopped and began to erect a tent almost exactly opposite the one in which Private Clint sat in his solitude and close to the bend in the lazy almost-dried-up little river that ran alongside the post. The tent went up quickly and was pegged tight. Into it went a cot, a chair, a washstand made of a box set on end with a cloth covering the open side, and Miss Ellen's trunk.

The squad was gone. Even Sergeant Peattie, who had lingered long, was gone. The flaps of the newly erected tent were closed. "Can't any more than shoot me," said Private Clint. He crawled under the rear canvas of his tent and set off on a wide circuit, bent low and crawling at times, taking advantage of all possible cover. He came up behind Miss Ellen's tent. He lifted its rear canvas and poked his head under. "Good morning, ma'am."

Miss Ellen was busy at her trunk. She jumped around, startled. She stared at the broad face peering up turtlewise. "Oh, it's you," she said.

"It's me all right," said Private Clint. He crawled the rest of the way under and perched himself on the chair. "I'm mighty peeved too. If you'd only had sense enough to keep your yap shut—"

"Mr. Buckner," said Miss Ellen, "all I have to do is yell and you'll be—"

"Go ahead and yell," said Private Clint. "Another charge or two won't mean much to me now. I want to know what in perdition and-I-won't-ask-pardon-for-that-either is going on over here."

"Why, Mr. Buckner," said Miss Ellen, very sweetly. "I don't know as you have any right to know but I'll tell you. Everybody's being so nice to me. That Lieutenant Henley's taking good care of my cat and he says it's just a marvelous mouser. And this tent is all my own and I'm to have a better place soon as more buildings are up and it'll be fixed real nice and I'm to be the officers' laundress and have my meals with the McKays and get right good pay too."

Private Clint groaned. He tried to make his voice plaintive. "But what about me?"

"You?" said Miss Ellen. "I don't know as that's any concern of mine. I have myself to worry about, seeing as you got me in such a fix. I think I'm doing right well." Miss Ellen reached up and fluffed her hair. "Maybe you've not noticed, being a man, but that Sergeant Peattie is a fine-looking man himself."

"Peattie," moaned Private Clint. "You watch out for him, I've been on leaves with him and I'm telling you—"

"He's told me plenty about you," said Miss Ellen. "Now I remember what he's told me I think it's time you crawled out of here and stayed away."

"Shucks," said Private Clint. "Peattie always did stretch things too far. How about you remembering those nights when the moon—"

"I will not!" Miss Ellen stamped one foot and glared at him. "You get out of here now or I really will yell!"

"Blame woman," muttered Private Clint as he crawled under the canvas. "Always being so blamed womanish." The last he saw before he let the canvas drop and departed on his return circuit was Miss Ellen standing straight and glaring at him and prettier than he'd remembered her all through the previous night. What he did not see and what Mrs. McKay did see five minutes later, as she pushed through the tent flaps with her arms laden with blankets and a mirror, was Miss Ellen slumped on the chair and crying.

Captain McKay stomped into his office hot and dusty from his afternoon jaunt to inspect his work crews at their labors. For an instant he thought he had been hearing voices from behind the canvas partition as he entered but now there was no sound. He listened. A soft melodic humming began and he relaxed. His wife indulged in that silly humming only when she was alone. He sat behind his table desk and wiped dust from his face. The canvas partition folded back at the front edge and Mrs. McKay's face appeared around it followed by the rest of her.

"Mac," she said, "you've left that Buckner boy sweating in that tent and wondering what you're going to do all last night and most of today. Don't you think it's time you had him over here to speak up for himself?"

"Speak up?" said Captain McKay. "He spoke up so confounded much yesterday I've a mind to let him squat over there the rest of the summer. If we were back anywhere near civilization and he behaved like that and I didn't have his hide there's plenty other officers'd think I was losing my grip."

Mrs. McKay simply looked at her husband and smiled a small smile. "Oh, I know," he said. "We're way out here the end of nowhere and I'm top dog and I can do about anything I doggone well please. So I'm just letting him sit there a while meditating on his sins. It'll do him good."

"Mac," said Mrs. McKay, "he's the only one out here, yourself included, ever thought to find me flowers. He's talked a girl you've been making sheep's eyes at yourself into coming here to marry him and now he's talked himself under arrest and into having her think mighty small of him. Sometimes I think you're not the same man I married twenty-too-many years ago." The canvas partition folded back again and Mrs. McKay disappeared behind it.

Captain McKay sat still, drumming his fingers and remembering many things. He rose and went to the doorway and out a short distance. "Buckner!" he bellowed across the level space and remembered bellowing that same name in that same voice when he and his command were pinned down in small scattered groups in a dry stream bed by many times their own number of hostile Indians and he needed a man who might be just reckless enough and tough enough to get through with a message for reinforcements. The thought flashed through his mind that likely he'd be bellowing that same name again when the settlers his post and others were supposed to protect began coming in real numbers to populate the Territory and the Indians got worried again about losing their lands and made trouble. He returned and sat again behind his table desk and made himself look stern and official.

Private Clint Buckner stood before him with that what's-coming-now look on his face.

"Buckner," said Captain McKay, "how much of my fifteen dollars have you got left?"

"Four dollars and thirty-seven cents, sir."

Captain McKay thumped a fist on the table. "Better'n ten dollars gone and you didn't spend a nickel on cats. I've heard the girl's story. By rights I ought to skin you alive and hang your hide out to dry. Maybe I will yet. First I want you to tell me how you got yourself in such a fool fix."

"Well, sir," said Private Clint, "you wanted cats. I couldn't find cats. Well, sir, I found one and it was attached to that Miss Ellen woman and she wouldn't sell it. I figured the only way to get it here was get her here. I figured the only way to get her here was to marry her. You're a man, sir. You know how it is. It seemed a kind of good idea at the time."

"Cursed if I do know how it is," said Captain McKay. "It's never crossed my mind to marry a woman to get a cat."

"That's only how it started, sir. More I saw of her the more I figured it was a good idea all by itself. She's a mighty attractive woman, sir."

"In a sort of way," said Captain McKay, conscious of Mrs. McKay behind the partition. "But she says it's plain you've been interested mostly in that cat all the time. Says you paid more attention to it coming here than to her. Says you were willing to about knock her out of the wagon to save that cat from a little water."

"That's all backward," said Private Clint. "That cat gives me a pain just thinking of it. You see, sir, when we headed here I got to thinking. I got to thinking what a real chunk of woman she is. Nerve enough to leave that wagon train and the only folks she knew and go to a place she didn't know a thing about and take a chance on a cross-branded Army mule like me. That's my kind of woman, sir. I got to thinking the only way I'd ever keep up with her and take care of her the way I ought was being a sergeant. That's the cat. I had to keep it safe. You promised me if I—"

"So-o-o-o," said Captain McKay. "A devil of a soldier you are. Conducted your campaign without thinking through to the finish. Forgot till too late how your fine talk would sound to her when she found out about the cat. Walked right into what I'd call a verbal ambush. Now you've lost out all around. Lost the girl. Lost the sergeantcy. I distinctly told you cats. Plural. You brought just one."

The partition folded back and around it came Mrs. McKay. Behind her and moving up beside her came Miss Ellen. Miss Ellen's head was held high and her eyes were bright. "Captain McKay," she said, "that cat is cats." Miss Ellen blushed very prettily and looked at Private Clint and looked away and blushed even more prettily. "That cat had an—well, an affair with another cat back in Springfield when we came through. It won't be long now. She always has four or five at a time."

Captain McKay looked at Miss Ellen blushing so prettily. He looked at Private Clint Buckner, who was looking at Miss Ellen with his head at a jaunty angle and a grin on his broad face. He looked at Mrs. McKay who was looking at him with that expectant expression that meant he had better do something and it had better be the right thing to do. He cleared his throat. "Sergeant Buckner, you will report back here directly after mess in the neatest uniform you can beg, borrow or steal around this post. You may regard the fifteen dollars as a wedding present. The ceremony will be at seven o'clock."

Out of the Past

This is a story of revenge. But revenge is an ugly word. It carries suggestions of hatred and personalized viciousness that may or may not be involved. There are times when revenge is more accurately a plain balancing of accounts, an expression of one man's loyalty to another. It is a balancing of accounts, an expression of loyalty bridging many miles and many years, that is chronicled here.

This is a story, too, of three parts. Three happenings. Three individual bursts of violent action separated in time and place. I will not tell you whether these happenings were true in literal fact. That is no longer important at this date. But you should know that they could have been true. Such things happened in this America in the years of westward settlement. I will not even insist that you accept these three happenings as parts of the one same story. I am content to present them in the hope you will understand them. And I will present them as you might come upon them searching, as I have often done, through the records of that westward settlement, the old letters and books and newspapers that remain as a legacy to us out of the past.

First, a letter. A letter written from a military post in the parched badlands of southern New Mexico in 1885.

This letter was written by a soldier, a sergeant, a cavalry man, to his mother back home in Missouri. He wrote it lying on a cot in a curtained-off section of an adobe and log-walled barracks marked with a sign that said "Hospital." He was a badly wounded, badly shaken man, profoundly grateful that he was alive and that he would live. The tone of his letter and a few hints in the text suggest that he was young without being youthful, maybe in his middle twenties, reasonably well educated for the time and the territory, a serious, capable man and a good soldier. He wrote the letter in segments on several different days, probably because he was too weak to do it all at once. His narrative of what had happened is rambling and understandably confused but the main outline is clear and direct.

Geronimo was off the reservation again, he and his renegade Apaches off on their last and bitterest raiding campaign. Troops were out after them and this soldier, this sergeant, was with those troops. The Apaches were up to their usual trick of scattering to strike in many places at the same time and the troops were spread thin in small detachments combing the territory. The detachment this sergeant was with had penetrated some rough country. The enemy smell was strong. The Indian scout leading the way slowed the pace till the horses were barely moving and said the signs spoke trouble. The lieutenant in command had the sense to figure that was warning enough and called a halt where rocks gave good cover in case of an attack. He sent the sergeant and the Indian scout on forward. There was no way of knowing whether the Apaches in the area had spotted the detachment yet. The plan was for those two to look over the ground ahead and try to locate the enemy, if possible without being seen. They were to go maybe three miles but no further. If nothing developed they were to look for another easily defended spot and one of them slip back to bring up the full detachment. The lieutenant was a cautious man, a good officer. He was going to move now only from strong position to strong position, not risking his whole command in a possible ambush.

That's the picture to hold in mind. Two men riding forward. Two men obeying orders and riding forward into rough country with the enemy smell in the air around. One of them is the sergeant, the letter writer, a good soldier who is serious about the Army as a career and has won his stripes early in his second enlistment. The other is an Indian, a Miniconjou Sioux from the northern plains, a man well into middle age who has fought the white men in the vigor of his youth and seen his tribe dwindle in defeat and has wandered far and has served now several years as a scout with the men he once fought. It is the letter writer who remains a shadowy figure, featureless, known only in character as revealed by his letter. It is the Indian who emerges in fairly clear focus, seen as the sergeant saw him, not to the sergeant just an Indian obscure in the anonymity of his race, in which all seem the same because of their very difference, but a man distinct and individual with the marks of a hard life upon him. He is a man of medium height, thick in the body with shoulders not wide but thick through and a heaviness around the hips. His eyes are small and black in a flat face pitted with old smallpox scars and he limps with his right leg from a stiffness in the knee joint and two fingers of his left hand are missing. He is a man hidden behind the blank wall of his flat expressionless face, nondescript in appearance in castoff Army-issue pants and shirt faded past color, yet a man on whose word an oldhand lieutenant would set the safety of his command and not think twice about it.

They rode forward. They went cautiously, holding to cover, working upward as the land rose toward a long ridge athwart their course. They stopped. Ahead and beyond the ridge they saw a thin streamer of smoke floating upward. A signal? A campfire? They moved forward again, even more slowly. They dropped into a hiding gully that led toward the ridge top. The Indian was in the lead, head up, eyes alert, nostrils wide in the slight wind. Suddenly he whirled his horse and waved to the sergeant to do the same and drove back down the gully at full gallop. As he passed the sergeant in the act of swinging his horse, the first shots came from up the gully among rocks along the sides. A bullet smashed through the sergeant's left leg above the knee and into his horse and the horse went down and he was thrown free and rolled headlong, striking against a stone that tore a jagged gash along his jaw, and as he rolled in the turning he saw the Indian scout diminishing into distance down the gully and then the Apaches scrambling out from among the rocks up the gully and starting toward him. He did not know where his rifle was. It had been jarred from his grasp and lay somewhere beyond the dying horse. He could not stand but he pushed up, leaning on his left arm, and clawed at his service revolver and had it in his right hand when another bullet smashed into his shoulder and he was flat and helpless on the ground.

Curiously he felt no pain in the shock of that moment. But everything about him was immeasurably clear and distinct, the hard ground beneath and the clear baked blue of the sky overhead and beyond and above all else the utter aloneness. He could hear the shouts of the Apaches coming and somehow the sounds did not penetrate the silence that surrounded him. And into that silence and that aloneness came another sound that could penetrate and that hit him as even the bullets had not. It was the sound of hooves and he could move and raise his head and twist it to look back down the gully. The Indian scout had whirled his horse again and was racing toward him, low-bent along the straining neck, reaching with one arm to lash the frantic animal to greater speed. The Indian scout pulled the horse spinning on its hind legs to a stop by the sergeant and leaped off and scooped up the sergeant like a limp sack of grain and flung him over the horse's withers and leaped again into the saddle and the heaving animal struggled into a gallop beneath the double burden.

How long they rode that way the sergeant could not know. The pounding of the horse's foreshoulders under him was an unbearable torment. He had time only to think that it was hopeless, that this horse was carrying double and the Apaches would have their own horses hidden near and be after them and overtake them, and then the jolting was too much and he dropped into darkness.

That was early afternoon. It was late afternoon when he regained consciousness for a few moments. He was lying in a tight crevice between two big rocks. All he could see was the sheer stone sides rising and the patch of deepening blue of sky between. Then he was aware that an Indian with a flat pitted face, naked to the waist, was bandaging or rebandaging his shoulder with strips of a faded old Army shirt. Again he had time for only one thought. He was thinking that this Indian was doing a good job considering the fact two fingers of his left hand were missing, when the darkness rose and overwhelmed him. Much later his mind flickered for a few seconds out of that darkness into another, into the darkness of the moonless star-pointed night, and he was aware that he was being carried, lying limp and doubled down, not now over the withers of a horse, but over the thick shoulder and tensed upper arm of a man. He could hear the slow strained breathing of the man carrying him and then he knew nothing and then drops of some raw stuff, rum or whiskey, were raking his throat and he was lying on the ground about thirty feet from a small fire and the lieutenant was kneeling beside him. He tried to move and sit up, fighting the pain that streaked through his stiffened body, and the lieutenant clamped him to the ground. "Easy," the lieutenant said. "You're not going anywhere. There's a lot of them out there. They've got us pinned down tight." And still the sergeant tried to move, to turn his head and look about, and the lieutenant understood. "He waited till dark to bring you in. But he's gone now. He slipped out again to make a try for reinforcements."

There it is, all that is needed. The rest of the letter is unimportant. What it chronicles is, in a sense, anticlimax. Reinforcements came and the Apaches sighted them and faded further into the badlands. The sergeant and two other wounded were sent back in a quartermaster's wagon. He was out of the campaign, out of the long later days of fighting and hard hectic riding and knew only by hearsay what those days brought. He was on a hospital cot with two bullet wounds which the doctor said would heal nicely and with a gash along the side of his jaw which the doctor said would leave a neat scar to remind him of what he had been through.

Lying there, writing his letter, this sergeant had plenty of time to think over what he could remember of what had happened and to wonder what must have happened during the hours he was lost in the darkness and an aging Indian with a limping leg got him away from Geronimo's Apaches and took him through to the safety of the detachment's rock barricade. That impressed him deeply and he wrote about it at length. But what impressed him more was the sudden shattering of his aloneness as he lay helpless on the ground in the gulley. His mind returned to that again and again. Three times the same brief sentence leaps out of the letter. *He came back.*

Second, an account of a court trial cited in a paper-bound local history of a Kansas town. The trial occurred in 1898. That is a jump of thirteen years in time and several hundred miles north-westward in place. But the mind can make it in an instant if interest holds.

This trial is cited in the town history as an example of lingering frontier conditions, of the kind of excitement that could still break forth in that part of Kansas near the turn of the century. The historian himself offers no hint of his sympathies in the case. He simply offers the facts established by the evidence and summarizes the testimony taken. Out of these facts and the varied testimony comes a plain picture of the event at issue and the reasons for the verdict given.

Background is important here. The town was close to an Army post, a cavalry headquarters and supply depot. Some people liked that, those who made money out of the soldiers, especially during the first week after each payday. Other people didn't like it, those with short memories who could forget the time when the presence of troops was a reassurance for settlers and those afflicted with the urge to impose their brand of respectability on their fellows. There were periodic complaints about brawls and noisy disturbances in the saloons and disorderly houses supported chiefly by the soldiers and the inevitable collection of rough and often unsavory individuals who congregated in the neighborhood of an Army establishment. A particular annoyance to many people seems to have been a small batch of Indians, most of them well along in years, who lived, or in the usual local phrase, squatted near the post with the apparent permission of the commanding officer and loafed in and out of town with no visible means of livelihood.

That was the situation when a drastic change took place. Far off in Havana harbor the battleship Maine was sunk. The United States declared war on Spain. The troops at this Kansas post were ordered east en route to Cuba. Within ten days the post was deserted except for a small squad left to dismantle it. An unnatural quiet settled over the outlying section of the town that had annoyed so many respectable citizens. And out of that quiet came the sudden violence that precipitated the trial.

The key character was a bartender, a reckless, redheaded, ready-tongued man. He must have had a quick temper to go with the hair and a streak of cruelty in him, because his wife had left him and had been trying to divorce him on precisely those grounds. Yet he was well liked in the district, among the men at least, well enough for some of them to chip in a few dollars apiece and pay his lawyer when he was brought to trial. And apparently he was a good hand at his job. His employer had kept him on month after month even though he was constantly overdrawn on his pay. It was a better than average bartending job too. He worked at the one saloon that had rarely been a target for complaints, not so much a saloon as a semi-club, a place where sandwiches as well as liquor were available to order and where the officers of the post had been accustomed to gather when they came to town.

On this particular morning the bartender had much on his mind. He was brooding over his family troubles—or so he said later. He was worrying about losing his job—which certainly could have been true. Business had all but died with the departure of the troops a few days before. These morning hours were dull. They edged toward noon and the only customers there were two beer drinkers fiddling with a deck of cards at a rear table. And an old Indian wrapped in a mangy old buffalo robe despite the warmth of the weather came in the door and sat down at one of the front tables near the bar.

The bartender knew this Indian, knew him by frequent sight and serving at least. It was unusual for an Indian to be in that saloon, but this Indian had been there often during the previous months, always with a group of middle-aged officers, had sat at that same table in that same chair, not exactly a part of the group yet with it, sitting silent there with the officers and drinking when they drank and sometimes nodding his head gravely at what was said. Now he was alone. The officers were hundreds of miles away, riding the rails toward the port from which they would embark for Cuba.

The old Indian sat stiff and still on the chair and the bartender watched him and a familiar anger began to burn in the bartender's mind.

That was one thing the bartender hated, serving drinks to a lousy Indian. What right did one of those smelly thieving old relics with his dirty coppery skin and ugly face have to come into a white man's place and drink a white man's liquor and expect a white man to serve it to him? The way to handle Indians was to throw them the stuff by the bottle, sell them the cheapest and make them pay plenty and go drink themselves into a stupor outside in some gutter.

The old Indian moved on the chair. He raised a hand to catch the bartender's attention as the officers had always done. "Whiskey," he said as the officers had always said. "The best."

For a moment the bartender fondled the thought of jumping over the bar and grabbing hold of the Indian and heaving him bodily out into the road. No. His employer was somewhere in the back room and would hear the noise and his employer was in no mood to tolerate the loss of a customer, any customer. The bartender took a whiskey glass and reached under the bar to the slop-jar on the shelf there in which the dregs left in used glasses were dumped. It had not been emptied for several days. He dipped the whiskey glass in and brought it out dripping with the foul mixture. He walked around the end of the bar and to the table and set the glass on it. Fifty cents was the top price for a single drink. No one was ever expected to settle his score until ready to leave. But the bartender stood there looking down at the Indian. "One dollar," he said. "Now."

The old Indian looked up at him. Slowly he fumbled with one hand inside the discolored old buffalo robe. He took a long time finding what he sought. A slow satisfaction began to build in the bartender and then suddenly faded as the Indian laid a silver dollar on the table. The bartender reached for it and the anger rekindled in his mind made his hand shake and he fumbled the coin and it fell to the floor and rolled. He bent to pick it up and as he did so he heard a chuckle from back by the rear table and the sound fanned the fire in his mind. He grabbed the coin and went again behind the bar and leaned against it staring at the old Indian and the whiskey glass filled with the slopjar dregs.

The old Indian lifted the glass in his right hand. He looked around the empty table and raised the glass a little higher as if in salute. He put the glass to his lips and took a first swallow into his mouth and his head bobbed forward and he spat the stuff out and then was still, sitting quiet in the chair, staring at the glass in his hand. He sat there motionless for perhaps a full moment. He rose, still holding the glass, and went straight to the bar and set the glass down and looked over it at the bartender. "Not good," he said.

Those were the last words the old Indian ever spoke for the anger in the bartender flamed upward and destroyed all restraint and he reached and took the revolver that lay on the shelf beneath the bar and brought it up for the purpose, he said later, of forcing the complaining old fool to drink the stuff anyway, but the Indian read more than that in his eyes and knew and dropped below the bar level clutching his old robe about him to escape and the bartender leaned and reached over and fired. The bullet drove angling downward through the Indian's neck into his body. He crumpled to the floor and rolled over and was still. He was dead before the two beer drinkers at the rear table had risen to their feet to come running forward.

There had to be a trial so there was a trial. A man had been killed and in the presence of two witnesses. But no one was very enthusiastic about it. The prosecution was less than vigorous, simply went through the formalities. The old Indian was as alone in death as he had been those last moments in the saloon. His officer friends were far away, traveling toward a new military frontier. Even those of his own race quickly, and perhaps wisely, disappeared from the neighborhood of the town when they heard what had happened.

It was a peculiar trial in one respect. The original charge was murder. That was changed to manslaughter, then raised to murder again—at the request, no less, of the bartender's lawyer himself. But that lawyer knew what he was doing. He was aiming at a direct acquittal. He pleaded self-defense for his client. He brushed aside the fact that the old Indian was unarmed. How could his client have been certain that the old scarecrow didn't have a gun or a knife concealed under that buffalo robe and wasn't crouching down to pull it and then come after him? The jurymen jumped at that lead. They were out less than ten minutes. Not guilty. "There was nothing to get excited about," one of them said later. "It was just an Indian. What's another one of them more or less."

Just another Indian. The almost casual opening testimony establishing some identity for this Indian offered a few facts bearing on that point. When he was younger he had served as an Army scout. He walked with a stiffness in his right leg and two fingers of his left hand were missing.

Third, an article in a small local weekly newspaper published in a

Montana mining camp in 1901. The jump this time is three years and more than half a thousand miles. But again the mind can make it if the will prompts.

The man who wrote the article, probably the editor of the local weekly because the paper could scarcely have supported more than a one-man staff, really cut loose in the writing. He filled nearly two columns of the single-sheet issue with it, wordy, bombastic, strongly personalized in the tradition of western journalism of the period, well larded with high-flying phrases about the up-and-climbing qualities of the enterprising settlement in glorious Montana in which he was privileged to live and hold a position of civic responsibility in the opening years of the bright new century called the twentieth. He was variously shocked, amazed, disgusted, startled, outraged at what had happened. He was thunderingly insistent that something should be done about it but not quite certain what. It is quite possible that he wrote to some extent with his tongue in his cheek. That boom camp in Montana, even in 1901, was not exactly a quiet humdrum community.

A man had been killed.

Everyone knew him, so the writer said. Everyone knew everyone else in that tent-and-shack settlement so new that the census of the year before had passed it by. He was the man who tended the bar in the larger of the camp's two emporiums devoted to the dispensing of liquid refreshment. Breathed there a citizen of the camp who had not gone into that emporium tired and thirsty from grubbing gold or copper out of the stubborn unyielding rock and been grateful to see that redheaded talkative man waiting behind the bar to dispense that liquid refreshment? What if the name he used was likely not the name his parents had bequeathed him? He served good drinks. What if he had come up to Montana from down Kansas way with a somewhat vague reputation of being a dangerous man in anger? He served good drinks and with a flourish. He was free, white, and well past twenty-one, with the usual supposedly inalienable right to life, liberty, and the pursuit of happiness. And he was dead. Ah, the shifting fluctuations of fate.

So much for the journalistic rhetoric. What had happened was in itself short and simple. And deadly serious. This man, this bartender, had opened the place as usual about ten o'clock in the morning. Most of the men of the camp were out at the diggings and had been for hours. He was fussing around behind the bar, wiping glasses and arranging them on a shelf. One customer was there, almost hidden in a corner, a miner whose wildcat claim had petered out and who was already starting the new day's drowning of his misfortune. And a man wearing an old slouch hat and a shapeless old overcoat came in and went straight to the bar and spoke to the bartender in a low voice. The bartender whirled from the shelf and stared at the man and dropped the glass he was holding and the man took a revolver from the right-hand pocket of the old overcoat and fired and drilled the bartender neatly through the heart. The man turned and saw the miner in the corner half out of his chair and staring. "Don't be in a hurry to follow me," the man said. The miner wasn't. The man went out the door and around the side of the shack and was gone. The only trace of him found afterward was a neatly rolled bundle under a bush a half-mile away, the revolver and the hat tucked inside the rolled overcoat. They offered no identification. Hoofprints of a horse were found nearby, but the trail faded out in the rocky country.

There is only one more point important. That miner was the sole eyewitness. The killing had happened so quickly and the man's hat had shadowed his face so completely that the miner had difficulty trying to describe him. It seemed to him, the miner said, that the man walked and stood very erect like someone who had seen a lot of military service. And he thought, he wasn't certain, but he thought the man had a scar along the side of his jaw.

Of course that man had a scar. He had to have it. A scar made by a stone in a gully in New Mexico sixteen years before.

Prudence by Name

Some folks wonder why I've stayed on here at Cubb's Crossing all these years, deputy sheriff at the start and still the same, just handling the fussy little cases and the office routine and tending the jail. Some seem to figure that if I'd pushed myself at the right times I might have been sheriff. I know myself better'n they do. I'm not big enough for that and I don't mean in size because I'm close to six foot in my socks and not too long ago could still hoist one end of a solid wagon without grunting extra much. I'm not complaining. I've been a fair average deputy and I've kept a nice jail on the little tax money squeezed out for that and I've found the job a good spot to get to know people and what goes on around town and in the country hereabouts. Some of the best friends I've had have served time in my jail. People are what count anywhere and you might not believe it but in this work you get to know a few worth knowing. Like Amos Birdsall and his wife Prue.

They came to the Crossing on a Monday. They could have got here on Sunday but Prue wouldn't travel on the Lord's day so they camped out along the trace a ways and waited for the day to pass. They came on in Monday morning, the whole family, Amos and Prue on the front seat of their wagon and the two kids riding on the lowered tail gate beside the crate of chickens and their skimpy belongings piled between with a tattered old canvas pulled over and lashed down.

Quite a few people were coming in those days, off and on over a stretch of months. A parcel of sections west of town had been opened to homesteading and the people were coming to stake claims. The land wasn't much, middling fair for cattle grazing but not for quarter-section farming, but a promotion outfit had been sending out the usual fancy-talk fliers back through more settled areas and the people had been coming. Some stayed and stuck it and some didn't. My first bet was the Birdsalls wouldn't.

You could hardly blame me on that. They sure didn't show much when I first saw them. This was back in Sheriff Godbee's time and the two of us were sunning on the porch of the building where we had our office and my jail when the wagon came along and stopped smack in front of us. They were a queer pair sitting on the wagon seat, big rawboned knuckly Amos in faded old over-alls and patched plaid flannel shirt with a straw hat pulled down over raggedy hair, and long thin wispy Prue, all stiffness and angles, in a bebuttoned back-east dress so long it came down and hid her feet and so high and tight up around her neck it made her chin jut out sharp and stern. She had that laced-in hardshell look a woman gets when she wears a whalebone or wire-rigged corset and she had a back-east hat on her head, round and lopsided with fake flowers and a birdwing sewed on it and two big hatpins stuck through it. I saw her and I saw the two kids pecking around the wagonload from the tail gate and I couldn't help wondering how a woman like that ever managed to have kids. She didn't see us, not so you'd notice. She sat there, prim and stiff, with her lips pulled in to a thin straight line and her eyes fixed straight ahead. It was Amos spoke to us, bobbing his head and grinning like he felt he had to be kind of apologetic and soothing or someone'd start snapping at him.

"The Birdsalls," he said. "That's us, whole kit and caboodle. Me here, called Amos, and my wife, Prudence by name, and a couple of sprouts, boy and girl." He pushed the straw hat back a bit and scratched through the raggedy hair around one ear. "This the sheriff's place, ain't it? Was thinking, I was, maybe you could tell me the way to the Jenkins claim. Bought it, we have, in hard cash and hopes." He pulled the hat down again, hard. "There's a claim locator back at the hotel, there is, but he wants ten dollars. I ain't got ten dollars." He shuffled some on the wagon seat and pushed the hat up again and leaned toward us. "You see, sheriff, we had some extra, cash I mean, and two days ago at evening camp and the dark coming down, it was, this gent rides along with those two guns showing on his hips and—"

Amos stopped talking. Prue had turned on the seat and was looking at him. He shrank about two sizes in two seconds. He grinned again in that apologetic way. "Forget it, sheriff," he said. "I was just blowing. Fact is we didn't have much left and I lost that, I did, back at Twin Forks bucking a faro bank. Can't figure what went wrong, I can't. My system ought—"

He stopped again. His wife, Prudence by name, was clearing her throat with a little rasping sound. She looked at us on the porch and away. "It was my fault," she said. "I let him go into that town by himself. The children were tired and I couldn't leave them and everything was so dirty we had to have some soap. So he did it again."

She sat still on the wagon seat looking straight ahead and Amos sat beside her bobbing his head and grinning in that apologetic way and Sheriff Godbee uncrossed his lean old right leg from over his left leg and crossed them again in reverse order and looked at me. "Howie," he said, "your jail's empty. Your desk's clear. Your middle's plumping. Saddle a horse and show these folks the way."

So there I was ambling along in the saddle beside the wagon and there Prue was jolting silent on the seat and there Amos was holding the reins in his big knuckly hands and squinting sideways at me and asking questions about the territory and telling me something about the two of them. They'd had several places, back in Iowa the last one and a mortgage on it and they kept missing payments, maybe bad luck, as he said flipping a quick glance at Prue, maybe faro as he didn't say, and they'd had to sell out and take whatever was left over and start again. They were heading west out our way when they met Jenkins heading east and they linked the notion of a claim with some buildings on it already and pulled him down on his price and paid him. "Too bad, it was," Amos said. "Him in poor health like that and having to leave. Good luck too. For us, that is."

"Poor health?" I said. "Jenkins? The only poor health he ever had came out of a bottle."

Prue turned on the seat and they both looked at me and the wagon jolted along and they both stared at me. "Buildings," Amos said. "There's buildings on it, there is. There's got to be."

I couldn't look at them. I watched the road ruts sliding past under the wheels. "Well, yes," I said. "Yes, there's buildings." I nudged my horse ahead and led the way off to the right down the wagon trace along the section lines and across the creek branch and up over the first rise beyond. I stopped and Amos brought the wagon along beside me and they could see the buildings, all the ramshackle three or really two and a half of them, the single-room tarpapered and slab-roofed shack and the split-log pole-and-sod-roofed shed with the open lean-to spreading out from one side.

They sat still and stared at the buildings. The two kids climbed down off the tail gate and stared too. "Anyway," I said, "there's a well. A good one."

Prue turned on the seat and looked at me and then at Amos. "Men," she said. "Why did God have to make men." She climbed down over the wheel on her side and marched straight to that ugly rough shack and through the door hanging on one hinge and the two kids looked accusing at me and Amos just as she had and followed her.

Amos bobbed his head at me but he didn't grin. "Edgy, she is," he said. "Been angry, she has, ever since out of blankets this morning and all because I wouldn't put on my Sunday clothes, I wouldn't, for coming into town. Knew I'd be unloading, I did, and starting work right away. Wasn't going to be changing back and forth." He pushed the straw hat back on his head and looked around. "Ain't much. Ain't much at all." He climbed down his side of the wagon and started toward the shack and Prue was in the doorway and her voice was high and shrill. "There's no floor," she said. Her legs seemed to crumple under her and she sat down on the big stone that was the doorstep and bent her head and put her face in her hands.

Amos stopped still, rocking on his big clumsy feet "That man lied to me," he said. He raised one big knuckly hand and clenched it into a fist and smacked it into the palm of the other hand. "There ain't no floor," he said. "All right, there ain't. But there's a roof, there is. We can rig a partition in that house. That shed'll make a fine chickencoop, it will. That lean-to'll take care of the team. We've got food in the wagon. Got our health too. We'll make out, we will, till I get a crop in and some more building done."

For a moment he seemed big and almost impressive standing there and then Prue raised her head and looked at him. "You promised me a board floor," she said. "It isn't decent without a board floor. Only the good Lord knows what it is to have to live with a man who doesn't even care if things are decent." And the little girl in the doorway behind her spoke up, with the boy trying to shush her, and her voice was an exact copy of her mother's. "He doesn't care. He just doesn't care." And Prue stood up, all stiff and angles, and marched past Amos standing there and past me still sitting quiet on the horse, and pulled a broom out of the wagon and marched back and into that house.

Amos sighed and came over by the wagon and began to unlash the load. I slipped down and helped. Together we hoisted everything out and piled it on the ground. The kids came running and scurried like packrats carrying small stuff and I helped Amos carry the heavy things into the house where Prue was bustling and raising dust. That was easy for her to do because the top layer of the packed dirt that was the floor was dry and crumbly. She didn't say another word but it wasn't long before I had the feeling too I ought to step careful and watch how I behaved or someone'd start snapping at me. I was glad when there wasn't much else I could do to help and I could head home to town and my jail.

That was late spring. By early summer the talk drifting around was that the Birdsalls were queer folk, unfriendly and plain peculiar. After a while I began to notice that when people talked like that they were really talking about Prue. Amos was just there, a hard worker when he worked, which was irregular, and a talker when anyone would listen, but just a man roundabout bobbing his head and being apologetic when people were near. Prue was the dominant one. She made the sharp impression. She made one plenty sharp on Sheriff Godbee's wife Martha.

It took a lot to rile Martha Godbee. She was just as broad and ample in spirit as she was in body, which was more'n enough for any one person, but she was riled when she drove back to town in the old buggy that day. The sheriff and I, up on the porch, saw her coming along the road at quite a clip. She pulled in close and climbed out before I could jump down to help her and she heaved up the two steps and pushed herself into the extra-wide chair we kept there for her. "That woman," she said and blew out her cheeks with a puffing noise.

We didn't say a thing. We knew we'd get it all and in a rush. "That Prudence Birdsall woman," she said. "And I was only trying to be neighborly. Things being said around town and by women I respect and I wondered were they true and went out to see and get acquainted, and they are. She can't even say hello like ordinary folks. Puts her nose up and says how do you do in that silly voice supposed to be refined and it's a pleasure meeting a person and she stands smack in the doorway blocking it and won't ask a person in. Oh she would she says but it wouldn't be decent not having a board floor but just plain dirt and she'd like a person to know she wasn't raised to walk around indoors on dirt and she wouldn't have to if she didn't have a man doesn't care one way or another about things being decent and is so shiftless and plain no-account he can't even put boards under the feet of his wife and children."

Martha Godbee puffed out her cheeks again and took in a big breath and started again. "Her talking like that and him standing right there and hearing it and the whole place looking so much better with the work he's done on it and him standing there trying to look friendly and like she's really only joking and her going on and on with more of the same talk in that silly voice that's not joking at all and sneaking looks at him to see him wince. And what she's doing to those children is a crying shame, with her letting them stand around hearing her and making nasty remarks too and referring to their father like he was a thing and call him 'he' and 'him' like he didn't even have a name and her not slapping them even once for it. Who does she think she is running down her man like that and with people listening and her putting on airs out here where we're all just folks and proud to be and don't care what kind of floor a person's got long as she's really folks too."

Martha Godbee took in another breath and jutted her chin at the sheriff. "What kind of floor did we have when we first came out here? Speak up now, Fred, and tell Howie here. What kind was it?"

Sheriff Godbee looked at her with his old eyes bright. "Dirt," he said. He chuckled. "Whole damn house was dirt. Sod walls. Sod roof. Dripped water two days after a rain." He jutted his own chin a bit. "But why ain't you peeved at him too? If he was the man he ought to be he'd shut her off soon enough. He'd whale her backside the way I'd've yours had you gone around nagging and complaining."

"Humph," Martha Godbee said, making her extra-size chair squeak. "It wasn't worrying over any whaling you'd do kept me from complaining."

"Well, now, Martha," Sheriff Godbee said and his old voice was soft and gentle. "You tell me what it was kept you from it."

"Because I'm not the complaining kind," Martha Godbee said and then she pulled in her chin till it was about lost in the folds of her ample neck and her voice was soft and gentle too. "And because I knew soon as we had a little over from things we needed more, getting started, you'd get me a better house."

"Well now, Martha," Sheriff Godbee said again, "maybe that's just the difference. Maybe that Prudence woman doesn't know what you knew."

I expect that was it. Prue couldn't know whether Amos ever would get her a floor or any of the other things she nagged about because there wasn't much he'd ever done to show he was the getting kind. He had good intentions maybe but he couldn't seem to follow through on them. He'd start something and then he'd want to finish it the easy way. He worked hard, irregular as I said before but hard when he did, and he put in a crop and didn't run too big a bill at Rudy Ferebee's store for seed and for food when what they'd bought ran out. The season was good that year and he had a fair crop and he sold his stuff, mostly corn and other truck, through Rudy to the Army post back near Twin Forks and he paid off his bill and laid in supplies right careful according to Prue's list and he had thirty-three dollars left. Prue was there with him when he got the money and bought the supplies. She was with him when they loaded the supplies and drove around to Luke Wagaman's place, where Luke did blacksmithing and handled what building materials were freighted into town. Amos climbed down and went inside the shop to talk to Luke about boards and he didn't come back out, and after a stretch Prue climbed down and went in after him and he wasn't there.

So there was the Birdsall wagon stopped again by our office-and-jail porch, only Prue was alone on the seat this time looking mad and worried all at once and talking but not in any high-toned voice. So the sheriff and I climbed up on the seat with her and I took the reins and we went around to see Luke and found out what happened.

Lumber was high around here in those days. The nearest timber and a sawmill were a long ways off and the railroad hadn't come through yet. Freighting costs pushed prices up. Amos didn't want rough boards either, green and likely to warp. He wanted finished boards seasoned right. He went in the shop and got to figuring with Luke what he'd need for a floor and even though their house was small it tallied eighty-seven dollars. Amos took out his money and counted it over again and it still was only thirty-three of those dollars and then while Luke was scratching around in his head what kind of a deal he might fix to help these new Birdsall folks Amos lit out the back door. "Didn't say another word," Luke told us, looking up at us on the wagon seat. "Jammed the money in his pocket and scatted out the back way."

Sheriff Godbee reached and took the reins out of my hands. "The lop-eared jackass," he said and he smacked the team on their rumps with the rein ends. I had to grab Prue and hold her from jouncing off as we swung in a half-circle. "Have to ask your pardon, ma'am," Sheriff Godbee said, slapping steady at the team to keep them stepping fast. "But it's the truth. Any man thinks he's got a faro system is a lop-eared jackass."

We pulled to a quick stop in front of Clem Rickey's saloon. The sheriff and I piled down and hurried in and straight through to the back room and there he was, chewing on a big knuckle and slumped in a chair across the table from the dealer with the box. He saw us and he knew what was doing right away. He bobbed, his head and grinned in that apologetic way. "Lost again, I have," he said. "And it ain't right. Should have run it up to more'n enough. Played my system, I did, but something went wrong and—" His voice died away. I expect we looked peeved. At least the dealer thought so because he put in fast with his own words. "It was straight play, sheriff. I don't run it crooked." And Sheriff Godbee fixed the dealer with a cold look. "Ain't arguing that," he said. "You wouldn't be in my district did I think different." He swung to

Amos again and I thought he might let loose with some chilling comments but he just looked at Amos a moment and sighed. "Better go on out. Prue's waiting for you to take her home." And Amos pushed up and walked out front slow and heavy on his feet and climbed up on the wagon seat beside her and took the reins. She didn't look at him, not once after she saw him coming. She didn't even speak to him. She didn't need to. She knew. She just sat silent, jolting as the wagon moved, and stared straight ahead and they went on along the road growing smaller and smaller in the distance.

That was a tough winter, snow often and staying and choking the roads. We were busy in town what with people sort of jammed together, not able to get out and around much. Sheriff Godbee had to spend a lot of time at Clem Rickey's helping Clem keep the boys behaving right and heading off fights when nerves were jumpy and since he couldn't always head them off my jail had boarders fairly frequent. I couldn't know much what went on at the Birdsalls' except that they were making out with Amos hustling to keep the house warm and Prue teaching the kids out of some schoolbooks she'd brought in her trunk. I expect no matter how big a fire Amos had inside the house it was still cold in there for him because people who happened by when the going was passable said he always seemed to be outside even in the coldest weather, puttering and wandering around all bundled in an old overcoat.

Then it was spring and everyone was buzzing busy while the good weather held and of a sudden Amos was standing in the office where I was helping the sheriff catch up on paperwork. He hadn't driven in. He'd hiked it. He had a bundle under one arm and he was about busting with his plans. "Going to get her that floor," he said. "Got my crop in. Boy and the team can do the cultivating, they can. Me now, I'm heading for the railroad camp. Forty and found, they're paying grading crews. Two months'll about make it. Appreciate it, I will, if one of you'll stop off at my place now and again and see everything's all right."

Two months he said. Two months, add a few days, it was and he was back. He came back the way he went, hooking a ride on a freight wagon, and hiked straight on home and drove into town again with his own wagon and to Luke Wagaman's and paid cash for good lumber and loaded it and stopped to push his head in our door and thank us and drove home. There was something wrong about the whole business and that wasn't just the fact Prue wasn't with him when he came in for the lumber. It was the fact he wasn't the least bit happy about what he was doing. He'd gone off tickled silly and proud he'd figured a way to get Prue her floor. He came back tight-faced and quiet, hardly speaking to anyone, staring down at the ground in front of him when he walked along.

Maybe a week later, maybe longer but not much, I found Sheriff Godbee in his office chewing on a pencil and wanting to talk. "Howie," he said, "I never did like arithmetic and don't like the way things add up now. That Birdsall woman's invited Martha out to call tomorrow afternoon."

"Why not?" I said. "She's got her floor. But what's arithmetic got to do with that?"

"Not much," he said. "Not direct. But there's a couple other things. One's what Lewis told me when I was over at Twin Forks the other day. They had a little ruckus over there, a week, ten days ago. Man tried bucking a faro bank. Had a little luck and was winning. Began blowing what he'd do with it. Put a floor in his place, build it bigger, maybe ship in a piano. Luck turned and he lost, all he'd won and what he started with. Took it hard and had to be bounced into the road."

"I'll be doggoned," I said. "What's the other thing?"

"This in the mail today," he said, poking at a letter on his desk. "From Bowlus over at the junction on the freight route. Little trouble over there too. Figures about the day after the other. Somebody nipped a fistful of cash out of the drawer behind the bar in the saloon there. Probably did it while everybody was out watching a dogfight but wasn't noticed till a while later. Bowlus's been checking and can't find a trace. Now somebody's remembered seeing someone come out the door while the fight was on. Didn't know him but think's he's seen him over this way sometime. Big man. Overalls and a straw hat."

"How much did he take?" I said.

Sheriff Godbee grunted. "What would you expect? They don't know exactly. Money hadn't been checked. But they figure it eighty-some dollars. I figure it eighty-seven."

I sat down in the other chair and stared at him and he stared back at me and after a while he sighed and pushed up. "Come on," he said. "Waiting never made any of these things any better. We'll go have a talk with Amos."

He wasn't in sight but Prue was when we stopped the buggy by the house. The door was open and she was standing in the doorway with a broom in her hand and past her we could see the floor, good boards well fitted together, smooth and already almost shining like it had been swept and scrubbed half a dozen times a day. She didn't act at all the way she had that first time. She looked right at us and she almost smiled. "Oh, do come in," she said. "I can have coffee ready in a minute."

"No, thank you, ma'am," Sheriff Godbee said. "We haven't

time. Just want to see Amos on a bit of business. Want to see him alone if you don't mind."

She was so still she seemed almost to have stopped breathing and her face began to change, getting pinched and tight again. "He's around somewhere," she said. "He was cleaning the chicken shed."

We started toward the shed and Amos came around the side of it and Sheriff Godbee took him by the arm and we went around the side together out of sight of the house and Prue in the doorway, and Sheriff Godbee started asking questions, making them more pointed as he got a little peeved, and Amos just looked at the ground. "I don't know what you're talking about," was all he would say and in a voice we could hardly hear. And sudden another voice, high-pitched and sharp, said the one word "Amos" and he jerked up straighter and Prue came around the corner of the shed. She must have been hiding there, listening to what went on.

"Amos Birdsall!" she said. "You can lie all you want to other people but you've never lied to me. Did you lose that money like all the rest?"

He tried to look at her and couldn't and stared down at his big knuckly hands. "Yes, Prue. I lost it, I did."

"And did you steal money from that saloon?"

"Yes, Prue. I took it, I did."

Prue turned to Sheriff Godbee. "All right," she said and her voice was harsh and bitter. "That's what you wanted to know."

"No," Sheriff Godbee said. "I knew. But that's what I wanted Amos to say."

There was a moment of quiet while we all were thinking our own thoughts and the two kids came running from somewhere calling out for their mother, and right away they sensed something was wrong and they ducked quick toward her and stood beside

148

her, clutching at her skirt. The boy just scowled at Amos and scuffed the dirt but the little girl began a sort of whimpering chant. "He's been bad again. I just know it. He's been bad again." And Prue shushed her by gathering her in closer with one arm and looked over her at Sheriff Godbee. "Well, anyway," she said, "you tell your wife to stay home now and walk around on her own floor. But there's one thing you'll have to let him do before you take him to jail."

Sheriff Godbee's old voice snapped. "Watch your words, woman. In front of these children."

"I will not," she said. "If their father's a thief, they might as well know it."

"All right," Sheriff Godbee said. "But there's thieving and there's thieving and stealing a man's self-respect is a damn bad thing too. Who but you's said anything about jail? It ain't our way to jail a man's got family responsibilities if that can be helped. What we've got to do now is figure a way for Amos to square this thing."

"I don't care what you do with him," Prue said. "But before you do whatever you do with him you'll have to let him get things out of the house for me. The children's cots and some blankets and the stove and all the food there is. I want them in this chicken shed."

"Chicken shed?" Sheriff Godbee said and that was one of the few times I ever saw him really surprised.

"That's where," Prue said. "You don't think I'm ever going to set foot on that floor again. Not on a floor that's not really mine and that's been paid for with thieving money. Not my children either."

Sheriff Godbee stared at her and started to speak and thought better of it. He turned to me and Amos. "A damn funny world," he said. "Maybe there's something to that woman after all. Come along. We'll tote those things out here and then see what can be done in town."

Plenty could. Plenty always could be done when Sheriff Godbee put his mind to it. He talked Luke Wagaman into handing back the eighty-seven dollars Amos had paid for the lumber. More than that, he talked Luke into letting Amos work out the price by helping at the blacksmith shop. That wasn't too big a favor Luke was doing because he had more work than he could handle fast as people wanted at the shop, and finding a helper could swing a hefty hammer like Amos during the busy summer season wasn't easy. In a way Luke wasn't really handing back the money. He was just paying that much in advance for work Amos would do. Then Sheriff Godbee took the eighty-seven dollars and put them in an envelope with a letter to Bowlus at the junction, and just what he wrote in that letter I never knew but it stopped any further action in the case. So after I posted the letter and came back by our office-and-jail building and went in to have supper with the Godbees at their house next door I was thinking this Birdsall business was working out all right. Amos would get his meals at Luke Wagaman's and sleep in the shop till his stint was done and if Prue wanted to be stubborn and live in that chicken shed till her floor was really paid for that was her lookout. She was about as much to blame as Amos. It was her nagging drove him to do what he did.

That's the way I was thinking at the supper table, so I was somewhat surprised when there was a knock and Sheriff Godbee called a come-in and it was Amos pushed in through the front door. I wasn't so much surprised at seeing him as at what he said. "Mr. Godbee," he said. "Sheriff, I mean. I want you to lock me up in your jail, I do."

"Well now, Amos," Sheriff Godbee said and he didn't seem to be much surprised. "That's an interesting idea. Why?"

"Seems to me, it does," Amos said, "I ought to do some time for what I did. Can't do it while working, I can't. But nights and Sundays I can."

"Amos," Sheriff Godbee said and his voice was a little stern, "have you been out home and got that idea from Prue?"

"I have not," Amos said. "But it's thinking of her in that shed's helped me think of it for myself, it has."

"Howie," Sheriff Godbee said, "lock this man up. Tight. Let him out breakfast time weekday mornings and lock him up again smack after supper. Sundays you'll have to feed him like you do other boarders. Any time he doesn't show when he should, you go after him."

So there I had Amos in my jail, off and on, nights and Sundays, most of the summer. That's when I got to know him, not just the way you know somebody who happens to live in your district and calls you by name and passes the time of day with you, but the way you know a man who sleeps under the same roof for a while and sees you close and gets to talking personal with you when a lantern's burning low. I'd come over after supper from the Godbees' and he'd be waiting on the porch and I'd take him in the building and lock him up, not in the waiting-for-trial quarters with bars all around but in the cooling-off quarters with the barred window and barred door and the old phonograph I had there to help boarders pass the hours. He'd stretch out on one of the bunks and like as not, evenings when he had no company, not even a drunk sobering up, I'd bring a chair and set it by the barred door and we'd talk till time for me to head for the cot I kept in my office. Talking with him like that got to seeming quite natural but I never did get used to him saying, as he did last thing at night, "Appreciate it, I do, you locking me up like this."

Not many nights and he was telling me a lot about himself and his early days. He'd been a farm boy in eastern Iowa and after his mother died and he was growing some size he skipped for a couple years and was a cowhand on a middling big ranch. Trailing with the older hands he had his first taste of faro. He had luck that first time and ran up a roll that went soon enough with the other hands' help but the memory of it stuck. Then his father died and since he was the only child the farm was his and he went back there and tried working it. Along about then he got married and began having bigger ideas and he slapped a mortgage on the farm to stock it with purebred cattle and then when payments were coming due he never seemed to have quite enough and he took to remembering his faro luck. I could fill in the rest easy.

It was while he was talking that way I asked the question that was bothering me. "Amos," I said, "back east where you were women aren't so scarce. How'd you ever hook on to one like Prue?" He didn't get mad at me. I expect he knew what I meant, at least how it looked to me. He scratched around in his raggedy hair and tried to answer me straight. "She's from New England, she is," he said like he was proud of that. "Had to earn her living so she came out to teach school. Had a hard time, she did, book-taught woman like that. Big boys wouldn't behave in school. Made fun of her and her ways. I whopped a few and she called to thank me, she did. Come summer we called on the preacher." Amos looked at me, a little red in the face and defiant. "She was pretty then, she was. Kind of soft and—and womanlike." He rolled over on the bunk and wouldn't look at me anymore and that was the only night he didn't thank me for locking him up.

A couple more weeks and I was beginning to nurse a worry. I was right fond of Amos by then and I could see this Birdsall business wasn't working out too well after all. There was Prue out in that chicken shed and there was Amos spending all his time working and being in jail and she hadn't come in once to see him. She knew what he was doing. Sheriff Godbee had been out special to tell her. But she'd been into town twice, driving their team, and got whatever she needed each time at Rudy Ferebee's store and gone right home again without stopping at the blacksmith shop and without even looking at my jail, when she went past on the road. And Amos was fretting about her. He wouldn't say anything more about her, but he was getting to look more like a big raggedy lonesome dog every day. I didn't know what to do about that but Sheriff Godbee did. He did it quick and direct and almost brutal the way he could be when he felt a need.

It was the next time Prue came to town, on a Saturday. She went to the store and would have gone on out of town again past our building but Sheriff Godbee stepped down into the road and grabbed the bridle of the near horse of the team and stopped the wagon. "Prue," he said, "you're a damn stupid woman. Why haven't you been in to see Amos?"

She reared up some on the seat. "Don't you dare talk to me like that!"

"I'll talk to you any way I've a mind to," he said. "You, a woman running out on her man a time like this."

"I'm not running out," she said. "I'm staying right there at that excuse of a home he's given me. Oh, I know what he's doing. He's trying to get back at me for nagging at him and now for living in that shed. Putting himself in jail. Working days and being locked up nights. Making himself look like—like a chain gang criminal."

"No," Sheriff Godbee said. "Like a man paying his debts. Working to pay for some boards for a silly woman. Serving time to pay the rest of us for breaking one of the rules of living we call laws." He let go the bridle and swung around and stomped up the steps and into his office.

Prue sat on the wagon seat staring after him. She saw me watching and jerked herself straighter and clucked to the team. But the next day, Sunday, she was back, all decked in her eastern dress and hat, bringing a clean pair of overalls and a clean shirt and some biscuits and a jar of her jelly in a basket. She waited in my office and I went and got Amos and pushed him in where she was and had enough sense to close the door quick.

That's how things went along until close to harvest time, Amos working and being locked up and Prue coming every Sunday, always with something tasty in her basket. She was just as prim and sharp-faced as ever and Amos acted some Sundays when she left like she had worked him over mighty thorough with her tongue but at least she was coming to see him and he didn't have that lonesome-dog look anymore. Then one day, midweek, Amos came along from the shop just after noon and up on the porch where the sheriff and I were soaking sun. "Paid up, I am," he said. "Every last cent. Own that floor now. Every last board. Got a new deal with Luke, I have, starting next week. Two days' work a week for ready cash. Now I'm going home and move Prue back into the house and watch her walk around on those boards and feel good." He pushed his old straw hat up a bit and bobbed his head and grinned at us. "Ought to be some celebrating, there ought. Why'nt you two come along. Best friends we have around here, you are. Be the first visitors on Prue's floor."

Sheriff Godbee squinted at the sky, thinking his own thoughts. "Might be interesting," he said. "Howie, get the buggy out. Beats walking any day."

So there the three of us were bouncing along in the buggy following the road and then off to the right and down the wagon trace and across the creek branch and all the way Amos was talking and humming and bobbing his head in anticipation. Right then that floor and going home to tell Prue she could walk on it now was the biggest thing in the world to him.

The two kids saw us coming and ran out to see who it was and looked startled at his shouts and scurried back and around the house and when we swung in near the chicken shed there Prue was waiting and the two kids were behind her peering around at us. Amos jumped out and I started to follow and Sheriff Godbee stopped me. "No hurry," he said. "Maybe there's more to this thing."

There was. I don't know how he knew there would be but there was. Amos hurried straight to Prue and she kind of backed away and didn't seem happy to see him coming. He was too full of his own feeling to notice and he grabbed her by the waist and picked her up and whirled her around and set her down and she stood quiet with a funny flat frightened look on her face. He still didn't notice. He took her by the arm and hustled her toward the house, talking steady how the floor was all paid for, every board, and how much better things were going to be all around, and she just stumbled along beside him with the two kids tagging and keeping her between them and Amos. He stopped by the doorstep and reached and pushed the door open and she pulled back away from him.

"No," she said. "I can't. I just can't." The words faded away and the silence was a strange feeling all about with Amos caught in it and the two kids crouched by the house wall now afraid to move.

Amos seemed to sag all over. "Why, Prue. I don't understand, I don't."

She just stood there, all stiffness and sharp angles, and she couldn't look in through the doorway and she couldn't look at him. "Prue," he said, his voice getting an edge. "What's wrong with you?"

"I can't do it," she said. "All these weeks I've been out here knowing that floor was in there and how silly I've been. I can't go in there. It wouldn't ever seem right."

Amos looked in through the doorway at that floor that represented two months' railroad work and two more months' blacksmithing and a lot of nights and Sundays in jail to him. He stood straighter and he drew in a long breath that seemed to fill him out to full size. "Prue, girl," he said, "would you feel better if that floor just wasn't there?" She nodded, a bare little bobbing of her head, and he marched over by the chicken shed and took the rusty old ax leaning against it and marched hack and in through the doorway and the whole house seemed to shake with the sounds of splintering wood. He came out and his arms were full of smashed pieces of those good boards. He threw them on the ground and with the ax he sliced shavings off one and huddled these in a little pile and put a match to them and when they were blazing he began to lay the pieces of board across the flames. And all the while Prue stood still and watched him and the two kids crept close to her and held to her skirt and watched him too and she stood still and a flush of color climbed up her cheeks.

Amos rose tall from squatting by the fire and looked across it at her and the silence was a taut tight feeling there between them and it broke with the sound of the little girl's whimpering voice. "He's being bad again, bad again, bad—" And Prue's hands moved sudden and sure and she had the girl by the shoulders and shook her. "Don't you ever," she said, "ever once again let me hear you speak about your father like that." She looked back across the fire at Amos and her face was all twisted and crinkled from the effort not to cry. "Amos," she said. "My Amos." She came around the fire reaching out toward him and he put out a big arm around her shoulders. She raised her head toward him and for a moment there in the line of her throat arching upward and her face open and eager to him you could see it. It was there and it was gone but it had been there. She was almost pretty and she was kind of soft and womanlike.

"There now, Prue," Amos said. "No more worrying now. Not ever again." He looked over her head at the two kids standing sort of lost and alone on the other side of the fire. He left Prue and went around and he scooped the little girl up in the crook of one big arm and held her high so her head topped his own and you could see this was something that hadn't happened to her for a long time and she was frightened at first and then kind of excited and pleased and he reached with his other arm and took the boy by the hand. "Sprouts," he said, "we have work to do, we have. Your mother doesn't want that particular floor in her house and she's right about it. Let's get busy. I'll do the chopping and you do the carrying."

Sheriff Godbee and I sat in the buggy and watched the four of them working together. The ax was thumping in the house and the kids were scurrying in and out with pieces of board and Prue was chucking these one by one on the fire. "You know what I'm going to do?" I said. "I'm going to kick in some myself and take up a collection in town. I'm going to get them another board floor."

"No need to do that," Sheriff Godbee said. "Prue's all right now. They're both all right. She's got something better'n a board floor."

She had. She had all right. Because sudden she remembered us and noticed us swinging the buggy quiet as possible to slip away and she came hurrying to stop us a moment. "Mr. Godbee," she said, "I want you to tell your wife to come call on me again soon as convenient for her." And Sheriff Godbee looked at Prue with his face seeming stern but his old eyes shining. "Prudence Birdsall, ma'am," he said, "I ain't so sure I ought to let my wife call on people that've only got a dirt floor for her to walk on." And Prue gave him look for look with her own eyes snapping and she snorted just the way Martha Godbee would. "Humph," she said. "A lot of difference your letting or not letting would make. It was me and not any dirt floor made her mad when she was here before. We'll be having a board floor again and it won't be because I nagged about it and maybe that'll be soon and maybe it won't because there are other things we need more but that won't have anything to do with her coming to call. She knows a floor isn't nearly as important as the people who walk around on it." And then Prue said what knocked all words out of Sheriff Godbee and made him fumble for his old bandanna to blow his nose. "Maybe she was born knowing that the way I wasn't," Prue said, "or maybe she's just lived so many years with you she couldn't help learning it."

We were mighty quiet, me and the sheriff, all the way back to town. But it was a nice warm good-feeling quiet.

Old Anse

O ld Anse Birkitt sat on the worn log doorsill of his cabin and looked down the slope and across the creek and watched Sid Jenkins and the stringy woman Sid called his wife pile their few belongings in a rickety buckboard. The morning sun was warm on his face and he wriggled his old bare feet in the warm dust of his dooryard and watched the Jenkinses drive away without a glance back at the shack in which they had lived for better than four years. Footloose, he thought. Would be the first to go . . .

The sun made its circuit overhead and dropped into the mountains behind the cabin and in the morning Old Anse sat in his doorway and looked down and across and watched workmen pull apart the plank building that had been Bartlett's store. He scrooged in a pocket of his faded jeans and found a remnant of tobacco quid and gnawed off a small chew. He watched John Bartlett fuss about and shout directions as the workmen loaded the planks on a pair of flatbed wagons. Greedy, he thought. Got a price for it and carting it away too . . .

The sun climbed past noon and what had been Bartlett's store building went away on the wagons along the lower valley road and darkness swept out of the mountains and Old Anse lit his lantern and prepared his evening meal. In the morning he sat on his log doorsill and looked down and across the creek at what remained of the little road-fork town and watched the people departing. The flies were bad and he slapped at them and let the sun's warmth soak into his old bones and watched the people go, family after family in wagons or buggies and the Crutchleys with their stairstep line of kids on foot and the blacksmith with his anvil and heavy tools on an oxcart and the schoolmaster on horseback with saddlebags full of books. The sun swung on its high arc and the afternoon rays beat against the back of the cabin and across the creek on the almost empty town and when darkness took it the only other light in the valley outside the cabin was in the big frame house rising above the others on the town side of the creek. Old Anse stood in his doorway and studied the yellow-patch windows of the big house across and almost level with his cabin. He blew out his lantern and shed his jeans and lay on his bunk. *Waiting to be the last of them, he thought. But he'll go like all the rest . . .*

Light crept over the eastern valley rim behind the big house and broke free and streaked across the sky and the sun shone warm on the cabin doorway. Old Anse rinsed his frying pan and coffee cup and settled on the log doorsill and watched the Peabodys strip the big house of its furnishings and load these on their big freight wagon. He slapped at the flies and watched Luke Peabody and his two big sons lash the load tight and harness the big work teams in double tandem and bring out the surrey with the tall trotter in the traces. The womenfolk came from the house and climbed into the surrey and the men swung up on the wagon and Old Anse sat still and watched them go.

The wagon stopped and the surrey behind it. Luke Peabody swung out on a wheel hub and to the ground and walked back and stood in the road dust looking at the big house. He turned and looked across the creek at Old Anse. He walked to the creek edge and made a funnel of his hands at his mouth and shouted. Old Anse caught the voice with ears that could still catch the rustle of deer hooves in grass at more than fifty paces, but he sat quiet and waited and watched Luke Peabody shake his head in exasperation and shout again and at last stride across the creek through water above his knees and come up the slope.

"Birkitt," said Luke Peabody, "seventeen years I've lived here and not once known you be neighborly. Could be my fault some. I've thought you an opinionated, shiftless old fool and said so many a time. That doesn't matter much now. I'd like to leave with a friendly word. Here's my hand on it."

Luke Peabody put out a big hand with the fingers stretched and reaching and Old Anse sat still and looked up with eye corners tightening. Luke Peabody let his hand drop. "So be it," he said. "All the same I'm asking a favor." And Old Anse tightened his eye corners more. "Thought there'd be a ketch to it," he said.

"Do you think I'd ask you was there anyone else left around?" Luke Peabody raised his hand and wiped it palm flat across his face. "I want you to set fire to my place." And Old Anse's eyes opened wide and he looked down at the dooryard dust and up again sharp and quick. "Why?"

"Because I don't like to think what'll happen to it if it just stands there."

Old Anse looked down at his feet in the dust and pulled them in close under him and stood up and held out a hand. "Changed my mind." And Old Anse Birkitt and Luke Peabody shook hands, both of them slow and solemn, and Luke Peabody started away and swung his head back without stopping and spoke fast. "You'll wait till we're out of sight around the bend?"

Old Anse sat on his doorsill and slapped at the flies and watched the wagon and the surrey fade in a dust haze around the bend of the lower valley road. *Got some of a man's feelings*, he thought. *But can't do the hard things himself . . .*

The sun arched overhead and Old Anse went inside and opened a can of beans. After he had eaten he went down to the creek and rolled up his jeans and waded across. He went along the lane by the squat stone piers on which Bartlett's store had rested and on by the deserted houses and shacks to the big house. He made a slow circuit of the place, peering in at the stripped-empty rooms. He took an armload of old straw from the stable and pushed this under the jutting rear porch. When the flames were licking at the wood he went back to the creek and waded across and on up to his cabin. He sat in his doorway, legs out drying in front of him, and watched the flames leap into view over the rear roof of the house and eat their way forward on the shingles. The wood of the house was dry with the years and the season and the fire reached and ran till the whole structure was blazing. Old Anse sat quiet and watched and it was his alone. There was no one else in the whole section of the valley to see it.

The uprush of flames slackened and the charring shell of the house shuddered and collapsed backward and the flames leaped again then settled down to steady gnawing at the wreckage. Old Anse stirred and swung his head to study the wide view before him. Shadows were long now, stretching away from him, and the deserted town and sweep of valley were hushed in the silence of their emptiness. *Breathing's easier*, he thought. *No people crowding a man's elbows . . .*

He looked down the valley to the right where the lower road curved away and ran on beyond vision around the bend to where he knew the crews of men were at work and the heavy stone-wagons were rolling and the carloads of gravel and cement were shuttling on the railroad spur. His eye corners tightened and he looked away with a quick jerk of his head.

The shadows merged into the overall darkening of dusk as the sun dropped into the mountains behind the cabin and he straightened and went around the corner to the left and to the near stand of trees where the tall square stone of white mountain marble still showed plain against the dark ivy on the ground. He stooped to pull away an ivy sprig starting up the stone. *Just you and me again, Marthy*, he thought. *Like it was in the beginning . . .*

A thin sliver of moon passed low over the horizon and the stars wheeled above and an hour before dawn Old Anse rolled out of his bunk and pulled on his faded jeans and a pair of moccasins. He was restless with a renewed eager spryness oiling his old joints. He took from the wall the old Colt repeating cylinder rifle that had never failed him in almost forty years' service. When the sun broke over the eastern valley rim he was three miles up the creek and over the first side ridge, heading into the rocky highlands toward the small hidden canyon that he alone knew.

Three hours later he was headed homeward with the dressed carcass of a small whitetail buck draped over his shoulders. His knees gave him trouble now and he stopped often to rest. Several times the fingers of his left hand holding the legs locked together in front grew numb and could no longer grasp and the carcass slid from his shoulders and he had to flex the fingers till strength returned to them, then kneel and stoop to get the carcass in place again and use the rifle as a cane to lever himself to his feet. Once he fell and rolled twenty feet downslope, bruising against stone, and lay still for a while breathing in short gasps and cursing soft to himself. The sun shone on him with the remembered friendliness of long past days and warmed his old bones and he rose and retrieved the rifle and gathered up the carcass again. He made the final stretch to the cabin with a sustained stumbling rush because he was afraid that if he stopped he might not get started with his burden once more. It dropped to the dooryard with a soft thud and he sank on the log doorsill and kicked off the moccasins to wriggle his old toes in the warm dust. *Knew it*, he thought. *Knew I could still do it . . .*

Old Anse reached inside the cabin for his ramrod and a piece of greasy rag. Quiet and serene in the sunlight he began cleaning the rifle. He was polishing the worn stock when his ears caught the sound and his head lifted and he saw the small wagon coming up the lower valley road. He rested the rifle across his knees and watched the wagon approach and turn to ford the creek below him and stop on the near side. His eye corners tightened into a squint as he watched the broad homely gray-topped figure of Sheriff Jesse Whitfield climb to the ground, followed by another man, bigger even than the sheriff, taller and wide-shouldered and handsome in his city clothes. He squirmed a bit on the doorsill and froze to stillness as they came close.

"Morning, Anse," said Sheriff Whitfield and nodded at the deer carcass. "So you can still find 'em when nobody else can." And Old Anse sat quiet. The carcass itself was his response.

Sheriff Whitfield wiped the sweat beads from his forehead and ran the hand on back through his thick gray hair. He sighed and pushed himself to his task. "Anse. You're being honored today. This is Hanson J. Powell. Engineer. Boss of the whole works. The whole blooming project. Insisted on seeing you himself."

Engineer Powell stepped forward and unleashed a rich voice, hearty and confident. "Delighted to meet you, Mr. Birkitt." And Old Anse looked at him with one quick glance and away and sat quiet.

Engineer Powell stepped back a pace and rocked on the soles of his trim new boots. "No reason for hard feelings, Mr. Birkitt. I came myself because I'm sure our agents failed to put the proposition to you in the proper light. Everyone else is co-operating. They have been paid good prices and have moved out. They are not standing in the path of progress. They know what we are doing is big. Really big. Why, when we finish the dam and this valley is filled we will have a reservoir that will irrigate fifty-seven thousand acres of that dry land out on the level. Fifty-seven thousand acres, Mr. Birkitt. Enough to provide prosperous living for hundreds of healthy farm families. More than that. We will have shown the way for the whole territory. There will be other projects like this. We will be making the desert bloom—"

Sheriff Jesse Whitfield shifted his weight from one foot to the other. "I told you, Powell," he said. "You're wasting breath."

"No," said Engineer Powell. "I refuse to believe that one man would be so stubborn as to try to block the will of many others. I refuse to believe that any man would cling so tightly to a scrubby little cabin like this and a few poor acres he doesn't even try to do anything with." Engineer Powell rocked again on his boot soles and his voice dropped to a lower, more confidential tone. "Mr. Birkitt, I will give you double the last price offered you and that is a final figure."

Old Anse rubbed one hand along the rifle barrel and back and sat quiet and Sheriff Whitfield spoke, dry and disgusted. "Get on with it, Powell. Tell him what's happened."

"Very well," said Engineer Powell. "I made that offer, Mr. Birkitt, simply to satisfy my own conscience. There was no need for it. Your property here has been condemned by court order and taken over by rule of eminent domain. You are being paid the assessed value only plus a small sum for the supposed inconvenience caused you.

A check has been deposited in your name at the county bank. This property, along with all the rest, now belongs to the land development company. We drove out this morning to tell you and move your belongings, if you have any, to the county seat. What you do thereafter is no concern of mine."

Old Anse sat still but his hands moved and the rifle swung until its barrel pointed at Engineer Powell. "Get off my land," he said.

Engineer Powell put his hands on his hips and rocked on his boot soles, bringing the toes down firm. "This is no longer your land." And Old Anse pulled back the hammer on the old rifle with a little snap. "You heard me," he said. "Ain't in the habit of speaking twice." And Sheriff Whitfield spoke, his voice crisp. "Go back to the wagon, Powell. I'll handle this."

The wagon creaked as Engineer Powell climbed to the seat and silence settled up the slope over the cabin dooryard. Sheriff Whitfield stood, big and broad, and his shadow covered Old Anse on the doorsill and his voice was mild. "The gun's empty," he said. "You were cleaning it." And Old Anse shrugged his shoulders a bit. "Can't talk to that bedamned easterner," he said.

"You're up against the law now," said Sheriff Whitfield. And Old Anse looked at him, eyes wide and clear. "Remember when your father came here," said Old Anse. "Walking with his oxcart up this valley. Staking a claim over that first ridge. Remember when you were born. Remember Marthy feeding you biscuit in this cabin afore you shed your first teeth. Remember showing you how to find deer. Remember when you married. Remember when your kids were born. And their kids too. You'll not put me off."

Sheriff Whitfield drew a long breath and let it out sighing and leaned against the cabin wall. "But why? You're too old to be living off here alone. You can't have much time left. Should think you'd want to spend it where things are easier."

Old Anse stretched his legs and reached to scratch a toe with the end of the rifle barrel. "Don't want things easy. Want them like now. Better with all those newcomers gone. Was too bedamned crowded. Came here afore anyone else. The first. Now the last." He set the rifle across his knees and looked down at it and ran one hand over and over along the barrel. "Moved all around these territories way back then. Always trying it over the next hills. Marthy took it long enough. 'Always settling,' she put it, 'and never settled.' Made me promise to find a place and keep it. Found this. Kept it."

The voice of Engineer Powell rose in a shout, impatience driving it up the slope. "Doesn't that old fool know his place'll be under twenty feet of water soon as the valley is filled?"

Sheriff Whitfield gave no sign he had heard. He looked down at Old Anse. "Martha's been dead a long time," he said. And Old Anse gave a small jerk of his head toward the left corner of the cabin. "She's here," he said.

"They'll move her for you. Just say the word and they'll move her down to the cemetery at the county seat." And Old Anse whipped his head up quick and his eye corners tightened sharp. "Move her? Moved her too often when she was alive."

The voice of Engineer Powell drove up the slope. "Sheriff, are you going to bring him along?" The voice of Sheriff Whitfield drove down the slope with a sudden snap. "No. I'm an old fool too." And the voice of Engineer Powell became cold and contemptuous. "Come along then. My time is valuable. Let him stay there and rot. He'll get out fast enough when the water starts rising."

Dust rose along the lower valley road again and Old Anse sat in his doorway and watched the wagon disappear around the bend. The flies were gathering and he rose to tend to the meat. *Always could handle Jesse,* he thought. *Being sheriff hasn't changed him any . . .*

The sun arched overhead and dropped into the mountains and the night breeze talked in the trees and the days passed and the nights between and Old Anse endured them with slow satisfaction in his solitude. Several times on a Sunday curious people from the work camp in the lower valley came up the road, but when he sat on his doorsill with the old rifle across his knees they kept a wary distance and went away soon. At odd intervals Sheriff Jesse Whitfield appeared, ambling in from various directions on his big bunchy roan, to bring a fragrant tobacco quid and lean against the cabin and look out over the valley and speak after long moments of memories of the old days. The rest of the time Old Anse was alone and the quiet independent serenity of other years crept back and sat with him on the doorsill as he watched the weeds take the cleared places around the deserted houses across the creek or went with him as he wandered the neighbor hills, rifle in hand, and saw the small game working back into long lost territory. Sometimes, sitting still in the doorway, his old ears caught the rumbling down valley that must be dynamite blasts and rock-car unloadings where the valley narrowed and the side walls came close and the dam was rising and these were the times he pushed to his feet and went off on long tramps over almost forgotten trails.

The days passed and the nights between and haze began to fill the shortening afternoons as the edge of fall sharpened the air and he killed another deer and strained to pack the carcass home and smoked the meat and dragged fallen timber to the cabin to be cut and stacked close against the walls. Then all rumbling ceased in the distance and days passed and the silence in that direction deepened and he found himself unable or unwilling to leave the cabin and the almost unconscious expectancy gripped him and the waiting began. Day after day he sat still, bundled now in his old buffalo coat, and his head turned ever more often to the right toward the lower valley and at last he saw it, the slow widening of the creek where it followed the road around the bend.

It was no more than a gradual swelling at first, a broadening of the lazy late-fall creek where this curved around and out of sight. For hours at a time he saw no difference at the distance then with a start he realized the water had slipped sidewise into another hollow and spread its hold on the land. By evening of the third day he saw the upward-inching line clear across the valley bed and the solid sheen of water behind broken only by clumps of bushtops and the lonely boles of trees whose roots were engulfed. He sat still and was so sunk in the watching that he did not hear the horses coming down the old trail behind the cabin until they moved around the side toward him.

Sheriff Jesse Whitfield let drop the reins of the empty-saddled horse he was leading and swung down from his big roan. He leaned against the cabin wall and looked down valley at the edging sheen of water. "Winter's being hatched in the mountains," he said. "Get your things together, Anse. We've fixed a room at my place."

Old Anse pulled the buffalo coat closer around him. "Bedamned about it," he said in sudden irritation. "Why're you so all-fired keen on taking care of me?"

Sheriff Whitfield pulled a sliver of ancient bark from the cabin wall and chewed on it in slow thought. "Maybe because you mean something to me," he said. "You sort of stand for the way it was when I was a kid." And Old Anse looked at him and away and down at his moccasined feet. "Maybe that's why I won't go." He waved an arm at the water down valley. "Can't rise much during the cold. Got plenty of food and wood. Intend to see it through." The sound of one horse stamping a hoof was sharp in the long silence and Old Anse stirred on the doorsill. "One more winter," he said. "Not much for a man to want." And Sheriff Whitfield smacked a fist into the cabin wall and stepped out and scooped up the reins of the other horse and swung up on his big roan. Old Anse sat still and heard the sound of the hooves fading on the trail behind the cabin. *Still the same Jesse,* he thought. *Raised them right in those days . . .*

The landscape browned and the now endless wind strengthened and stripped the trees till only the evergreens held their color and the water crept forward, measuring its advance by almost imperceptible degrees according to the ground confronting it. Old Anse sat and watched it every daylight hour till the cold drove him inside and then he kept a fire blazing and sat on his barrel-stool and watched through the window in the south wall. Ice formed in the creek and thickened and the flow dwindled and the first snow floated down from the mountains and the days passed and the snow came again whipping into a blizzard that packed the low places and piled the drifts. He could see only driving white through the window and when the weather cleared the valley was wrapped for winter and the edge of water was lost beneath the blanket of snow spreading unbroken from the frozen ground on over the surface of ice.

Old Anse stayed inside now and the days passed and the weeks. Daylight and dark were the same to him and he waked and dozed and ate when hunger prompted and fed the fire, with no attention to time. Outside the winter held its course rigid and with repeated snowings and inside he lived through other winters in his mind. Remembrance ran back into the far years and he sat by the fire and talked to Martha and he knew she was not there but outside under the tall stone and yet he talked to her and the old cabin was filled with her quiet listening. He dozed and woke to feed the fire and dozed again and he came over the high slope behind the cabin with the tireless energy of youth in his legs and the valley reached untouched before him and he turned to call her to hurry beside him. He stirred and brought in more wood and the fire leaped again and the muscles of his back and shoulders ached with a satisfying weariness as he drove his ax deep into the trunks of stout trees and felled them and lopped away the branches and dragrolled the logs to the cabin site and she helped him notch them and set them in place. He let the ash-choked fire go out and cleaned the fireplace and coaxed new flames into leaping action and he stood outside with the sunset behind him and the contentment of a man's full-day work upon him and she was beside him and they looked down the valley where people passed along the trail by the creek he had made packing in supplies, and the people fanned out to settle in the surrounding hills and he knew them all and was one of them and their neighborliness was a good thing with no pressure in it and they gathered to help him bury her and the stillborn child under the white stone.

The endless wind rushed with rising strength outside and beat through chinks in the cabin wall and fought with the fire and he kept this well fed and pulled his stool close and he sat on the log doorsill alone in the round of the days and one by one old neighbors over the hills faded out of knowing and the trail broadened into a road and the town grew house by house and the people were strangers who kept away from him, afraid of his long silences and sudden sharp speech, and told themselves strange tales about him and he watched them and their hurryings and let time glide past in the inevitable moving of the years.

The days grew longer and the wind slackened and rose and slackened and rose again, coming now in gusts and sighing with a new softness. The snow settled during the days to harden only at night and the ice became spongy and at last the creek broke through all covering and cleared its bed and raced with rising vigor, tumbling slush and ice chunks with it. The sun beat down and the snow settled and faded and clear spots appeared on the high slopes and Old Anse stood in his doorway and saw the water stretching in a vast sheet from the small rise at the edge of the empty town on down the valley and out of sight around the bend below.

The creek rose, shouting in spring exuberance, and poured the water from the melting snow far up its course in the mountains down into the growing lake. The level of the stretching sheet climbed by visible hourly stages and Old Anse sat on the doorsill and watched it top the rise by the town edge and run like a reaching finger along the road and spill into the cellar hole where Bartlett's store had been. Down valley the trees surrounded in the fall stayed brown and bare but up the high slopes the small buds burst and a tinge of green flushed along the boughs and he sat still and shed his old buffalo coat in the sun and watched the water take the houses, inching upward board by board.

It coiled around their lonely walls and slithered through cracks to explore the barren rooms. It swirled around their eaves and rolled up their roofs and over and they were only dark shadows fading into the overall sameness under the smooth wet sheen of the surface. It washed over the charred remnants of Luke Peabody's place and that blackened scar on the opposite slope was gone and the lake held it a lost secret. There was no semblance of the creek now. It fed into the lake far on up the valley and the widening water crept up the slope toward the cabin. The sun shimmered on it by day and the slice of growing moon by night and Old Anse wore away the hours on his doorsill and watched it move in and across his dooryard. Eating and the little necessities were mechanical habits, and with the apparent unthinking indifference of an old rock he watched the water rise and erase all that was familiar before him. When the first ripples reached his feet he straightened and stepped up and stood in the doorway. When they lapped against the log he stepped back and closed the door. He looked all about him, studying every object in the cabin, and shook his head. Empty-handed he went to the small rear door that gave on the rising slope behind, and opened it and hesitated and returned by the fireplace to take the old rifle from its pegs. Holding it in the crook of an arm he went out the rear door and kicked this shut after him. Fifty feet up the slope he stopped on a small outcropping ledge and lowered himself to sit on the rock.

The water edged along the sides of the cabin now, feeling about the base logs. Old Anse sat still and watched it slide to the left and finger through the grass and slip under and through the ivy leaves to curl slow and relentless around the base of the white stone. The sun swung far overhead and the water crept up the stone and the sun dropped into the mountains behind him and the moon rose and silvered the lake and filtered its pale light through the trees by the cabin and the soft shimmering of the water was halfway up the stone. The night cold sank into his joints and the white shaft seemed to sway in the rippling sheen and he stared at it and toppled in a slow descent on his side in the sleep of exhaustion.

In the first light of morning Old Anse woke with a start and fought the chill stiffness of his old muscles to get back to a sitting position. He peered forward through the clearing grayness. Only the pointed tip of the white stone showed above the water and ripples raised by the freshening breeze washed over it. He watched and the water seemed to hold back from the point and then closed with a soft swish over it and the stone was a gray-white shadow under the surface. Old Anse shivered and swung his head to look at the cabin. The water surrounded it and was high up the sides, and through the top panes of the side window he saw his stool floating past inside. The water rose and gurgled under the eaves and started its climb up the low ridge of the roof. The ripples sent their small wettings ahead and the abiding edge of the water followed. Only the hump of the ridge remained and this dwindled and became no more than the line of the center peak and then this too was taken and the lake spread untroubled from slope to far slope.

Old Anse stirred and shook his head and the slow accumulating anger of the months came forward in his mind and broke and left him empty and old beyond reckoning. He pushed to his feet and staggered and caught himself and as he looked around in a strange indecision he saw the broad figure standing ten yards away.

"All right, Anse," said Sheriff Jesse Whitfield. "It's finished. Come along now. I'm taking you home with me."

Old Anse Birkitt sat on the top step of the porch of Sheriff Whitfield's house and looked out over the front hedge at the streets framing the central square of the county seat and the row of buildings beyond. The late spring sun was warm upon him and he was grateful for it. Somehow he was never warm clear through anymore. Across the way the stores were busy and people passed up and down the courthouse steps and wagons moved along the street. Behind the buildings where the railroad cut through to the station, an engine whistled and its heavy breathing and the clatter of cars drifted across the square. Old Anse fidgeted on his step. *Bedamned lot of goings on,* he thought. *Makes a man tired just watching . . .*

He pushed up and went around the house across the back yard

to the stable. He took a manure fork off the rack and went in the big roan's empty stall and began pitching the dirtied straw through the window to the pile outside. There was no snap left in his muscles and he grunted with each forkful but he kept at it with grim satisfaction. Footsteps sounded in the stable and he stopped. Sheriff Whitfield's dull-witted handyman stood in the stall doorway bobbing his head in slow rhythm. "That's my work, Mr. Anse. Sheriff says you don't have to do anything around here."

Old Anse dropped the fork and let it lay though the prongs were up. He pushed past the handyman and out of the stable and swung on a circuit of the big yard just inside the hedge where his frequent tramping had already worn a path. He caught a movement of curtain at a house window and a glimpse of the sheriff's wife peering out. He stopped short. *Somebody's always checking on me,* he thought. *Seem to have the notion I'm off my rocker . . .*

Back on the front step he opened his old knife and began whittling aimless shavings from a small piece of wood he had picked off the main stovepile. They flowed from the blade and fell around his feet cluttering the bottom step and at last he was conscious of them. He stopped whittling and stared at them a long moment. He reached and picked them up one by one till the step was clear. He looked around and there was no place along the neat house front to put them and he jammed them with the knife into the pockets of his faded jeans. He sat still and watched the people and wagons across the way. *Don't belong here,* he thought. And after a while his eye corners tightened and his old lips folded in to a firm line. *Jesse's wrong. It's not finished. Not yet . . .*

The sunset glow bathed the house and died away into dusk and Old Anse sat at the supper table and listened in friendly attention to Sheriff Jesse Whitfield telling of the day's doings and thanked the sheriff's wife for a good meal though it still seemed strange to him to be eating food prepared by someone else, and at last was upstairs in the room they had fixed for him. He sat by the window and watched the late moon rise and waited till long after the whole house was dark and silent. With the old rifle in his hand he slipped into the hall and down the stairs. His moccasined feet made no sound as he eased out the back door. He took the ax from the block by the woodpile and an empty feed bag and a coil of rope from the stable. *Jesse won't mind*, he thought. *Won't grudge me these . . .*

By sunup he was past the dam and working along the valley rim. Through the trees he could see the lake below him stretching broad and strange and beautiful on beyond the upper bend. He came on the faint trace of the back trail that had led down to the cabin and pushed on without stopping. A third of a mile farther he slipped down the slope to where a shoulder of land pushed out into the water. Sitting cross-legged by the water's edge he studied the whole scene. The shimmering expanse of the lake seemed to throw the whole wide view out of focus and for a time everything appeared unfamiliar to him. At last the water barrier began to fade in his mind and he grasped the valley again, complete and as it used to be. Turning his head in slow scrutiny he scanned the entire valley rim and fixed his landmarks for imaginary lines spanning the lake from side to side and lengthwise, and where they crossed was the spot he sought. He picked up a twig and tossed it into the water and watched it move away. There was a current, slight and almost imperceptible, but moving and in the right direction.

A few feet into the water nearby he found three trees of manageable size and dead, water-killed and bare. He stood in the shallow water and swung the ax and some of the former snap seemed to flow into his old muscles. He felled two of the trees without halting and rested and the third took longer then it too lay ready, partway into the water, and he trimmed away the branches and lopped off the thin upper ends. Tugging at the logs he got them farther into the water, floating with only the inner ends grounded, and with part of the rope he lashed them into a crude raft. He was panting now and soaked and had to sink on the shore to rest. As he lay full length on the ground he heard, down valley, the sound of a horse whinnying and in the following silence he listened and caught the faint far-off shouting of several voices. He pushed up from the ground, hurrying now, and took the feed bag and filled it with stones and tied the mouth shut and struggled with it until he had it on the near end of his raft. He paused to ease the breath fighting in his chest and heard the voices coming closer, and frantic in haste he laid the rifle on the raft and splashed through the water to the outer end and heaved until it was floating free. Careful not to tilt it, he crawled aboard and lay flat along the logs and paddled with his hands over the sides until his arm muscles bunched and refused to move.

Time passed and boots crashed through brush along the lake shore and voices shouted and these were meaningless sounds to him. His muscles relaxed some and his breath eased and he raised his head, straining it back on his neck like a turtle. He was well out into the lake and the slow current was drifting him down and out toward the middle. He slapped against the water with his left hand and arm in a desperate flurry and relief ran through him as the forward end of the raft swung in a gradual arc in the right direction. He turned his head back and there were figures running on the shore and one broad figure standing motionless on the shoulder of land watching him. *Don't care a bedamn about anyone else*, he thought. *But Jesse'll understand . . .* And then he forgot them all and concentrated on steering his raft toward the crossing of his landmark lines.

The slow, almost imperceptible movement brought him closer and closer and peering ahead and down he saw shifting shadows that steadied and became the clumped branches of a stand of submerged trees. Peering down with his face almost touching the water he saw and saw not and seemed to see again a glimmering of white far down among the tree trunks and ahead the big humped shadow of the cabin roof. Inching around on the raft he sat up and reached and took the free end of the rope from the bag and looped it around his waist and knotted it tight. He held the old rifle firm in one hand and hunched along the logs until his feet touched the bag and began to push it. His weight and the weight of the bag together tilted the raft and water washed over the end and the bag slid and dropped in silent descent and the rope tightened taut to his waist and he heaved himself forward and down into the dim water. Cold engulfed him in a downward rush and his limbs thrashed and he did not know it and his fingers remained clamped around the rifle. It's finished, he thought, and all thinking ceased in an endless nothingness and the disturbed water rocked above and the small waves spread and died and the cool surface of the lake spread serene and untroubled from slope to slope of the valley.

Takes a Real Man . . .

That's fair cussing, gents. Stings the ears a bit. But it's mule-team cussing. Might do to make the rope tails move along. Wouldn't push a yoke of oxen ten feet on a downgrade. Now if you could hear Big Jake Bannack . . .

Never drove an oxteam did you? Slowest critters in harness ever grew hooves. Outpull anything else on four feet and do it on a little dry grass for fodder. But slow. I've seen a turtle come up behind a three-yoke freighting outfit and swing wide and go past without even hurrying. And they're stupid. And stubborn. And aggravating in endless ways. Maybe all that because, being oxen, riling folks to fury is about the only kick they can get out of life. Just one thing they understand. Strong language. Strong and stinging with smoke coming out of it. That'll make them move. Takes a real man to do it . . .

Big Jake can do it. Big Jake can make the slowest oxen step along so fast for them they look almost alive. He's big with near the heft of an ox himself. Chest like a hogshead. Mouth like a megaphone. Mind made for cussing, chockfull of all the words plain and fancy any man ever knew and plenty more he's thought up for himself. When he rears back and uncoils his whip and sucks in air till that chest's ready to bust out the oversize shirt he's awearing, timid folks with tender ears run for cover. He starts easy, voice just arumbling in his throat, but all the same oxen that'll stand sleepy through the best cussing another man can do'll perk their ears and begin to blow a bit They know. He's talking their language. In no time at all he's really aroaring and the echoes bounce through the hills and the air gets hot and a blue smoke rises and the oxen move. They move all right. They haul the heaviest wagon out of the deepest mudhole and plod up the road with the wickedest whip in the world picking flies off their rumps and the most sulphurous cussing this side the devil's fireplace roasting their hides every step . . .

Yep. Big Jake can do it. Big Jake freights supplies from the railroad up the slopes to my town. Nothing's too big or too heavy for him to haul, not with those six big oxen of his and the two biggest under the lead yoke. Garfield and Hayes he calls those two. Big Jake's a Democrat Gives his critters Republican names so his cussing can do double duty.

Once a month he makes the round trip up from the railroad. It's quite an event when he arrives. We know he's coming long before he's in sight. There's a bad stretch about half a mile out of town where the grade's particular steep and the road runs narrow between two cliffs. Springs from the rocks keep the ground soft. When he hits that stretch he lets out the last notches in his cussing and just about plain blasts those oxen through. We're doing this and doing that around town and we hear the first hot echoes hopping through the hills and the womenfolk close their windows and stuff cotton in their ears and the rest of us gather to watch the road. First thing we see is the blue smoke floating up over the cliffs. Then we see Garfield and Hayes heaving and straining to top the grade and behind them come the other two yokes on the chain and then the wagons, four of them, the big-bodied lead and the two trailers and the small camp outfit tagging on two wheels, and beside them Big Jake himself snaking out the whip and aroaring. His cussing comes straight at us along the road then and we listen close to catch what he's saying and any new brand of profanity he's invented. But when he reaches town we scatter quick. For the first five minutes the main street's his. He needs time to celebrate and simmer down. He plants his feet firm in the dust and sends his forty-foot whip lashing out in every direction and cracking like cannon on the Fourth. He looks around to see is anyone fool enough to be within range so he can nip a hat off a head or a button off a vest. His oxen stop and stand sleepy-eyed chewing their cuds and maybe a mite proud that he's cussed them into doing it again but, being oxen, too cantankerous ever to let that show. The cussing dwindles to a kind of purring and the whip-cracking fades in a last few tickling pops and when he starts coiling the leather the rest of us come running out to see who'll be first to buy Big Jake a big drink . . .

Yep. That's the way he used to do it. That's the way he still does it. But there's a difference nowadays. Echoes still bounce through the hills when he starts aroaring. Smoke still rises and the oxen still move. The tone's the same and the tune's the same. But the words are different . . .

The Right Reverend Pemberton Willoughby's responsible. It's all his, the whole credit. He beats Big Jake at Big Jake's own game. Beats him fair and square, and that changes the words and likely the Right Reverend Pemberton Willoughby's the one man ever could do it . . .

Parson Pem we call him. The full name's too much in the mouth. He's big too, almost of a size with Big Jake himself, though he doesn't seem so at first in his pegleg pants and frock coat. Has a fine preaching voice too, deep and round and carrying far for outdoor services. He comes to town one day riding on his old mule and slides off and announces he's heard we need a church. He's decided our souls must be sickly from sojourning in a churchless town and require weekly applications of verbal mustard plasters in the form of sermons and he's arrived to see we get the same. If there are any objections, will the objectors please to step forward at once so he can take care of them right away without wasting any time. None of us really object. Anyone can come into my town any day and set up any kind of a shop he wants long as he doesn't step on too many toes too hard. But this gent wants objections and we're always obliging so a couple of the boys step forward to offer some and before they know what's happening he has them both by their necks and pops their heads together and there they are both sitting dazed on the ground and he's looking around bright and cheerful for more. There aren't any more. "Fine," he says. "Couldn't be better. This is Tuesday. There's no reason why, come Sunday, with you all working the way I'll show you, we shouldn't have a church built."

He's right. Come Sunday, he has his church up. No pews in it yet and no pulpit, but the walls are solid and the roofs almost on and there's the start of a little steeple sprouting in front Everybody contributes something, material or work, because he's that kind of a man. Makes you want to contribute. By time the next Sunday rolls around we're all convinced. He's our parson. Maybe we don't all expect to be too regular in attendance at his little church, but he's our parson and we're proud of him. His preaching's the right kind, simple and straight and scorching the sinners and short so the wooden seats don't get too hard. And he's the helpingest man ever lived. Let a neighbor be putting in some fence and Parson Pem is out there with his frock coat off adigging post holes. Let a woman have an extra heavy week's washing and like enough Parson Pem'll be coming along and rolling up his sleeves and plunging his hands into the soapsuds. Let a jam develop at the blacksmith shop with people waiting long for work and it's Parson Pem who'll be in there pumping the bellows and swinging the second hammer. Can't say he converts every one of us to every point in the dogma he likes to expound. Can say he converts plenty of people and some surprising at that to his way of being neighborly.

Yep. The Right Reverend Pemberton Willoughby's our preacher. I figure it's about the third week he's been with us and the tip's being put on the steeple and just about everybody in town is standing around watching, when we hear the first hot echoes hopping through the hills far down the road where it comes up between those two cliffs. Parson Pem hears them too but they're still too faint for him to make out the words. He stares in surprise at the womenfolk scattering to their houses and slamming doors and pulling down windows. He stares along the road with the rest of us and sees the blue smoke with sulphur edgings float up over the cliffs. He sees Garfield and Hayes come heaving and straining over the top of the grade and behind them the other two yokes and then the wagons and beside them Big Jake snaking out the whip and aroaring and filling the air with the smell of brimstone. The words come straight along the road now and Parson Pem can make them out. A look of horror settles over his face and he claps his hands to his ears. But that's not much protection against Big Jake's voice and brand of cussing and, anyway, the temptation's strong. He eases on the hands and then drops them and just stands there staring in a kind of unbelieving fascination at Big Jake acoming.

He's still standing there still staring when Big Jake hits main street and the rest of us skip for cover. The oxen stop and drop their eyelids and start chewing their cuds and Big Jake plants his feet firm in the road dust and starts cracking the whip. He sees Parson Pem standing there and out snakes the whip and off sails the parson's hat. Big Jake is some surprised when Parson Pem still stands there astaring and out snakes the whip again and off comes the top button of the frock coat. Still the same. Out snakes the whip again, tip flicking neat and precise for the next button, and up comes one of Parson Pem's big hands and grabs the tip and yanks hard on it and forward and down into the dust goes Big Jake. He comes to his feet aroaring and arushing for the tussle and sudden he sees what he hasn't seen before, the hindside-foremost collar around Parson Pem's neck. He roars and he bellows and he simmers down to a gurgle. "A rev'rend," he says in disgust. "A big one and the best chance for a ground-thumping in a month of freighting and it's a rev'rend." Parson Pem looks at him in equal disgust. "A heathen," he says. "A foulmouthed and profane and benighted heathen." Big Jake lets loose again. Beats even his own best previous cussing. The oxen open their eyes and look startled and the blue smoke rises with fiery edgings and Big Jake finally gets it out "Take off that collar," he roars. "I'll show you who's a heathen!" And Parson Pem reaches up and unhooks the collar in back and tosses it over on the board sidewalk.

They meet with a thump that shakes buildings both sides the street. They wrap their big arms around each other and butt with their chins and heave and grunt and heave again. Parson Pem's a tough one at this kind of tussling but Big Jake's a tougher. He's used to wrastling oxen in and out of yokes and hoisting freight in and out of wagons. He heaves extra hard and swings Parson Pem off his feet and lifts him and thumps him down on the ground so that the air goes out of him in a big whoosh and he can't move for a minute or two. Big Jake looks down at him and grins some.

"You're a mealymouthed rev-rend," Big Jake says. "But you're quite a man too." Parson Pem looks up at him grim and determined and fights for breath and gets some. "You're a heathen," Parson Pem says. "A cursing profane heathen and an abomination to men's ears. But when I've knocked that out of you, you'll be a mighty man of the Lord." Big Jake plain can't believe what he's hearing from the man he's just beat and he shakes his head and snorts and stomps off into Willie Lord's saloon to clear the dust out of his throat . . .

That's the way it goes. Every month the same. The echoes bounce through the hills and the blue smoke rises strong with sulphur and the smell of brimstone and Garfield and Hayes appear straining over the grade and Big Jake comes along the road snaking out his whip and aroaring and there in the middle of main street is Parson Pem reaching up to unhook that collar. Every month Parson Pem lands thumping on the ground and the air goes whoosh out of him and Big Jake stands looking down and shaking his big head in wonderment and stomps off for liquid comfort. Rest of us don't mix in. This is between those two big men and we let it be. That's how we do things in my town. Not saying we don't have bets running on the outcome. But Parson Pem is our preacher and Big Jake is our bull-whacker and we're proud of them both. Only interfering we'd do would be to stop any outsider from interfering with them.

Then the month comes when Big Jake can't take it anymore. The blue smoke is sort of thin this time and Garfield and Hayes just about crawl over the top of the grade, maybe out of habit much as anything else, and Big Jake doesn't even let a little pop out of his whip when he reaches town. Coils it slow and careful and hangs it on the lead wagon and walks over where Parson Pem is standing collarless in the middle of the street. "Rev'rend," he says, almost plaintive, "ain't there anything'll stop you tackling me every time I get here?" Parson Pem beams at him bright and cheerful. "Certainly. When you stop poisoning the air with your profanity, why then I'll put my collar on and keep it there."

Big Jake shuffles his feet and runs a big hand across his forehead and down over his face, wiping off the dust. "Rev'rend," he says, "you just don't know. In your business freighting souls to where you think they ought to go, there's no call for strong language. Not that kind anyway. But a man who whacks bulls has just plain got to cuss them. I'll lay you a straight proposition. If you can drive those critters of mine five miles and up that last grade without cussing, I'll quit it and never cuss again."

Yep. That's what turns Parson Pem into a bullwhacker for the first and maybe the only time in his life. It's early evening when Big Jake puts that proposition. It's late evening by time the rules are ready. The two of them start discussing the whys and wherefores of this cussing-no-cussing contest right there in the middle of main street. Rest of us come out from cover and join in. Look at it first as kind of a joke but see how strict earnest those two are and soon we're all the same. We name old Sandburr Sam Claggett, our sheriff, to be judge of the proceeding. With him in charge we know it'll be run right. He sets eight o'clock the next morning for the start so the oxen'll have a chance to rest and not be asked to be hauling again after already doing a day's work. Big Jake allows that seems fair to him. Old Sandburr says next he thinks there ought to be a time limit. Parson Pem agrees that's only fair and suggests two hours and Old Sandburr looks sorrowful at him and announces firm he's making it four hours, which is still less than he'd want if he was trying this himself. There's to be only one wagon but a load on that to give it heft and they argue a bit over that. Not over the weight but over the cargo. Willie Lord offers ten barrels of whiskey but Parson Pem balks at that and they settle on ten barrels of flour. Near the end Parson Pem is squirming a little. Wrastles with his conscience and at last says he believes in doing the Lord's work by whatever means come to hand but still it only seems fair to him to let Big Jake know he's handled a whip some in his time and had experience making critters move. "What kind of critters?" Big Jake says. Parson Pem explains he's busted sod with a four-horse span when he was agrowing and he's been a helper on a mule train heading west after graduating from his preacher-school. "Horses," Big Jake says. "Mules. It's the same's before. You just don't know . . .

Come morning we're all out there to watch at the five-mile mark Old Sandburr's measured off, just about all of us including the women, who are set to do some yipping and huzzaing because they look on Parson Pem as their champion in this. He's wearing a pair of overalls borrowed from Big Jake because they're the only ones in town of a size to fit. He's bareheaded and his eyes are aglowing and the only thing preacher-like about him is that hindside-foremost collar he's kept on, maybe to remind him to watch his words if or when the going gets rough.

Wagon's there, ready loaded with ten barrels of flour from Jed Durkin's store. Oxen's there too. Been out there all night, pegged by good grass. They're rested and they've grazed and it's just another day to them. Big Jake's yoked them and Old Sandburr's inspected the yoking and they're standing there placid and quiet chewing their cuds and, being oxen, paying no more attention to all of us buzzing around than to a flock of flies.

Parson Pem takes the whip and uncoils it. "Got the time?" he says. Old Sandburr checks his stemwinder and nods. "Stand back," Parson Pem says. He snakes out the whip and he does know how to handle it. Gets some nice sharp cracks out of it near the oxen's ears. "Gee, Garfield!" he shouts. "Haw, Hayes!" he yells. They don't even know he's there. He chirrups at them. Clucks at them. Tries all the starting noises he's ever heard. He whistles. Shouts. Stomps his feet. Makes the whip hum and crackle mean. Those oxen chew their cuds sleepy-eyed and don't pay any mind to him at all. He stands looking at them and there's a faint pink flush coming up his neck above that collar of his.

He walks around front and puts a rope on the lead yoke to try leading them. Pulls. Pulls hard. Garfield and Hayes grunt a bit and go on chewing their cuds. He wraps his big hands tighter around the rope and digs in his heels and heaves. Garfield opens one eye a little wider and blows soft and Hayes knows the signal and sudden they both stretch their necks forward and the unexpected slack catches Parson Pem off balance and down he goes on his rump. He sits there staring at those oxen and the pink above his collar is darkening red and spreading on up over his face. Garfield and Hayes look at each other and to show what they think of his little annoyances they double under their front legs and plop down in the road dust to take a nap.

Up the slope where we're all standing awatching there's a snort and something like a mixed cackle and bellow. It's Big Jake near busting his ribs with the merriment inside pushing out. Old Sandburr fixes him with a cold eye. "Rules are," Old Sandburr says, "no outside meddling of any kind. That burbling of yours adds insult to the injury those critters are doing the parson." Big Jake pushes a big fist in his mouth and subsides sort of strangling, all the same enjoying himself more'n he has since the first time the parson shed his collar to tackle him.

Parson Pem gets to his feet. Sweat's showing on him and he's breathing deep and fast. He goes up to Garfield and Hayes and unfastens his rope and you can tell by the way his fingers fumble with the knot that already he's madder'n a man who can't let some out in cussing has a right to be. He squats down on his heels in front of them and stares at them two, maybe three minutes. Then he begins.

His voice is low at first, but it's his preaching voice, the one that can carry against any wind for outdoor service, and it grows and swells deep and round as he talks and he hits each word harder and harder. "You're naught but benighted heathen too," he says to those oxen. "Benighted heathen dwelling in the darkness of ignorance and your sins testify against you. But that's not your fault. Your education's been neglected something shameful. No one's told you and no one's taught you. But it's there in the Book for all to read and for all to know. Genesis One: Twenty-eight. *Subdue it*, the Lord said to man, meaning the earth and all things upon it. *Have dominion over the fish of the sea, and over the fowl of the air, and over every living thing that moveth upon the earth.* That means you too, you four-footed loafing benighted heathen beasts of the field. There's no escaping it for you. Stupid you are and stupider you'd like to pretend to be even than the Lord made you, but you can't mistake the meaning of those words." Parson Pem's voice is rolling out like a roaring thunder and righteous anger is putting wisps of smoke around the edges and Garfield and Hayes open their eyes and look at him. "No excuse for you now!" he roars. "I'm telling you and now you know! Dominion it is! Dominion it'll be! I'll smite ye in wrath with a continual stroke! I'll dominion ye if I have to kick each and every one of ye the whole five miles!"

Parson Pem stretches up straight and goes around and steps in by the chain behind Garfield and Hayes. He applies the toe of his right boot with plenty of power to Garfield and to Hayes in special tender spots and they both grunt surprised and lumber up to their feet. He goes back by the wagon and takes the whip and whirls it around his head and sends it out with a crack that near tears off the tip. "Dominion!" he roars and a puff of smoke floats upward. "Dominion over the beasts of the field! Get amoving, ye benighted bulls of Balaam afore I punish ye seven times seven for your sins!" And Garfield and Hayes heave reluctant into their yoke and the others follow their lead and the wagon moves and the women with us on the slope start yipping and Parson Pem throws back his head triumphant and strides forward and Big Jake pulls his fist out of his mouth. "Sounds suspicious like cussing to me," he says. But Old Sandburr fixes him again with a cold eye. "Kind of strong in spots," Old Sandburr says, "but I listened careful. Caught nary a cuss word."

Yep. Parson Penn has those critters amoving. Keeps them moving without too much trouble. Not at first, that is. Load's light alongside what they're used to hauling and they're remembering the town's not far ahead and when they reach there they always get a grain feeding, so they plod along fair enough for them. He strides along beside, putting his feet down deliberate and matching pace to theirs, and he's recalling that the Book mentions oxen often and feeling good and sort of biblical himself because of that and cracking the whip and roaring "Dominion!" every now and then when he thinks they're hesitating some. He's so tickled with having them moving that it's quite a spell before he realizes that, being oxen, they're amoving almighty slow. Cocks an eye at the sun and does some figuring. It took him all of half an hour to get them started. He's been a full hour, maybe a mite more, on the way and he hasn't even reached the halfway mark. He notches up the whip-cracking and the roaring and tries to hurry the critters. That's when his troubles start again.

Making oxen move is one thing. Making them hurry is flour out of another barrel. One thing they don't take to, that's hurrying. They'll work when blasted into it, but they'll work in their own way and their own time. Parson Pem tries to hurry them and they won't hurry and the sweat starts dripping off him and he gets madder by the minute and the madder he gets the stubborner they get and they begin trying tricks on him. No sense telling all they try. Anyone's ever watched them knows the slow deliberate devilment they can do. Just a sample's the time they give him when he has to pull out so the morning mail coach with the right of way in the road ruts can go past and they pull out for him surprising willing and in doing it manage to tangle their feet over the chain and just stand there looking disgusted at a driver that'll let that happen to them. Takes him better'n fifteen minutes to straighten that out and another five to get them moving again. He's a patient man but by then all the patience he packs is worn out and when he dominions them on along the road his hair's waving wild and his face is dark red and he has to send out smoke puffs mighty frequent.

All the same he's moving them along. Doing it so well that Big Jake is getting worried. He takes Old Sandburr off to one side. "Sandburr," he says, "dry weather we been having. Ain't much mud on up that grade. Would you say there was anything in the rules to stop me hurrying ahead and toting some buckets and sloshing some water in a few places?" Old Sandburr just looks at him and Big Jake shuffles his big feet. "Ain't no harm," he says, "in a man asking, is there?" Still Old Sandburr just looks at him and Big Jake shuffles his feet some more. "Well, anyhow," he says, "you keep listening close. He's building up a head of steam that's plain got to bust out in cusswords."

Big Jake's not the only one thinking that. About all of us figure the same. Then we're certain because those oxen hit the beginning of the grade and start up and feel the wagon dragging hard and they stop. Stop dead. Hunch down and droop their heads and start chewing their cuds placid and determined showing they've stopped to stay. The dominioning they've been getting's enough to move them along the near level but it won't push them up that grade and they think they've got the measure of this man driving them and he hasn't got what it takes. For a while they're right.

Parson Pem works on them. Works hard. Tries what he's been doing right along only harder. Tries it with variations and new angles. Blasts at them. Blows at them. Sends up puffs of smoke that're acquiring a bluish tinge. They don't even twitch their ears. Tries the toe of his boot again and has to quit because he's only hurting himself. Lays the whip right onto their hides and they hunch their shoulders a bit and go on chewing. His face gets a bright purple and his neck is so fiery red you'd think that hind-side-foremost celluloid collar'd bust into flames. He throws the whip to the ground and jumps on it with both feet and tears at his hair with his hands. He glares at those oxen and he rears back his head and draws in a mighty breath and opens his mouth to let the roaring out and Big Jake and Old Sandburr lean forward intent to listen and already there's a grin starting on Big Jake's face. But the words he hears aren't what he expects. Parson Pem's voice rolls out like a thunder. "Job Six: Two and Three. *Oh that my grief were thoroughly weighed, and my calamity laid in the balances together! For now it would be heavier than the sands of the sea!*" He stretches taller and his voice rolls even louder. "Job Seven: Eleven. *Therefore I will not refrain my mouth; I will speak in the anguish of my spirit; I will complain in the bitterness of my soul!*" He swoops down and grabs up the whip. His voice roars forth and the echoes begin to bounce through the hills. "Isaiah Twenty-nine: Six. *I shall visit ye with thunder, and with earthquake, and great noise, with storm and tempest, and the flame of devouring fire.*" He sends the whip humming and cracking at Garfield and Hayes and his voice roars up and a tinge of brimstone edges the air. "Jeremiah Seven: Twenty. *Behold, mine singer and my fury shall be poured forth upon this place!*" Garfield and Hayes lift their heads and their ears perk and Parson Pem's voice fills all the wide spaces with its roaring and the smoke comes not in puffs but in a steady cloud. "Chronicles One: One through Four," he roars. "*Adam, Sheth, Enosh! Kenan, Mahalaleel, Jered! Henoch, Methuselah, Lamech! Noah, Sham, Ham, and Japheth!*" And those oxen heave into the yokes and the wagon moves and they go almost jumping up that grade and Big Jake looks at Old Sandburr who shakes his head and Big Jake trudges after the wagon into town to shake Parson Pem's hand and admit he's beat . . .

Yep. That's our preacher, the Right Reverend Pemberton Willoughby. But that's our bullwhacker too. Big Jake Bannack. Maybe you ought to know how he comes out on that proposition too. Not so good at first. We don't realize that till another month's gone by and it's time for him to be in with another load. We're waiting for it and Parson Pem in particular because a barrel organ's coming for his church. The day passes and Big Jake doesn't show. All the next morning and still he doesn't show. The mail coach driver says he saw Big Jake down the road a piece and thought he seemed to be having trouble. Old Sandburr saddles up. Rides out to see what's doing. Back in less than an hour looking thoughtful. "Jake's there," he says. "Bottom of that last grade. From the look of him he's just about been pulling those wagons himself. Says he's been subduing and dominioning those critters all the way and it's mighty slow going. Can't get them to budge up the grade. He's sitting on the ground turning pages in the Book he's bought and can't find the right place."

Old Sandburr looks around for Parson Pem but that's not needed. Parson Pem is already out climbing bareback on his mule. He goes down the road whacking it with his heels. Rest of us gather outside and watch him disappear between those two cliffs and go on down the grade. We wait. It's worth waiting for. First thing we hear is the echoes bouncing through the hills and the rumbling as they shake stones loose and start rockslides off in the distance. Then we see the smoke rising, thick and blue and floating up over the cliffs. And heaving forward in positive leaps come Garfield and Hayes over the grade and behind them the other oxen and the wagons with the organ lashed and swaying on top the lead load and beside the wagons those two big men, with the mule tagging. They're striding along each with an arm over the other's shoulders and their heads are back and they're aroaring: "*Adam, Sheth, Enosh! Kenan, Mahalaleel, Jered! Henoch, Methuselah, Lamech!*"

Hugo Kertchak, Builder

In America, people said, there was work for anyone willing to work. A man with a trade could make his way there and freedom would be a real thing freshening the air he breathed.

Four years Hugo Kertchak saved for the passage money. He had the few coins that remained from his mother's burial fund and the small amount that had been left to him by his father. He had the smaller amount that had come to him with his wife. He had the gold piece given to him by his uncle at the birth of the first child because it was a son and would bear the uncle's name. He had these and he saved in many ways. He saved though he had work only about one week in three. He put away his pipe, out of sight and out of mind. He drank only one mug of beer and that only on Sunday and after a time none at all. He fed himself and his family on bread and potatoes and occasional green vegetables. The money that would have bought meat joined the rest in the old leather purse that had been his father's and that was kept behind a stone of the fireplace.

After four years and two months he had enough. He sold the few pieces of furniture that were his in the rented cottage. He led the way for his family. Under his left arm he carried the long narrow toolbox that had been his father's and his grandfather's. His right hand held the small hand of his seven-year-old son. Behind him came his wife. On her left shoulder she carried the bundle of extra clothing wrapped in a blanket with a strap around it. Her right hand held the small hand of their five-year-old daughter. They walked the nine miles to the station, where they waited for the train that took them west across Europe to the port and to the ship that took them west across the Atlantic.

Hugo Kolchak walked the streets of New York. He left his wife and children in the boardinghouse run by a man from the old country and walked the streets of the strange city. He knew fifty-three words of English, useful words learned the last days of the crossing from another steerage passenger on the ship. He could not learn them as fast as his wife, for she was quick at such things, but he was learning much more each day, learning them slowly and thoroughly so that he would never lose them and so that he could pronounce them clearly, with only a small trace of accent He walked the streets and times were hard. Even in America times could be hard. There was no work.

There was plenty of work in the new lands, people said, in the new settlements westward with the afternoon sun. A country was growing and a man could grow with it, even a man already in his middle thirties.

Hugo Kertchak talked to the boardinghouse man, who could speak to him in his native tongue. He talked to a patient man at the railroad station, using the words he had learned, and had difficulty arranging in right order. He counted what was left of the money. It was enough.

Hugo Kertchak and his wife and two children rode upright on stiff railroad coach cushions west to Chicago. All one day and one night they rode. They walked across the sprawling city to the other station. They carried the toolbox and the bundle and they walked asking directions. They rode upright on other slat-backed seats west across Iowa into Nebraska. They leaned against each other and slept in snatches as the train jolted through the darkness of night. The sun rose and they sat up straighter and divided and ate the last loaf of the bread and the last piece of the cheese bought in Chicago. They looked out the train windows and saw the wide miles reach and run past them. It was a new and a strange and a big country. But in the side pocket of Hugo Kertchak's jacket was a letter from the boardinghouse man addressed to a friend out in this new and strange and big country.

The train stopped at the town. Hugo Kertchak and his wife and two children stepped down into the dust of the road that was the town's one street, flanked on one side by the single line of track, on the other by a brief row of false-fronted frame buildings. The wind that blew over the wide country, tireless and unending, swirled the dust stirred by their feet up around their legs and made the children cough. The train moved on and the sun beat down and the wind blew and they were alone in the road dust. The few sparse buildings of the town seemed lost in a circling immensity. Distance stretched outward and on and beyond grasp of the eyes in every direction. They walked through the swirling dust across the road and up the two steps to the platform along the front of the building whose sign said "Store & Post Office." Hugo Kertchak set the toolbox down on the platform and went into the building.

At the rear of the store two men sat hunched on stools playing checkers on the squared-off top of a barrel. They raised their heads and looked at him. Behind a counter at the right another man leaned back in an old chair with his feet up on the counter reading a newspaper. This one lowered the paper and looked over it at him like the others. Hugo Kertchak took the letter from his pocket. He went to the counter and held the letter out so that the name on it could be seen. "You know?" he said.

The man behind the counter raised his feet and set them carefully down on the floor. He folded the newspaper and laid it carefully on the counter. He leaned forward and took the letter and held it at arm's length to read the name. He handed the letter back. "Sure I know," he said. "Or aiming it a mite better I'd offer I used to know. That there particular person ain't inhabiting these parts anymore."

Hugo Kertchak frowned in the effort to understand. "You say what?"

The man behind the counter smacked a hand down upon it. "I say hightailed out of the county. Skedaddled. Vamoosed. To put it pretty, he ain't here anymore. He's gone."

Hugo Kertchak understood the final words. "You say where?"

The man behind the counter shouted a question at the checker players. "Back east somewheres," one of them said. "Didn't name a place." The man behind the counter shrugged his shoulders and spread out his hands. "Reckon that's that. Anything else, stranger?"

Hugo Kertchak shook his head. He could think of nothing else, only the fact that confronted him. Slowly he turned and went out again to the front platform. He stood staring into the far reaches of distance. He tore the letter into many small pieces and let these fall fluttering around his feet. Slowly he sat down on the platform edge with his feet on the lower step and his head sank forward until it was almost between his knees. In the old leather purse in his pocket there was thirty-seven cents of the strange American money. And a woman and two children were staring at him in a stricken silence.

The tireless wind of the wide country blew upon him, hot and dry. The wind brought with it a sound, the sound of a hammer driving a nail.

Hugo Kertchak's head rose. He stood, erect on the step. He reached and took the toolbox. "Anna," he said to his wife, "here you wait."

Hugo Kertchak walked along the road through the swirling dust. The sound led him to the last building westward. Around the far side, out of sight before, a man was constructing a small shed. The framework was already up, the rafters for the flat, slightly sloping roof already in place. There was a pile of lumber on the ground with a small keg of nails beside it. The man had cut several side lengths of board and was nailing them to the corner posts. He stopped and turned to look at Hugo Kertchak. He seemed glad of an excuse to stop.

"Am carpenter," Hugo Kertchak said. That was wrong. He made the correction. "I am carpenter."

"Cursed if I am," the man said. "This beswoggled hammer has a mind of its own. Likes my thumb better'n the nails."

Hugo Kertchak was not certain what all the words meant. But here was work, the work he knew. "I show," he said. He laid down the toolbox and opened it. He took out the hammer with the new handle that he had whittled and sanded long hours on the journey until the balance was exactly right for his broad, square hand. He dropped some nails from the keg into his jacket pocket. He lifted the next side board and set it in position. He swung the hammer in smooth, steady strokes, short arcs with clean power in them. It was good to be using a good tool again. But the framework was not solid. The whole skeletal structure quivered under the strokes.

Hugo Kertchak forgot the man watching him. He was intent

upon the problem before him. He walked around the framework, examining it from each side. The joints were not well fitted. They did not lap each other so that they would share and subdue the strains. The braces were in the wrong places. This America needed good workmen.

Hugo Kertchak took his wooden rule from the toolbox and unsnapped it to full length. He made his measurements. He selected several boards and marked them off, using a nail to scratch the lines. The saw was in his hands, the saw that had been his father's and that he had filed and refiled on the long journey until its teeth yearned for good wood to cut. It sliced through this wood swiftly and sweetly. Here were his braces. He nailed these into place. He put a shoulder against a corner post and heaved. The framework stood solid. It was not as firm as it would have been if it had been built right from the beginning, but it was much better. He reached for the next board and stopped. The man was making a noise.

"Hey!" the man was saying again and again, each time louder, trying to catch his attention. "Hey, carpenter. What'd you stick me to polish off this thing?"

"Stick?" Hugo Kertchak said. "Polish off?"

"How much to finish it?" the man said. "Do the job up right."

Hugo Kertchak looked at the framework again. The shed would have no windows. There would be only a door to make. This work was nothing, just nailing boards in place. He tried to estimate a price, one that would not be too low because this was America and yet would not be so high that the man would be unwilling to bargain. "Four dollar," he said.

"Well, now," the man said, rubbing a hand up and down along one side of his chin. "That's a reasonable fair price, I reckon. But cash is mighty scarce in these parts around about now. Tell you what. I'll make it two dollars cash and toss in whatever stuff's left, boards and nails and the like."

Hugo Kertchak's mind worked slowly over the words. "I can do," he said. "Done," the man said. "Reckon all else you'll need is some hinges and a latch for the door. I'll go rustle some." The man swung away and Hugo Kertchak stared after him in amazement. There was no arguing back and forth. There was no talk about how much wood he should use and how many nails. There was no talk about how good the work must be for the price or how long he must wait for the money. There was no writing about the business on paper so that there could be no argument afterward over what had been said and promised. A man said "done" and it was settled. Hugo Kertchak shed his jacket in the warm sun and began sawing board lengths and the endless wind of the wide country sent the sawdust swirling as he sawed.

The sun climbed high overhead and the shed sides climbed with it. The man came back with a pair of big hinges and a latch and screws to go with them. He set these down by the lumber. "Lunchtime," he said. "Better go wrastle yourself some food." He disappeared into the nearby building.

Lunchtime. Suddenly Hugo Kertchak remembered his wife and two children alone on the store platform. Thirty-seven cents would buy bread if bread could be found in this strange place. He started toward the road. He had not gone ten steps when around the corner of the last building came his wife. She walked proudly with her head high. In one hand she carried two fat sandwiches made of thick slices of bread with meat between them and in the other hand she carried a tin pitcher of cool water. "The store man gives," she said in English and then she began talking rapidly in their native tongue, but she had no chance to say much because the store man himself came around the corner close behind her and he was talking so loudly that he almost shouted. He talked straight at Hugo Kertchak. He was very angry. He thought that Hugo Kertchak was closely related to an animal called a polecat with maybe a dose of rattlesnake thrown in. What kind of a horned toad was Hugo Kertchak anyway to leave a woman and two kids in the hot sun breathing road dust when decent neighbors were around that would let them come in and sit a spell and stay as long as they liked? Why hadn't he spoken up like a man with a chunk of backbone and said he had a family with him and was flat busted and didn't have a place to stay? What brand of mangy miscreants did he think people in that state were that they couldn't provide food and shelter for a family that needed same till they could provide their own? He, the store man, was going to tell this Hugo Kertchunk or whatever crazy name he called himself what he, this Hugo Kerchunkhead, was going to do and he'd better do it. This ringtailed baboon of a Hugo crazy name was going to set himself and his family down in the extra room of the living quarters back of the store and he was going to pay a stiff price. How? He was supposed to be a carpenter, wasn't he? So his wife said anyway. Well, he was going to prove that. He was going to slap some decent shelves in the store to take the place of the rickety ones there and they'd better be good shelves or he'd find himself with a sore backside from being kicked all over a quarter section. And maybe he wasn't such a hollow-head of a bohunk as he looked because he seemed to have rustled himself a hammer-and-saw job already but the shelf proposition still stood and was he man enough to rear up on his hind legs and say would he do it?

Hugo Kertchak understood only part of the words. But he understood that the store man's anger was a good anger and that there was more work for him to do. What exactly it was did not matter. It was carpenter's work. He was a good carpenter, almost as good a carpenter as his father had been. He looked straight at the store man. "Done," he said.

The store man was not angry anymore. He chuckled. "Talking American already," he said. "When you're through here, come on down to my place." He turned abruptly and disappeared around the corner of the building.

Hugo Kertchak nailed the last roof board in position. He was worried about the roof. It should have some other covering to make it waterproof. He would talk to the man about that. He slid to the ground and cut and shaped the last side boards to fit up snugly under the eaves. He ran neat finishing strips down the corners. There was still a nice pile of wood left and the keg of nails was only half empty. It was not really fair. All this good wood and all these nails and two dollars too for a little sawing and hammering finished with the afternoon only half gone. There was still a door to make. It should be a good door.

He selected the wood carefully. The door grew under his hands. He cut and mortised the pieces for the outer rim. He planed and fitted the pieces to be set in these and give a paneled effect. The wind of the wide country set the shavings dancing. This was the kind of work that showed what a good carpenter could do. He was so intent on it that he did not hear the hooves approaching, the sound softened in the dust. He was startled when he looked up and saw a man, a new man, watching him about thirty feet away. It was a horseman and he had a pistol in a leather holder on his hip. Hugo Kertchak saw the horse and the pistol and was afraid. It was an instinctive fear out of old memories deep in his mind. Then he saw the face of the horseman and he was no longer afraid. It was a young face, serious and sunburned, with many small wrinkles around the eyes from much squinting into the endless wind, and the expression in the eyes and on the face was wide and open like the country around.

"Man oh man," the horseman said. He pushed his hat up from his forehead and wiped at the dust there. "You sure can wrangle those tools." He turned his horse and went out of sight around the building.

Hugo Kertchak fastened the hinges to the door. He set the door in the doorway and slipped thin shavings under it for clearance and fastened the hinges to the door frame. He pulled out the shavings and tried the door. It hung true and swung easily out and back to fit snug and flat in line with the frame. He began work on the latch. This time he heard the hooves. The horseman appeared around the building. A tied bundle of letters and newspapers hung from his saddle horn. He stopped his horse and leaned forward in the saddle inspecting the shed. "Man oh man," he said. "That's what I call a door. Kind of like a fancy beaver on a roadside bum but there ain't no mistaking it's a door." He clucked to the horse and moved on, straight on out into the wide country, riding easily and steadily into the far distance.

Hugo Kertchak stood on the small rear platform or porch of the store building and saw the last tinges of almost unbelievable color fading out of the western horizon and the clear clean darkness claiming the land. There were two silver dollars with the thirty-seven cents in the old leather purse in his pocket. Behind him in the lamplit kitchen his wife and the store man's wife were clearing dishes from the table and rattling them in a tin washbasin. The two voices made a gentle humming. It was remarkable how women did not need to know many of each other's words to talk so much together. But there had been much talk too with the store man himself, who was still sitting by the table reading his newspaper as if he had to cover every word in it. This was only a small town, a very small town, the store man said, but it would not always be small. It would change, and quickly. Now there were only wide stretches of land around where men raised cattle for meat and leather and let them wander without fences to hold them. But soon the government would open the land for farmers and their families. They would come. Whole trainloads of them would be coming. They would settle all around and the town would grow and business would be good and there would be more work than men to do it.

Hugo Kertchak could hardly believe that what was happening was true. In one day he had new money and some materials for his trade and a friend who could be angry at him for his own good. This was a strange country and the people were strange but theirs was not an alien strangeness. It was only a difference that a man could learn to understand.

His wife was on the porch beside him. "Hugo. Think of it. In the cold time, in the winter, they have a school. Free for all people's children." She put a hand on his arm. She had not complained very much through the four years of saving. She had followed where he led on the long journeying. "We stay here?" she said.

The tireless wind of the wide country blew full in Hugo Kertchak's face. It was still hot and it was still dry. But there was a freshness in it that was not just the beginning of the evening cool. Hugo Kertchak put an arm around his wife's shoulders. "We stay," he said.

Hugo Kertchak was the town carpenter. He helped the town get ready for the coming land boom. He built new shelves in the store and a long new counter and racks for farm tools. He built and polished to a shining finish a bar in the biggest of the buildings that was a saloon and would be a dance hall. He patched the blacksmith shop roof and extended it out to form a lean-to addition where wagons could be kept waiting repairs. He built stalls in the broad shedlike structure that would be a livery stable. These were honest jobs well done and he could pay the store man board money and even save a little for the house he would build for himself with the materials he was assembling. But they did not satisfy him. They seemed so small in the bigness of the land.

He sat on the front steps with the store man and watched the western color fading out of the sky. A man on a horse came along the road, hurrying, stirring the dust for the tireless wind to whirl. It was the young horseman. He stopped and looked down at the two on the steps.

"Howdy, Cal," the store man said. "Climb off that cayuse and sit a spell. Could be there's a bottle of beer hanging to cool in the well out back."

"Man oh man," the horseman said, "you would think of that when I ain't got the time." He looked straight at Hugo Kertchak. "Reckon me and the other hands ain't so hot with our hammers. Barn we built's in bad shape. Haymow's collapsed with hardly no hay in it at all. And everybody's pulling out early morning for fall roundup. So I tell the boss how you wrangle those tools. So he sends me to put a rope on you for repairs."

Hugo Kertchak picked out the important words here and there as he had learned to do with these Americans. "Done," he said. "Where is barn?"

It was a big barn, casting a long shadow in the morning sun. Hugo Kertchak drove toward it, perched on the seat of the store man's light wagon. All the last miles he could see the barn bumping up out of the wide flat land and he did not like what he saw. It was too high for its width. It leaned a little as if the bottom timbers on one side had not been set right on a firm foundation. There were no neat slatted windows high up under the pointed eaves to give proper ventilation. The doors sagged and could not be closed all the way. Hugo Kertchak shook his head and muttered to himself.

He stood inside the doors and saw the remains of the haymow and listened to the boss, the ranchman, speak many words about propping it up again and perhaps strengthening it some. He did not listen to catch the important words. He was looking up at the fine big timbers that should have been cut to lap each other and fastened with stout wooden pegs and instead were simply butted against each other and tortured with long spikes driven in at angles that had already started splittings in the good wood. He did not even wait for the ranchman to stop talking. "No," he said in a loud voice. "Sorry is it to me I said 'done.' This work no." He sought for the words that would say what he meant and found them and as always in excitement he forgot the pronouns. "Is America," he said. "Has freedom."

The ranchman's eyes narrowed. His voice was soft and gentle. "What has freedom got to do with my barn?"

"Freedom," Hugo Kertchak said. "Freedom for work right." He waved his arms at the walls around. "You see? Bad work. Not strong. Cold weather come. Snow. On roof. All the time wind blow. One year. Two year. Not no more. Everything down."

The ranchman's eyes were wide open again. He sucked in one end of his mustache and chewed on it. "That bad, eh? I know it was slapped together in a devil of a hurry. Couldn't you fix it up some?"

"Fix bad work," Hugo Kertchak said, "makes better. But all the time still bad."

The ranchman chewed more on his mustache. He remembered that the range would be shrinking as homesteaders came in and he would have to depend more and more on winter feeding. He couldn't take chances on a rickety barn. The old days were slipping away and he would have to plan closer for the future. "Maybe," he said, "maybe you could build me a good barn?" He saw Hugo Kertchak's eyes begin to shine. "Whoa, now," he said. "Take it slow. I don't mean the best barn in the country. And no fancy doors. Just a good solid dependable barn. Knocking this one apart and using as much of it as you can for the new one."

Hugo Kertchak no longer said "I am carpenter." He said "I am builder." The land boom arrived and the trainloads and wagon-loads of settlers and they fanned out over the wide land and with them for miles in all directions went word that when it came to building, Hugo Kertchak, builder, could do a job right. Most of the homesteaders threw up their own shacks. Many of them simply squatted on their claims in tents and flimsy tarpapered huts waiting to prove title and sell out for a quick profit. Many others were too shiftless even to do that and drifted away. But here and there were a few and their number gradually increased who had capital or the competence to acquire it and could meet the conditions of the new land. They looked forward and they built for the future and Hugo Kertchak built for them. They paid what and when they could and sometimes he waited months and a year or more and longer for the last of the money but that did not matter because there was work for every working day and he was building and he had enough.

He built toolsheds and wagonsheds, sturdy and unshakable. He built barns, strong and solid, that seemed to grow out of the earth itself and settled firmly to the long competition with wind and weather. He built houses, small ones at first and then larger when times were flush and money plentiful and small ones again when that was all people could afford. No roof on these houses sagged when snow was heavy on it. The tireless wind found no chinks to whip through and widen. Sometimes he hired a helper or even two, but mostly he worked alone or when there was no school with his growing son as helper because that was the way to be certain that all the work was done right.

The town grew and spread out on both sides of the railroad track and other builders came, men who underbid each other on jobs and hired many men and had the work done rapidly, sometimes good and sometimes not good. They built a town hall and a hotel and a jail and a railroad station and some store blocks and some fine-looking houses and other things and how they built them was their own business. Always there was someone out across the wide land who needed a shed or a barn or a house built as Hugo Kertchak could build it.

Hugo Kertchak's son was a good carpenter. He worked on Saturdays and during vacations with his father and was paid what a helper would have been paid. Sometimes he seemed to think more of the money to be earned than of the job to be done and he had a tendency to hurry his work. But when his father was there to watch he was a good carpenter. When he graduated from high school, he did not work as a carpenter anymore. He worked at many jobs in the town, only a week or two at each. He was restless and irritable in the home. He talked with his father. He wanted to go to the state university and study to be an architect. "That is right," Hugo Kertchak said. "In America the son should do more and better than the father. Work with me until the school begins again and save the money." His son did and when the school began again what he had with what Hugo Kertchak had in the town bank was enough.

Hugo Kertchak's daughter was a good cook like her mother,

fine-colored and well-rounded as her mother had been at the same age. She was quick with words, too, like her mother and did well in her studies. She won a scholarship to go to the state normal school and study to be a teacher. But in the first year at the school she met a mining engineer who was leaving soon to work for a mining company in western Montana. She wanted to marry him and go with him. Hugo Kertchak comforted his wife. "Is she different than you?" he said. "Is it not she should go where her man goes?" There was only a little money in the bank now but there was enough for a wedding.

Times were slack. The town was very quiet. The opening of new lands had long since moved far on farther westward. The population of the town dwindled and dropped to a stable level. There was no more building.

Hugo Kertchak became a maker of barrels. He made them of all sizes for many purposes, from small kegs to big hogsheads. He made them firm and tight. He shaped the staves and fitted them together as he had shaped and fitted the timbers of his barns and houses. On most of them he used iron hoops, but he liked to make some completely of wood with wooden hoops fitted and shrunk so that they held better than the iron itself. He made them outdoors in the back yard of his house, where his wife could see him from the window, working under the high sky while the endless wind blew through his graying hair and made the shavings dance around his feet. He had a broad shed there for a workshop but he worked in it only when the weather was bad. He was building outdoors in the open, using his tools on good wood with the skill he had brought with him to this new land. He was building good barrels. But he did not call himself Hugo Kertchak, builder, anymore.

Hugo Kertchak's son was home for the summer vacation. After

one more school year he would have the parchment that would say he was an architect. Now during the summer he worked with his father, making barrels. He talked as a young American talked, fast and with much enthusiasm, and his talk was big with his plans for his profession. Hugo Kertchak listened and thought of the time when men who worked with steel and stone and concrete as he worked with wood would build the fine structures his son would design for them. And Hugo Kertchak's wife sat on the small back porch in the summer sun and watched the father and the son making barrels together.

Hugo Kertchak's son went back to the university and the winter was long and hard and when the spring arrived Hugo Kertchak's son and other young men at the university were given their degrees early so that they could enlist and fight in the war with Spain. There would be time enough for him to be an architect when the war was finished. But there was no time. The telegram came telling that he died in Cuba of the yellow fever. Hugo Kertchak tried to comfort his wife and she tried to comfort him. He at least had his work, his barrels to make, and she had nothing. Even her daughter was far away to the west in Montana. She sat on the small back porch and watched him work where their son had worked with him. She sat there too often and too late in the endless wind with no shawl over her shoulders and no scarf around her head. It was pneumonia with complications, the doctor said. Four days after she took to her bed she died quietly in the night. Hugo Kertchak stood by the bed a long time in the early morning light. He cranked the handle on the telephone in the hall and called the undertaker and made the arrangements. He went out to the back yard to his tools, old and worn but still serviceable like himself. Only with them in his hands did he feel alive now.

Two days after the funeral the letter came from his daughter telling why she herself had not come. Her husband had been hurt in the mine. His left leg was crushed and he would not walk again. The company was paying for the doctor and the hospital but even so there was no extra money. Her husband would not be able to do mine work anymore but in time perhaps with his training he could do office work of some kind. Meanwhile they thought of establishing a small store which she could run. The local bank might loan her the money she would need.

Hugo Kertchak sold his house. He kept the workshop and a small bit of land with it bordering on the rear alley and moved a bed and a table and some chairs and a bureau into the shop. It had a coal stove that gave good heat and on which he could do his small cooking. There was a mortgage on the house and the price he received was not high but when the mortgage was paid there was enough. He sent the money to his daughter and her crippled husband. He did not need it. He had a workshop and he had his tools.

Hugo Kertchak made barrels but they did not sell as they used to sell. They stood in rows and on top of each other along the side of the workshop and he had no orders for them. Tin and galvanized-iron containers were being used more and more. These were cheaper and more convenient and more easily handled. Hugo Kertchak became a maker of coffins.

The coffins Hugo Kertchak made were good coffins, built as the houses and the barns and the barrels had been built, shaped and fitted, firm and solid. Always, as he worked on them, he remembered the one he had made for his wife and worried about the one someone else had made for his son far off in Cuba. He did not make many, most of them only on order from the town undertaker, because good wood was becoming expensive and he could not have a big supply on hand and because working was harder now. He moved more slowly and there was a stiffness at times in the muscles. But the skill was unchanged, the sure strong touch with the tools.

People he had known in the first years died and were buried in Hugo Kertchak's coffins. People he did not know were buried in them too. The town was changing. New people and new generations walked the streets. Electric lights brightened many houses. Horseless carriages began to cough along the roads and their owners talked about the paving of streets. The new ways of the new century changed old habits. The undertaker came to see Hugo Kertchak. He could use no more of the coffins. People wanted the shiny decorated models that came from the manufacturing places in the cities. People wanted these and there was a nice profit in them. That was business.

Hugo Kertchak puttered around town with any little jobs he could find. Sometimes he built bookcases or pantry shelves or flower trellises when he found people who wanted these. Most of the jobs were tending people's yards, planting bulbs in the spring, cutting grass in the summer, raking leaves in the fall. His daughter wrote to him regularly, once a month. She sent him snapshots taken by a neighbor of the two grandchildren he had never seen. She wanted him to come and live with her. He could help in the store. There was not much money but it would be enough. But he could not do that. The thought of going so far now and of living in the mountains frightened him. He could not leave the town and the wide flat country that had welcomed film and the quiet grave in its half of the small plot in a corner of the town cemetery. Regularly he wrote back, laboring hours over his broad rounded script, careful of his spelling and to put in all the pronouns. He was well. There was plenty of work. Someday soon he would come on a visit, in the fall perhaps when the rush of summer work was done, or in the spring when the winter cold was past. And sometimes he managed to put several dollar bills in the envelope for the grandchildren. He did not need much for himself.

Days when there was no work and the weather was pleasant he liked to sit in the sun on one of the benches by the town hall and watch the two morning trains go past on the track across the way, the express that roared through without stopping and the local that puffed to a stop by the station for a flurry of activity there. Always people were arriving and people were leaving and new faces were around and things were changing and that was America. He could remember when a train could stop and only a single small family step down from it into a dusty little town that seemed deserted and yet they would find friendship springing up around them as if from the wide land itself. That too was America. He sat on the bench and remembered and people smiled at him as they passed and sometimes stopped to talk to him because he was a part of the town and of the past that had made the town and he did not know it but he was America too.

A woman from one of the county boards came to see Hugo Kertchak in his shop. She sat on the edge of one of his old chairs and talked in a self-consciously kind voice. She had a card in her hand that told her facts about him and she did not know these were not the important facts. He was an old man, living alone, with no regular work. The card told her that. It would be much better for him if he would turn over to the county any small property he still had and let the county take care of him. The county had a nice old folks' home where he would have companionship and would not have to worry about anything.

The woman saw the tightening of the old muscles of Hugo Kertchak's face and she hurried to say more. That would not be charity. Oh, good heavens, no. He had been one of the early settlers and he had helped the community grow. The county owed it to him to take care of him. "Wrong," Hugo Kertchak said. "All wrong. This America owes me nothing at all. It gave what a man needs. A home without fear. Good friends. A chance to work. Freedom to work right. If there is owing, it is for me. To take care of myself." He was indignant and this made his voice sharp and the woman flushed and stood up and turned to go. Hugo Kertchak was a little ashamed. "I have thanks that you think of me," he said. "It is good that you help people. But for me there is no need."

Hugo Kertchak sat on the bench by the town hall and the tireless wind of the plains country ruffled the dwindling gray hair on his bare head. People nodded at him as they passed but few people talked to him anymore. That was his fault. He talked too much. He said the same things over and over. He wanted to talk about the weather or politics or prospects for the year's crops or anything else another person wanted to talk about. But inevitably his voice rose, shriller and more querulous, and he would be doing most of the talking, telling about the old days when a man got angry at another man for his own good and a man said "done" and a thing was settled and a young horseman remembered a man he saw doing good work and people appreciated work that was done right, not slipshod and in a hurry, but right with every beam and board shaped and fitted and fastened to join its strength with the strength of the others in the solid firmness of the whole structure.

Hugo Kertchak remembered. His old hands remembered the feel of his good tools. He began going home by different and roundabout routes, walking along the roads and alleys and looking for stray pieces of wood. He gathered what he could find, pieces of old shingles, broken boards, boxes and crates thrown away. He carried them to his workshop. Day after day he worked in the old shop. Two days a week he did gardening and that paid for his food. The rest of the time he stayed in the shop and worked. When the wife of the man who had bought the house went out to hang her wash in the back yard near the shop, she heard the sounds of old tools in use, the steady striking of a hammer, the soft swish of a plane, the rhythmic stroke of a saw.

The day came when she hung out her wash and heard no sounds in the shop. When she took down the dry clothes in late afternoon there was no sign of activity. In the evening, when she stood on the back porch and peered into the darkness, there was no lamplight showing through the shop window. Her husband refused to leave his newspaper. "So what?" he said. "The old wind-bag can take care of himself. He's been doing it for years, hasn't he?" But in the morning, after a worrying night, she insisted and her husband went out to investigate. He came in again quickly and to the telephone and called the coroner's office.

The coroner and a deputy sheriff found the body of Hugo Kertchak on the floor where he had toppled from a chair in the last struggle for breath as his heart failed. The old pen he had been using was still tight in the fingers of his right hand. They picked the body up and laid it on the old bed. "Sometime yesterday," the coroner said. "That's the way it is with these old ones. One day they're fussing around. Next day they're gone."

The deputy sheriff was looking around the shop. "What d'you know," he said. "Take a look at these things." On a shelf above the workbench was a row of little buildings, small birdhouses, each delicately made yet sturdy with every piece of the old wood shaped and fitted and fastened with skillful care. The deputy sheriff put his hands on his hips and stared at the tiny buildings. "I'll be damned," he said. "You never know what these old bums'll be doing next, fussing around with things like that when anyone's a mind for one can get it for a quarter or maybe fifty cents at a hardware store. Wasting his time on those when likely he didn't have a nickel. Now the town'll have to bury him."

"Shut up," the coroner said. He was holding the unfinished letter that had been lying on the old table. He was reading the last words: "The town people will sell my shop and the land that is left and send the money to you. They are good people. It is for the boy. For help with a school. To study it may be for an architect . . ." The coroner folded the paper and put it in his pocket. He moved around the foot of the bed and pulled an old blanket from what lay between the bed and the wall. It was a coffin, firm and strongly built, the once rough planks cut and fitted and planed smooth and polished to a good finish. On the top lay an old cigar box. In the box were a title form for a small lot in the town cemetery and an old leather purse. In the purse were some crumbled dollar bills and a handful of coins. "No," the coroner said. "Not this one. He paid his score to the end."

The man filling in the grave in a corner of the cemetery shivered a bit in the chill sunny air. He finished the job, piling the dirt in a mound so that when it settled it would be level with the ground around. He leaned a moment on the shovel while he took a scrap of paper from his pocket and looked at the name on it. "Kertchak," he muttered to himself. "Seems like I remember that. Made barrels when I was a kid." He lifted the shovel over one shoulder and went away.

An automobile approached and stopped by the cemetery and two men stepped from it. One was the editor of the local newspaper. The other was tall and erect with the heaviness of late middle-age beginning to show in a once lean body. He wore a wide-brimmed hat and under it his face with the many wrinkles about the eyes was windburned and wide and open like the country around. Under his arm he carried a cross made of two pieces of wood. "Man oh man," he said to the editor, "I'd never have known if it wasn't for that article in your paper. Started me remembering things." He went to the mound of dirt and stuck the wooden cross into the ground at the upper end. He stood silent a moment, staring at the wooden cross. The upright was a piece of new two-by-four. The crossbar was an old board found in the old shop that had once been nailed over the doorway of the house in front of the shop. Carved into it in square solid letters were the words: Hugo Kertchak, Builder.

The automobile moved away and silence settled over the cemetery. The endless wind blew and whipped some of the dried earth of the mound in tiny dust whirls around the base of the cross and blew in soft whispers on out over the wide land where they stood, strong against weather and time, the sheds and the barns and the houses Hugo Kertchak had built.